continued...

Also by Molly MacRae

The Haunted Yarn Shop Series
Book 1: Last Wool and Testament
Book 2: Dyeing Wishes

SPINNING IN HER GRAVE

A HAUNTED YARN SHOP MYSTERY

Molly MacRae

AN OBSIDIAN MYSTERY

OBSIDIAN
Published by the Penguin Group
Penguin Group (USA) LLC, 375 Hudson Street,
New York, New York 10014

USA | Canada | UK | Ireland | Australia | New Zealand | India | South Africa | China
penguin.com
A Penguin Random House Company

First published by Obsidian, an imprint of New American Library,
a division of Penguin Group (USA) LLC

First Printing, March 2014

ISBN 978-0-451-24064-4

Printed in the United States of America
10 9 8 7 6 5 4 3 2 1

For the distaff side of my family

ACKNOWLEDGMENTS

I've taken liberties with this book by spinning a yarn about a livestock feud called the Blue Plum Piglet War. There is no record of any such incident occurring in east Tennessee's history and I hope I'll be forgiven for suggesting the outlandish notion. For real stories from the region's past, visit the Jonesborough-Washington County History Museum in Tennessee's oldest (and my favorite) town, Jonesborough. Information about the real Pig War—an 1859 border dispute between the United States and Great Britain—can be found in a quick Internet search. Many thanks to the spinners of the Champaign Urbana Spinners and Weavers Guild who answered the questions I asked and also the questions I *should* have asked. Thanks, especially, to Jackie Brewer, for introducing me to PVC and bicycle-wheel spinning wheels and to Kate Winkler for another wonderful knitting pattern. Thanks and admiration to my brother Jack, aka Dr. John Alexander MacRae, who let me borrow his brilliant creation, his Incredible Tent of Wonders. You can be awed and amazed by the real Incredible Tent of Wonders on Labor Day weekend each year at the Kline Creek Farm in West Chicago, Illinois. And, as always, thank you to Ross, Gordon, Milka, and Mike Thompson. I love to write, but you are my true loves.

No piglets were harmed in the writing of this book.

Chapter 1

"With guns?" I stared at the man standing on the other side of the sales counter in the Weaver's Cat, my fiber and fabric shop in Blue Plum, Tennessee. I'd only just met him—Mr. J. Scott Prescott as it said on the card he'd slid across the counter. He was slight and had a well-scrubbed, earnest face that at first glance put him anywhere from early twenties to midthirties. He wore an expensive suit and tie, though, and had the beginnings of crow's-feet at the corners of his eyes. Taken together, those details put him closer to the mature, successful end of that age range. He also came across as calm and operating on an even keel, despite the mention of guns. Unfortunately, much as I wanted to appear the competent, calm business owner so early on a Friday morning, I couldn't help sounding more edgy than even. "You're kidding, right?"

"Your town board already gave us—" Mr. Prescott started to say.

I interrupted, holding up my hand. "But they're running through the streets with guns?"

"Only some of them will be running." Again, the gravitas of his suit and tie helped.

"Okay, well . . ."

"Half a dozen. A dozen tops, and we reconsidered the burning torches and decided against them. Most of the rest of the actual participants will be posted at strategic points around town." He gestured right and left, fingers splayed in his excitement. Thank goodness for the suit; otherwise he was beginning to look and sound like an eager Boy Scout. "We already have permission to use the park," he said, "and the old train depot and the upper porch of Cunningham House. The main concentration will be in the two or three blocks surrounding the courthouse." His hands demonstrated several concentric circles, then came together with a ghost of a clap and he leaned toward me. "Oh, and we've been given access to the roof of the empty mercantile across from the courthouse. Those locations are for the visible men; the rest will be hiding. As I said, the plans and permissions have been in place for several months, but one of the property owners was recently obliged to back out and that's where you and the Weaver's Hat come in."

"Cat."

"Pardon?" He straightened.

"Sorry. I didn't mean to interrupt, but we're the Weaver's Cat, as in 'meow.' Not hat."

"Really? I'm embarrassed. Anyway, we'd love it if one or two of the men could sneak in here during the action and watch from the windows upstairs."

"Hmm."

"They won't get in your way. They'll watch at the windows and when they see the other men down in the street, they'll stick their heads out and shoot. They might also do the famous yell, but I'll tell them that's optional, sort of as the spirit moves them, if you see what I mean. But a bloodcurdling yell like that really whips up the enthusiasm of the spectators, and between that and the shots erupting from unexpected places, it'll keep things off balance in a realistic way so that the whole reenactment will have an incredible sense of authenticity and it'll be great." He stopped, eyes wide. I took a step back.

"At this point I should ask you not to divulge any of the details we've discussed," he said. "We're keeping the program under wraps. Looking for the big reveal, if you see what I mean. The wow. Also, I forgot to ask, do the windows upstairs open? Because there isn't any point in trying to shoot out of them if they don't."

I'd processed his words and understood his gesturing hands, and it would have taken a harder history-loving heart than mine to ignore the excitement of a good-natured reenactment. The tourists flocking to town for our annual heritage celebration—Blue Plum Preserves—would no doubt love it, too. But my mind kept skipping back to my original question. "With *guns*?"

J. Scott blinked.

"Sorry. I didn't mean to shout," I said. I surreptitiously wiped my mouth in case I'd also spit. "But the stories I remember hearing always made that whole episode sound more like a loud fuss between neighbors than a feud with guns."

"But a feud is more fun. Plus, there's historical precedent. A pig almost changed the course of American history in 1859. Look it up sometime. It's fascinating. Of course, we're switching the pig out for a piglet, because piglets are cute. People love them. I'd also like you to think of the marketing possibilities. If the event goes well this year, just wait until next. And I assure you it will be perfectly safe. No projectiles. No live rounds. No actual aiming at people. Your mayor and aldermen were extremely impressed by how thoroughly and carefully I've choreographed the event. It will be playacting at its finest. Verisimilitude and good fun. We're taking Blue Plum's worn-out skit and giving it the life it should be living. We're giving Blue Plum's history the voice and resonance it was meant to have. Believe me when I say this will take your festival weekend to the next level. Blue Plum Preserves is going to be on the map and on every heritage tourist's itinerary. The result will be more visitors, more fun, and more money in the merchants' pockets. Win. Win. Win. And here's something else that will interest you. If I'm not mistaken, one of the originators of the festival, a founding mother, if you will, was, like you, a knitter."

"Are you talking about Ivy McClellan?"

"Ivy?" He nodded. "Yes, that could be the name. I see you know your local history. That's wonderful. She might be the one who dabbled on the original skit, too. The records aren't entirely clear on that."

"Ivy McClellan was my grandmother."

"You're kidding. Is she still . . ."

"She died four months ago. This was her shop. She and a couple of friends wrote the skit based on their research."

"I am so sorry for you loss." He gave his sorrow half a beat. "But then this will be especially wonderful. It could hardly be more appropriate for the shop to have a role in this year's celebration. You will be honoring your grandmother's memory and her vision by letting part of

the action take place here. And that win, win, win I mentioned? It will go for you and the Weaver's Cat, too.
You'll see. People eat this stuff up." He smacked his lips
and smiled. "Frankly, I'm surprised you aren't already
aware of the reenvisioning of what I believe is a corner-
stone activity of Blue Plum Preserves."

I opened my mouth—but to say what? That I'd been
busy planning the shop's own festival booth and related
activities? Maybe. To tell him my life had been upended
and my mind otherwise occupied since Granny died?
Probably not, but it didn't matter, anyway. He was
primed and ready and got in ahead of whatever I might
have said.

"Also, if you stop and think, I feel sure you'll realize
you're focusing on the wrong component of the event."
He shook his head with a sad cluck of his tongue. "It
happens, though. Mention guns and there are people
who will misinterpret what you're trying to do. But I
think that, like the others, you're missing the educational
importance of this kind of event. You're focusing on a
small part of our tool set and missing the bigger picture
of our message."

"I could be." I nodded, trying to give him the benefit
of a snapless judgment. He was right. I was having trouble getting past the guns. Guns in the streets of Blue
Plum. Guns fired out my second-floor windows. Guns in
a little skit about a minor land squabble and wandering
livestock. I gave myself a shake to jar my focus somewhere other than guns. Then, to give my judgment more
time to flex and accommodate other interpretations, I
picked up his card and read the fine print under his
name. "You're a piano salesman?"

He tipped his head and smiled. "High-end," he said.

That probably accounted for the antique ivory color of the card and expensive feel of the stock. The name of the store and his position were expensive-sounding, too. He was vice president for institutional sales at the Copeland Piano Gallery in Knoxville, about a hundred and twenty miles west of us. Interesting. I glanced from the card to J. Scott Prescott for a quick comparison between him and whatever my preconceived notion of piano salesmen was, high-end or otherwise. Before I got further than thinking his hands were smaller than seemed optimal for reaching octaves, a question occurred to me.

"What's your interest in this, Mr. Prescott? Why are you involved in our 'worn-out skit,' if you don't mind my asking?"

He didn't seem to mind. In fact, his smile warmed and he slid a second card across the counter. This one was a richer, almost edible butternut color and glossy with an embossed seal in the center. I ran my fingertips over the words running around the seal's edge: "Prescott Preservation Realty."

"Also high-end," he said. "And I'll let you in on a secret. The empty mercantile there across from the courthouse? I'm brokering a deal for an exciting new business and an eager tenant-to-be. That's why we'll have access to the roof. As a favor to me. The owner has been trying to rent or sell the place for years and is very happy I came along. I specialize in at-risk vintage and antique buildings. I am all about preservation. Of our history, our heritage, our homes. Our *home*." He spread his arms wide, embracing the whole, heartwarming caboodle and with "our *home*," he gave a slight bow. "So you see? I fit

right in with the tenth annual Blue Plum Preserves celebration."

"Oh, I didn't realize you're from Blue Plum."

"Well, no, actually I'm not. I was using 'our' and 'home'
in the broader sense," he said. "I also suspect I'm preaching to the choir when it comes to antique buildings. This
whole row house is an architectural gem. Do you rent?"

"I own."

"The whole row?"

"This house."

"Well, the way you kept the feel of the original home
when you repurposed it should be written up in one of
the journals. No changes too drastic— it'll be a snap for
anyone to turn it back into a single-family residence.
And having this unit is a plus. Windows on three sides,
plenty of light. Are there any structural problems? Anything with the drains? The roof? If you ever want to
sell—"

"No."

He might have taken my interruption as a slap. I
might have meant it that way. I felt like a cat with fur on
end, claws exposed for a razor swipe across his nose if he
took another step closer to my mortgage-free deed. This
house had been my grandparents' home. Granny had
started the Weaver's Cat right there in the corner of the
room and let it grow and stretch until it had taken over
the whole house. Granny's inspiration and the love she
had for all forms of needlework were intricately and in-
extricably woven into every inch of the Weaver's Cat.
This building—and all its accumulated fibers and fabrics
and textures and colors and *memories*—this house was
not a repurposed unit.

"It won't be for sale anytime soon," I said after taking a deep breath.

"Message received." J. Scott Prescott held up a placating hand and smiled. "And you just proved my point about preaching to the choir."

"Huh. Okay. But I guess I'm still not following. How did you get so involved? Here, I mean, and in the skit? All the way from Knoxville?" It was tempting to add "in little old Blue Plum," but only because I was beginning to feel perverse.

"We're giving the skit a title, by the way," he said. "Apparently it's never had one, other than people calling it the pig skit. It's now, officially, 'The Blue Plum Piglet War.'"

He dipped back into his inside suit coat pocket and brought out a third business card. I reached for it, but he was ahead of me again, and he took my reaching hand, cupping it in his. If he'd actually gripped my hand, I would have yanked away from him faster than he could give a Blue Plum Piglet War yell. But all he did was lay the third card on my palm, tap it twice with a fingertip, and wink.

I ignored the wink and removed my hand from his. This third card was simple white cardstock with a stylized sketch of an ink bottle and a feather pen poised as though it had just finished writing the words "Prescott Preservation Plays." I put the card on the counter next to its friends.

"You're a man of many business cards."

"I'm a man of many interests," J. Scott said, "and by necessity a man of several streams of income. I blame the economy. But writing heritage plays for community celebrations is my true passion. If I may be allowed to put it in such high-flying terms, I feel a calling. I've written seven plays, to date, for communities from Darien in coastal Georgia to tiny Cumberland near Kingdom Come State Park in Kentucky. Each one has been well received and made a difference in the lives of the citizens."

"But the—"

"And you can trust me on the gun issue," he said. "The reenactors will not be just a bunch of good old boys playing with fantasies and popguns." He grinned, showing me his ivories and also showing me that he could laugh at a stereotype as easily as the next good old boy. "So, Miss Rutledge, Kath, I know this is short notice, but may we have your blessing and permission to stage part of 'The Blue Plum Piglet War' from the upstairs windows of your charming place of business next weekend?"

"No. I'm sorry, but no."

J. Scott Prescott finally accepted my answer with a shrug and a sigh. He departed, leaving behind his trio of cards and the dead silence of a shop with no browsing customers. "Dead" and "silent" were two words that should have made perfect sense when used together. They would have for most people I knew. But most people I knew weren't haunted. In fact, no one I knew was haunted. And although I didn't know much about the *life* of my dead friend, I did know "silent" wasn't the right word to describe Geneva in her current existence.

I never used to believe in ghosts. Why should I? My profession as a textile preservation specialist grounded me in science. I believed in physical attributes, chemicals, logical analysis, stabilization of fragile materials, and the eradication of pests. So how did I explain suddenly seeing, hearing, and interacting with a, um, er . . . a ghost? I didn't. I couldn't. More accurately, I hadn't "gone there" yet and wasn't sure I wanted to, although I knew that eventually I needed to.

"You spend too much time thinking," a voice said from on high.

I glanced up. Geneva was curled around the blades of the ceiling fan I hadn't turned on yet.

"I was thinking about you," I said.

She appeared to preen. It wasn't always easy to interpret her facial expressions or body language, owing to the fact that her body was less substantial than an Orenburg lace shawl I'd once had the pleasure of curating and she was never entirely in focus. But smug was easy to see. Anger, too. She billowed and pulsed in alarming ways when she was angry. And although it was hard on my nerves, it helped that she went in for melodramatics. The sound effects, alone, provided useful clues to her moods. Since making Geneva's acquaintance, I found myself less and less amazed by the odd things I could get used to.

"Were you eavesdropping up there?" I asked, bringing up a sore subject.

She huffed. I ignored it. She wasn't a fan of sore subjects or being ignored, so she huffed again and heaved her shoulders, behaving like a put-out teenager. I was pretty sure she *wasn't* a teenager, but she knew how to act like one.

Having a ghost in the shop didn't present as many problems as one might think. The most obvious problem—the whole boo factor with customers shrieking and running out—wasn't a problem at all. Except for Argyle, the shop cat, no one else saw or heard Geneva. This was my own, private haunting. And privacy was the main issue. Geneva could materialize and fade out and drift through walls so that, unless I saw her hovering like a wisp of smoke somewhere, I never knew if I was alone and couldn't ever be sure I was having a private conversation. Maybe she'd grown up in a two-room log house with thirteen brothers and sisters or maybe her sense of personal space had atrophied over the century or more since her death. But getting her to accept, gracefully, that she couldn't listen in anytime she wanted—or worse, join in— as an ongoing "negotiation."

I started tidying the baskets of impulse-buy notions near the cash register. She swooped down from the fan and popped up in front of me.

"We agreed," she said, "that you can have no expectations of privacy when you're interacting with customers."

"You're right. We did. But we also agreed that it's impolite if you don't make your presence known." I gave myself two points for being firm but calm and a third point for smiling while doing it. Sometimes it helped if I treated our interactions like a competition.

"It's hard to keep track of all your rules and restrictions," she said with a sniff. She floated over to perch on the shoulder of the mannequin standing near the counter and I gave myself a bonus point for not telling her she looked like a giant, cobwebby parrot.

"So, have you ever heard of this feud Mr. Prescott was talking about?" I was always looking for historical details she knew firsthand that might help pinpoint when she'd lived. She claimed she didn't remember much about her life and got upset if I pressed her to try. From her reaction to the deaths of a young couple earlier in the year, there was clearly something traumatic in her own background that she was blocking out. Her memory, otherwise, especially for dialogue and plotlines from fifty-year-old television shows, was unbeatable.

"He's calling it the 'The Blue Plum Piglet War,'" I said. "It happened sometime in the 1820s or 1830s during a boundary dispute that escalated when one guy let his pigs get into another guy's crops."

"What was he growing?"

"Something tasty to pigs. I don't know. Potatoes?"

"Potatoes, pigs, and pandemonium," she said with relish.

"Do you remember it?"

"I'm not *that* old."

"Well, no, I didn't think you were, but people have always told stories about it. My grandmother told them to me. Maybe your grandmother told them to you. Maybe *she* was there. Anyway, you might be interested in watching the reenactment next weekend."

"I'm more interested in your reenactment. You do the same thing every time."

"And what are we talking about now?"

"The way you rebuff every gentleman caller who shows the least bit of interest in you. Mr. J. Snot Big Shot. He was full of himself, but I saw the way he took your hand."

"That is absolute baloney."

"It's not. He's sweet on you and you spurned his advance." Her voice throbbed with pathos for J. Scott.

"I spurned his attempt to put good old boys with

guns in our upstairs window and his advance on the building. He's a slick salesman. He doesn't give a flying fig about me."

"No one would with that attitude."

"My attitude is fine."

"For a nun."

My outer thirty-nine-year-old was willing to pick up a dust rag and move away from that jab. But that went against everything my inner seven-year-old stood for. "Joe," I snapped. "For your information, I don't rebuff Joe. We're having dinner tomorrow night at Mel's."

"We *are*?"

"Not *you*. Joe and I."

"And there you go." She threw her wispy hands in the air. "Rebuffing again. But never mind. Loneliness is my lot in death. I'll never understand your need to exclude a lost soul from the warmth and gaiety of a simple dinner out. But I'll survive."

A customer came in while I was still clutching the top of my skull, and the last vibrations of my heartfelt "aaaaargh" echoed in the attic. I gave myself three points for telling the customer a credible story about banging my head against a brick. There was a quietly sniffed "so unprofessional" from the irritating ghost now sitting in the front window with Argyle the cat and I gave myself another two points for not throwing a large, firm cone of rug wool at her. That would have been so unfair to Argyle.

Chapter 2

The customer I'd lied to about hitting my head fell in love with the rug wool I so prudently hadn't sent flying through the ghost and the front window. The wool was a lovely mango color. The woman bought it and three other cones in shades of deep green, warm brown, and ripe tomato for a rug she said she would call "East Tennessee Curry."

Ardis Buchanan arrived in time to hear the woman tell me she hoped my head felt better soon. There was a noise like a raspberry from the window, but only I heard it. Argyle was sound asleep on his back, his yellow tabby tummy exposed for maximum radiant heat absorption. He took industrial-grade naps and none of Geneva's noise ever bothered him. Ardis held the door for the customer and raised her eyebrows in my direction.

"Headache, hon?" she asked. "You should take something for it before it gets out of hand."

I waved off her concern and she slipped into the small office behind the counter to leave her purse. I'd "inherited" Ardis when I inherited the Weaver's Cat and so many other things from Granny. She'd been Granny's business manager and good friend for as long as I could remember, and now I was lucky enough to say she was both those things to me. Lucky, because there was no way I would try running the Cat without her. Always smelling of honeysuckle, she was tall, rock solid, and sensible. I wasn't so tall and wasn't quite such a rock, although I did like to think I was steady and sensible. Or I *had* thought I was sensible. Until my world was turned cockeyed . . . in so many ways . . . interesting ways.

"Anything going on this morning?" Ardis asked the same question every morning. She had a knack for making it sound like idle curiosity or a bid for juicy gossip more than a check to see if I was floundering.

I started to tell her about J. Scott Prescott's visit, but she interrupted, her nose wrinkling.

"Do you smell that?"

"Smell what?"

"I don't know." She took tentative sniffs in several directions. "Something. Maybe nothing." She shook her head. "A whiff and now it's gone. Maybe something that woman tracked in?"

I dutifully scanned our hardwood floor, retracing the woman's steps between the counter and the door and back again. I didn't find anything obvious and didn't smell anything less pleasant than wool and honeysuckle.

Ardis walked over to the wall and flipped on the ceiling fan. "Let's move the air around anyway," she said, "just in case." She sniffed again, then made another face.

"You still smell it?"

"No, I'm on to the next topic. But first, are there customers?"

I shook my head.

"Okay, then, next topic. Reva Louise." She thumped her fist on the counter. "I cannot tell you how much I wish that woman was as easy to get rid of as that stink was just now."

"Wow, Ardis. You don't think that's a tad strong?"

"Strong is what we'll need to be to keep Reva Louise at bay. I stopped by the café to pick up coffee on my way here, and do you know what she had the gall to tell me? *Tell* me, mind you, not hint, or suggest, or in any other way inquire or ask. She told me that she knows the best way to run a demonstration tent and she has 'arranged her schedule' so she can give us the help we must surely need. Also, she wants to borrow a drop spindle so she can learn to spin and be one of our demonstrators next weekend."

"And after hearing all that, you forgot your coffee?"

Ardis thumped the counter again.

Reva Louise Snapp was the new baker at Mel's on Main, the café down the street from us. Reva Louise was also Melody Gresham's—Mel's—half sister, although there wasn't any noticeable family resemblance. Mel's energy was obvious in her compact, muscular frame and bristling personality, and that energy seemed to percolate out the top of her head and straight up through her spiked, mustard yellow hair. Most of her energy went into running her café, arguably the best eating establishment in a radius of many miles.

Reva Louise, in town for five or six weeks, was . . . less defined. Hair? A middling brown. Height? Not quite tall. Weight? Someday she might have to watch it. But if I were asked to recall distinguishing characteristics to identify her in a crowd, I couldn't have come up with any.

"Maybe she did events like this back wherever she came from and she's just trying to fit in," I said.

"More like trying to shove her way in," Ardis huffed. "Do you know what she said when I told her our demonstration roster was full? With a waiting list? She said, and I quote, 'In that case, I can cover the sales counter in your shop.'"

"I guess she's trying to be helpful."

"No," Ardis said. "Helpful is asking if we actually need help. Or stopping by with an offer of cold lemonade." She picked up a dust cloth and snapped it at an imaginary army of dust bunnies.

"Or bringing the coffee you forgot?" Reminding her of the caffeine she'd left behind was a mistake. I had to rescue the poor dust cloth before she wrung its neck. "So, what did Reva Louise say when you told her we didn't need her help in here, either? Was she angry?"

"Oh no, hon. I left that for you to tell her. She's bringing the treats for Fast and Furious this afternoon."

Chapter 3

Rock-solid Ardis said that leaving me to deal with Reva Louise was the sensible course of action.

"You don't see it as wimping out?" I asked.

"No, hon, because there is no telling what I might do when my dander's up. Trust me." She put her hand on my shoulder and gave it a trustworthy squeeze. "It is much better for customer relations and safer for all concerned if we stick to our normal routine. I'll mind the shop this afternoon and you go on upstairs to Friday's Fast and Furious and have a good time."

"Have a good time and also tell Reva Louise thank you but no, thank you."

"Tell her firmly, Kath. Be calm, but very firm. And don't worry. Debbie will be there to back you up."

Debbie Keith, who worked for us part-time, was a marshmallow.

Friday's Fast and Furious, a challenge knitting circle, was an offshoot of the fiber arts group that Granny had started called TGIF—Thank Goodness It's Fiber. Every Friday at four o'clock, anywhere from three to a dozen of us met in the TGIF workroom on the second floor of the Weaver's Cat to enjoy the company of other driven knitters and spur one another on toward our goal. The challenge the group had set was to knit one thousand hats for hospitalized babies and toddlers by the end of the year.

"That's two and three-quarter hats per day, for the group as a whole," Debbie had told me when I joined the group, "rounding up slightly."

"That's almost twenty hats a week."

"Twenty very small hats," Debbie said. "And there's no point in calling it a challenge if it isn't one."

Fast and Furious meetings were casual and the TGIF workroom contributed to the laid-back atmosphere. Granddaddy had made the space by knocking down the wall between the two back bedrooms on the second floor. He built shelves and cupboards along two of the walls for storage, and Granny lined the other two walls with sideboards and Welsh cupboards for more storage. Oak worktables took up most of the floor space, but there was enough room left for a circle of mismatched, overstuffed comfy chairs grouped around a low coffee table.

People dropped in and out of the Friday meetings as their schedules allowed. The only constants were time and place, background music to set the knitting mood, refreshments from Mel's, and two important questions. That Friday afternoon, Debbie put on a CD of instrumental jazz with some nice percussion, tossed the hats she'd finished onto the coffee table, and asked the first question.

"How many this week?" Her three hats were sweet little brown things with bear cub ears.

I hadn't been fair when I'd thought of Debbie as a marshmallow. She was a young widow, living alone, raising sheep on a farm that had been in her family for more than a century—hardly the work of a pushover. But at the Cat she wore long skirts and embroidered tops and with her blond hair pulled back in a loose braid she looked as though she'd stepped out of a delicate Carl Larsen watercolor. Now she looked expectantly at the rest of us. We were five so far, including Ernestine Odell, John Berry, and Mel.

"I'll see your three and raise you one." John laid out four navy blue hats, two with pink roses made of felted wool. John was one of Granny's oldest friends. He'd spent most of his eighty-plus years torn between his roots in the Blue Ridge Mountains and his love for the waves on the deep blue sea, and anyone who noticed his resemblance to the handsome sea captain in *The Ghost and Mrs. Muir* could guess the sea had always held the stronger hand. John had come home only occasionally in recent years, to see his brother and—so he said—to convince Granny to sail away with him after Granddaddy died. He was full of stories, and that might have been one of them, but the light in his navy blue eyes when he told it to me, and the pink in his cheeks, convinced me it was true even if he'd never been able to convince Granny to go. Now he was back in Blue Plum for good. He'd sold his boat and come home to care for his brother.

Mel added two hats in a soft shade of orange to the pile. "I'm in my melon period," she said. "Sorry. Maybe more next week." She picked up the honeydew green hat she was working on and went back to knitting.

"Are you sure it isn't your melancholy period?" Debbie asked. "Something wrong, Mel?"

"Not a blessed thing," Mel said. She didn't snap at Debbie, but her mustard yellow spikes were as eloquent as raised hackles.

"Ta-da!" I quickly added my hats to our collection, drawing curious eyes away from Mel's unsmiling face and aggressively clicking needles.

"Two!" Ernestine picked up one of my hats, held it close to her thick lenses, and admired it. Ernestine liked to encourage me. My knitting skills had atrophied over years of academic and professional pursuits, and these two hats, in simple stockinette, were absolutely nothing to exclaim over. "The sky's the limit now, Kath. Before you know it you'll be adding ribbing and bunny ears." Ernestine was a small, round woman who reminded me of a cheerful mole. She was probably in her seventies and though she squinted at the world through her glasses, she rarely missed the nuances of the conversations going on around her.

John rubbed his hands and asked the second of the two important questions. "What delicious sin did you bring us today, Mel?"

Mel kept knitting and didn't answer. But she didn't need to, because Reva Louise breezed in, her project bag under her arm and the answer to the second important question in a covered cake carrier.

"Was that you sounding greedy, John Berry?" Reva Louise asked. "Oh, don't worry. I'm just teasing, sweetie. Look, I brought rhubarb ginger upside-down cake, and there's enough so you can each take some home. I'll put it over here and we can have it after we get some work done. It'll be good incentive. Mel, I asked you to bring the coffee along. You didn't forget it, did you?"

"The coffee's right there, Reva Louise," Mel said. She continued to knit and didn't look up.

"Why, yes, it is."

It went through my mind that only Ernestine would be so blind as not to see the insulated coffee carafe already sitting on the sideboard where Reva Louise was setting out her cake. But that was the kind of unkind thought Granny would have tut-tutted over.

"Is Sally Ann watching the café?" I asked.

Mel nodded.

"Does she knit?"

"No, ma'am. The knitting must come from one of those wandering paternal genes," Mel said.

She was referring to the odd fact that while Reva Louise and she had the same father, Reva Louise and Sally Ann Jilton shared a mother and an upbringing down in Gatlinburg. Sally Ann and Mel were close in age, early forties, and maybe five years older than Reva Louise. Sally Ann, a thin, chain-smoking, hardworking woman, had been waitressing at Mel's for two or three years when she and Mel discovered their family connection one night over a couple of beers and a new recipe for sweet potato pie.

Looking at Reva Louise that afternoon, I had trouble seeing her resemblance to either of her half sisters, in looks or style. She wore a snug, dark green T-shirt and slacks in the same midrange brown as the hair she tucked behind her ears. As she studied the layout on the sideboard, her hands ran through a silent checklist, pointing to plates, napkins, forks, and cups. She picked up the insulated carafe, twisted the lid, and with her eyes closed inhaled a waft of coffee aroma.

"Mm, delicious," she said. "Do you think you brought enough, Mel?"

Mel probably didn't hear the question over the industrious clicking of her needles.

"Mel takes good care of us," I said. "And it was nice of you to bring extra cake, Reva Louise. We'll all enjoy taking some home."

"You're so welcome, Kath." She smiled and sat down in the faded chintz armchair next to mine. "Of course there might not be extra if some of our other members would bother to show up." She plopped her project bag on her lap and looked around at the group. "But this is fun, isn't it? How did we do this week?"

"We're still counting," Debbie said. "Ernestine, how many for you?"

Ernestine held up three daffodil yellow hats. "Three and—"

"Wonderful!" Reva Louise cut in. "That makes fourteen." Without giving Ernestine's hats a glance, she pulled the others toward her and spread them out across the table. "That means mine almost put us over twenty for the week."

"Wow, you made six?" I asked.

"Well, no, I said *almost*," Reva Louise corrected me, although she obviously enjoyed my astonishment. "I did make five, though, because I believe in pushing myself. There, now, aren't these fun?" She pulled five raspberry-colored pixie hats from her project bag and laid them on the table. "Isn't the color yummy? I got it at the most amazing yarn shop over in Knoxville."

The hats were pretty cute, but they would have been cuter if she'd bought the raspberry-colored yarn downstairs. Debbie blinked and looked at me but was too polite to say anything.

Ernestine was still holding her yellow hats, her mouth still open from being preempted. When Reva Louise sat back, she continued. "And Thea and Joe send their apologies for missing again this week, but they gave me their hats to bring along." She laid her three hats on the table and brought out two done in leaf green and three with red and white stripes. "There. That puts us four over the top for the week, and I can't think of a better reason to celebrate. Let's have that ginger cake and coffee. John, bring me a big piece, will you?"

"Cream, no sugar?" he asked.

"Exactly right."

Reva Louise rolled her eyes and shook her head, but joined the rest of us at the sideboard. When I looked back at Ernestine, she was peering closely at one of Reva Louise's pixie hats. She picked a small bit of something from the inside of the hat and tucked the bit into her skirt pocket. Then she ran her hand around the inside of each of the other pixie hats, put each one back on the table, smoothed her skirt over her knees, and sat back smiling myopically at a dress form in the corner. An odd but interesting old duck, Ernestine Odell.

Geneva chose that moment to drift into the room. She didn't often join us on Friday afternoons. According to her, the relentless clicking of knitting needles reminded her of so many mice clittering across the top of a coffin. "Clittering" was her word, and I wasn't sure it was one, but it was plenty descriptive.

"Why so quiet in here today?" she asked, and then, when I didn't answer, "What's the matter? Ghost got your tongue?" She never got tired of that joke. "Well, don't mind me. I'm just here because I thought I smelled gingerbread and, oh my, I *do* smell ginger. You can't imagine how that takes me back."

"It does?" I said, surprised.

"Yes, and I say bless the woman who made it. I don't ever want to hear a word against her." Geneva closed her eyes and followed her blissful nose to the sideboard, circling Reva Louise and making her shiver.

Mel looked at me over the rising steam of her coffee, spiked hair alert. "'It does'? What are you talking about, Red?"

"Did I say that out loud?" I tried to laugh it off, but my never having had a knack for the easy lie, the laugh ended in a "heh" and a shrug. "Sorry, Mel. That was part of a different conversation. I was sort of reliving it, I guess." Outright lies might not come easily, but shading the truth wasn't so tough.

"Different's okay, Red. Nothing wrong with different." Mel brushed past me and sat down with her coffee. No cake, I noticed. Too bad she couldn't give her share to Geneva.

I'd never seen Geneva react to a smell before. She was floating three feet above the sideboard on her back, looking like a sea otter gently rocking in the waves. No, come to think of it, except for the rocking she probably looked more like a body laid out on a slab. Strangely, that didn't put me off helping myself to a slice of the cake.

"I think I've died and gone back home to my mama's kitchen," Geneva murmured, "or maybe to heaven."

This was really very interesting. Had she ever mentioned smelling anything before? I couldn't remember. She'd said she couldn't feel anything but cold and she couldn't eat or taste. But smells—smells evoking memories—aroma therapy for ghosts? I wanted to ask her about her mother, her mother's kitchen. Could I use smells to jog her memory of who she was and finally get some answers?

"I know I'm charming," Geneva said, still floating on her back above the sideboard, "and you could stare at me all day, but don't. It's rude. Besides, your friends are wondering why you're so fascinated by that nail hole on the wall behind me. Go play with your knitty friends. Shoo." She closed her eyes and dismissed me with a minimal wave of her fingers.

I didn't want to lose the moment, but there wasn't anything I could do in a roomful of people, so I whispered, "Ginger, tell me later." If she heard, she ignored me.

As I turned around with my cake and coffee to rejoin the group, Reva Louise was saying something that sounded like "a little fey, I think." Her smile was friendly, though, and she raised a forkful of cake toward me in a toast, so maybe I misheard. None of the others looked suddenly abashed as though I'd caught them talking behind my back about odd, staring behavior. John and Mel were back to knitting. Debbie and Ernestine lingered over the crumbs on their plates. I sat down and Frank Sinatra started singing from someone's bag.

"That's your phone, Reva Louise," Mel said without looking up from her knitting.

"Is it?" Reva Louise looked unconvincingly startled.

"You're the only one I know with 'My Way' for a ring-tone," Mel said.

Reva Louise put her cake plate down and dug through her project bag for the phone. When she checked the display, a look of annoyance crossed her face. With a cluck of her tongue, she stood, dropping her project bag on the chair. She spoke one harsh "What?" into the phone before hunching her shoulders and walking over to the sideboard with it.

"How long do you think people have been cooking with ginger in this country?" I asked.

"That's an interesting question," John said.

"A nice diversion, too." Ernestine glanced toward Reva Louise. "She doesn't look happy with that phone call."

"Some people swear by ginger as a cure for mal de mer," John said.

"And I like it on my oatmeal in the morning," Ernestine said. "Oh no, that's cinnamon. I don't suppose it would hurt to try a little ginger, though, too. Kath, dear, you have your grandmother's knack for starting interesting conversations."

"Thank you, but I really would like to know how long we've been cooking with it in this country."

"George Washington's mother supposedly baked gingerbread for Lafayette," Mel said.

"Oh."

"That's it? 'Oh'? I throw out an interesting crumb of ginger trivia like that and you're disappointed?" For the first time that afternoon, Mel sounded and looked more like her usual self. "I don't know about you sometimes, Red." She shook her head, a spark of fun glinting in her eye.

"I'm very happy for Lafayette," I said. "Any idea when ginger became easily available around here? If it was commonly used or more of a luxury?"

"Nope," Mel said. "Your first question stretched my reserve of ginger trivia thin, and now it is depleted. But that's what the Internet and Thea were invented for."

"You're right. Thanks, Mel." Huh. Thea Green, one of our absent knitters, was also the town librarian. She lived to look things up. I picked up my knitting and then we heard Reva Louise raise her voice.

"I said not now!" Still with her back to us, she took the phone from her ear, obviously finished with her call. And from the rise and fall of her shoulders and the sound of repeated slow, deep breaths, she was just as obviously working to compose herself. When she turned around she appeared calm again.

"The problem with cell phones," she said, "is that there's no app for slamming a receiver in the other person's ear. We've lost that simple satisfaction. Isn't that a shame?" She laughed lightly and sat down.

"I think there is one," I said.

"If there is, it could not possibly be good enough," Reva Louise said.

Geneva, her floating ginger daze interrupted by Reva Louise's outburst, had followed her back to the group. She circled around behind Reva Louise, making mother hen noises. Reva Louise shivered and rubbed her hands to warm them.

"Troubles?" Mel asked Reva Louise.

"No."

"Oh," Mel said, and to my ears her "oh" sounded

more disappointed than mine had over the lengthy presence of ginger in the Americas.

"Poor Reva Louise," Geneva crooned, continuing to circle poor, unsuspecting Reva Louise. "Keeping a smile on her face. Putting her best foot forward. So strong after such a harsh exchange of words. So brave. She's so much better at lying than you are."

Chapter 4

"Do that thing you do," Geneva said, "and find out what our poor Reva Louise is lying about."

I touched my left ear. Geneva and I were experimenting with various cues for me to use when I couldn't openly communicate with her. Clearing my throat or coughing attracted too much attention, and touching my left ear was our latest effort. It was supposed to mean "shh," "no," or "not now." Unfortunately, Geneva preferred to think of the cue as a suggestion and sometimes chose to interpret it as "ask again."

"You know what I'm talking about," she said.

I touched my ear, then brushed it so she would notice and get the message. She paid no attention.

"Don't be a chicken."

I rubbed my ear and shook my head. I did know what she was talking about and I was surprised she *was* talking about it. It was something I'd never discussed with her or anyone else. In fact, this was the first time I knew, for certain, that she was aware of it. But it wasn't anything I "did." It was something that "happened" and, as far as I could tell, I had no control over it.

She was talking about a crazy sensation I felt sometimes when I touched someone's sleeve or shoulder—a sensation charged with that person's emotions. It had only been happening since Granny died. It was extremely weird. I didn't like it. And I couldn't explain it any more than I could explain the presence of Geneva in my life. Or a few other things. I was dealing with it by not thinking about it, more or less successfully. And by not touching people. And I wasn't about to oblige a pushy ghost by reaching over and patting Reva Louise on the back to see if I could tell what kind of personal stew she was in. Geneva was right; I was chicken.

"Go on. I dare you," she said.

I rubbed my ear so hard that I dumped most of the stitches from my needles, and what I communicated then, openly and more volubly than I should have, offended Geneva. From the askance looks they gave me, Debbie, Ernestine, and John were startled, too.

"My sensitive ears cannot bear that kind of language," Geneva said. "When you feel like apologizing, you will find me in my room." She huffed her way out, nose in the air. I rubbed my right ear, in case she looked back. The right ear was our sign for "yes" or "good." I hoped she would interpret it as "good riddance."

"Has that tricky stockinette got your panties in a twist?" Reva Louise asked. "Hand it over and I'll straighten it out for you."

I resisted the sudden urge to get up and tug on clothing and underwear. "I can get it, Reva Louise. Thanks, anyway. Sorry about the slip of the tongue, there."

"You should try knitting something more in line with your skill level," she said. "Stick to scarves or little washcloths. They'll be less frustrating for you."

"Kath is hardly a beginner." Debbie practically harrumphed in my defense. "She's rusty, as who wouldn't be after devoting her time and energy to her professional life?"

"Oh yes, I heard how you lost your job," Reva Louise said. "What a blow. I hope your professional ego wasn't too fragile, and I hope you don't think I meant to offend you about the knitting."

"It was nice of you to offer the advice."

"I'm always ready to help," Reva Louise said. "Mel can tell you." Mel might have told me, but she didn't get the chance. Before she could open her mouth, Reva Louise brought up the subject I'd been dreading. "And I am so excited about helping in our demonstration booth at Blue Plum Preserves next weekend. In fact . . ." She got up and went to one of the Welsh dressers where there was a salt-glaze crock holding a bouquet of hand spindles. She picked one with a blue-and-white ceramic whorl and held it up. "You don't mind if I borrow this, do you? I hear we're demonstrating spinning this year, so I guess I'd better learn."

"Ardis told you the demonstration schedule is full, though, didn't she? She's already got experts using wheels and spindles and working with wool, flax, silk, cotton. One woman even spins dog hair."

"My goodness," Reva Louise said. "How outlandish of her. But you can never have too many demonstrators at an event like this." She brought the spindle back to the coffee table and gave it a twirl. "Oh, fun! Look, it's like a top."

"Yes, we *can* have too many demonstrators," I said, making a grab for the spindle before it spun off onto the floor. "There's limited space and we want the visitors to have a good experience, so quality is better than quantity. Have you ever used a spindle before?"

"But it doesn't look so hard. They're like training wheels, right? You get the knack and then move on to a real spinning wheel. Ha-ha! Training wheels. Get it?"

Debbie, as skilled a spinner as Granny had been, kindly laughed at the joke she'd undoubtedly heard before. "But they aren't really, Reva Louise. Hand spindles are useful tools all on their own. Let me find a better one to start with." She took the ceramic spindle from me, put it back in the crock, and chose another. "Here. This is a good beginner's spindle." She handed Reva Louise a spindle with a plain, smooth, wooden whorl. "It's less likely to break if it drops."

"That's a great idea," I said. "And if you stop by tomorrow, Debbie can get you started. Then after you've had time to practice, we'll see about adding you to our file of demonstrators. For another event."

"That's so nice." Reva Louise put the spindle on the table without giving it a second look. "How are you set in the shop? I know TGIF helps out and I want to do my share, so why don't I help with sales inside?"

Be calm but firm, Ardis had said. The firmest answer would have been "No," but before being that blunt, I countered with a couple of my own questions. "Don't you have to be at the café, Reva Louise?" I turned to Mel. "Aren't you guys swamped during the festival?"

"I just love the way you call us all 'guys,' Kath," Reva Louise said. "It's so Yankee of you."

Calmly, firmly, I bit my tongue.

"But to answer your question," Reva Louise said, "I

keep baker's hours at the café. I'm in before the birds are up and home again by noon, which is how I'm able to accomplish all I do in any given day. I give one hundred percent to my job and have another hundred percent left over for my projects and my community."

"That's very industrious of you," Ernestine said.

"Industry pure and simple." Reva Louise nodded. "That's my secret, and that's why—"

"And that's why," Mel said, looking directly at Reva Louise, her needles still, "you should spend that afternoon enjoying the festival."

"*That* is a wonderful idea," I said. "There will be so much going on. Music on the courthouse steps, other demonstrations and exhibits to visit. It's almost too much to see in one afternoon, but it'll be a great way to relax and learn more about your new hometown at the same time. Really, it'll be a treat. Isn't that what we tell the tourists? 'Treat yourself to the sights and sounds of Blue Plum's yesteryear.'"

"Smells, too," John said, "if you visit the draft horses. I believe they'll be over by the post office."

"Aren't you just the sweetest things to suggest that," Reva Louise said. "But my husband and I already feel more like natives than tourists. In fact, Dan is playing one of the key roles in the festival's theater production." She touched her hair, laid her fingers against her cheek, and gave us a conspiratorial smile. "I'll let you in on a little secret, too. The director wanted me for one of the leads, but I felt obliged to turn him down because of my commitments."

"You know J. Scott Prescott, then?" I wondered what her take on him was.

"Wait a second," Mel said. "*Theater production*—you mean the pig skit? For heaven's sake, there aren't any lead roles in the pig skit except for the pig."

We didn't get to hear Reva Louise's reaction to Mel, because Frank Sinatra started singing "My Way" again.

"Mute it," Mel said. "Let it go to voice mail."

Reva Louise yanked her phone out of her project bag and checked the display. "For the ... I have to take it." She stood up fast, scraping her chair back several inches across the hardwood floor Granddaddy had sanded to a mellow finish. We all winced. She crossed to the back window overlooking the alleyway behind the shop and stood, her shoulders hunched, phone tight to her ear. She could have, should have, taken the phone out into the hall, but none of us were about to tap her on the shoulder and tell her so.

The rest of us exchanged glances and did our best to ignore the single, angry syllables Reva Louise spit into her end of the connection, but I was glad to see that Mel continued to watch and looked ready to go to her sister if she was needed. It was time to finish up for the afternoon, anyway, and we started packing up. The soft sounds of yarn and needles slipping back into bags weren't enough to cover the last part of the conversation, though.

"*No,*" Reva Louise said. "And, by the time I get home, it had *better* be." She obviously did need a phone-slamming app, and when she turned around after the call, she didn't seem the least embarrassed. "Honest to goodness," she said with a laugh, "they'd be helpless without us. Oh, is everyone leaving?"

The only further sour note came when Mel asked, as she had earlier, if there was trouble. At Reva Louise's snapped response, Mel shrugged, picked up the coffee carafe, and left. John and Debbie waved good-bye and followed Mel out.

"You go on, too, Reva Louise," I said. "Ardis will let you out the front door."

"Why don't I take the dishes down to the kitchen on my way?"

"Take the plates. I'll get the mugs. It's a lot to juggle otherwise."

"You're right and look how much I already have to carry. I'd better leave the plates. You don't mind, do you?"

It didn't matter whether I did or not. She wiggled her fingertips and took her cake carrier and cute project bag out the door and down the stairs. The only gingerbread she left behind was crumbs on the Welsh dresser. I was wiping them away when I noticed the salt-glaze crock of spindles. More specifically, the salt-glaze crock of spindles minus the spindle with the blue-and-white ceramic whorl. It definitely wasn't there, but that didn't keep me from looking again.

"It's gone. Reva Louise took it with her."

I jumped embarrassingly high for someone who should be getting used to unexpected voices and sudden appearances. It wasn't Geneva beside me, though. It was Ernestine.

"I'm sorry," she said. "I thought you knew I was still here. I made a quick stop in the restroom and came back to see if Reva Louise left any gingerbread. It's my shoes." She pointed at her feet as if that would help me follow the zig in her conversation. She was wearing thick-soled athletic shoes, black with turquoise and hot pink racing stripes. "My granddaughter went shopping with me. You should see the underwear she talked me into. But perhaps that's too much information. The shoes are very quiet, though, which I like." She peered at the Welsh dresser. "I was hoping to take a piece of the gingerbread home for a bedtime snack, but that's gone, too."

"She did say she brought extra, didn't she. Sorry, Ernestine. She must've forgotten."

"It was the phone call," Ernestine said. "That kind of rumpus could make extra gingerbread slip anyone's mind. It must have made her forget which spindle to borrow, too."

"It's nice of you to put that *spin* on it, Ernestine. Did you see her take it?"

"I saw both spindles when I peeked in her bag."

"Oh."

"Sneaky, I know. Me, I mean."

"And Reva Louise."

"I did have a reason," Ernestine said. She fished in her pocket and brought out a tiny scrap of paper. "I don't know that it matters, and I didn't want to say anything in front of the others or embarrass her."

"I saw you pick something out of one of her pixie hats. What is it?"

Ernestine put the scrap in my hand. It was a manufacturer's inspection sticker.

Chapter 5

The problem with meeting Joe Dunbar for supper at Mel's on Main was caused by the same reason we decided to eat there. It was the best place to grab a cup of coffee, linger over lasagna with wild mushrooms and fontina, descend into decadence over dark chocolate torte, or simply step inside and savor . . .

"You look nice," Joe said, holding the door for me.

"Really? Thanks." At the last minute I'd exchanged the flowered skirt and flats I'd worn at the shop for my favorite jeans and sandals. I'd kept on a green knit shell, throwing on a shirt with a watery pattern of blues and greens against the evening chill. And who knows, maybe to look a little like a trout for Joe the fisherman, too. "Wow, what are they cooking tonight?"

"Something with mustard?" Joe's nose was well educated. "Definitely barbecue."

But because Mel's was the best place to eat, it meant we'd probably run into people we knew. Not such a terrible problem, except we'd be taking a chance on people speculating about us as a couple while we were still speculating ourselves. Mel's food easily trumped worries about speculations, though, and we nodded and said hey on our way to the counter, placed our orders, then found a table halfway down the long room.

When our order came, Mel's food had to work a little harder to make up for another problem. It was Saturday night and the café was crowded, so we were also taking a chance on people, who didn't have enough imagination to speculate about us as a couple, pulling over a chair to join us. Joe's brother, Deputy Cole Dunbar, for example. Cole, whom I always thought of, but never called, Clod.

"Why can't Mel call a hamburger a hamburger?" Clod groused. He dumped himself in the chair next to Joe, so then I faced two Dunbars. "Who needs cute names for food? And what's that?" He pointed at Joe's plate.

"Wing Dings."

"Pfft. Speaking of which, how are you this evening, Ms. Rutledge?"

"Ecstatically enjoying my Bubble and Squeak." I wasn't eating Bubble and Squeak, but if he could assume it was okay to sit down without being asked, I could assume it was okay to be snarky without any other provocation. Joe really was eating the Wing Dings—boneless, skinless barbecued wings—and I was having Mel's Mustard-Roasted Vegetable Medley. And we'd been having a nice time, sharing cat stories starring Maggie, who lived with Joe and hated me, and Argyle, who loved everyone indiscriminately. Clod wasn't a cat person.

The Dunbar brothers were a study in similarities and contrasts. They were the same height. The same height as Ardis, in fact—call it six feet. Clod was muscled and mulish. Joe was lanky and more like an El Greco monk. Clod was older by a few years. Both had dark hair. Clod's was mostly gone. Joe's was wavy and stood up in tufts and

didn't look as though it was disappearing anytime soon.
Unlike Joe, who disappeared frequently. Mostly up mountain creeks with a fishing pole, either as a paid guide or
on his own. He told me he'd never met a stream he didn't
like and wouldn't try to fish even if it meant crawling
through a rhododendron hell to do it.

Joe was as dedicated to his fishing as Clod was to up-
holding the local law. And any mention of the law raised
one of the more interesting, and delicate, contrasts between the two brothers. Clod was a black-and-white,
straight-and-narrow, law-and-order guy. Joe was . . .

Joe was a man of several income streams, much like
J. Scott Prescott. Joe's streams weren't as high-end as
J. Scott's, and that might be why he had more of them.
He did odd jobs for us at the Weaver's Cat and taught
fly-tying classes in the shop. He was a decent watercolor-
ist and sold his paintings at another shop in town. He did
his fishing guide bit. And then there were other "jobs"
about which there were unanswered questions. To my
mind the questions were unanswered, anyway, because
although Joe gave a good *impression* of telling, the few
times I'd asked, his answers really weren't much more
than hedges. The whole thing was complicated. It was
even more complicated for law-and-order Clod, and I
got the feeling he'd erected a firm barrier against any
questions at all. As far as I could tell, they didn't spend a
lot of time together, but when they did they got along in
their own quiet way.

"You on duty for the festival next weekend?" Joe
asked.

"You know it. And we're calling in the auxiliaries. This

thing gets bigger every year. You fishing as far away as you can get?"

"Maybe." Joe took a sip of iced tea. "But I might stick around."

Clod made a noise that was either a laugh or skepticism.

"Here's your Humdinger Dangburger, Deputy." Sally Ann Jilton, the half sister Mel and Reva Louise shared from different directions, was the waitress that night. It wasn't any easier to see Reva Louise in Sally Ann than it was in Mel. Sally Ann had striking cheekbones and a long nose that Reva Louise missed out on. Sally Ann's hair was a darker brown, but just as thin as she was, and she kept it twisted in a tiny dancer's bun at the nape of her neck. She held on to Clod's plate and nodded toward the back of the café. "A booth's coming up empty. I can put this down there if you want."

"No," Clod said, "I'm good."

Sally Ann looked at me and shrugged. "I tried." She turned back to Clod. "Do you want your pie now or later?"

"When you get the time," said Clod.

Sally Ann shrugged again and left. Clod emptied half a bottle of ketchup onto his plate next to a mound of fries. He picked up a couple of the fries and swiped them through the red puddle.

"Tell me, Ms. Rutledge," he said, "did you ever come up with any more details about that mysterious antique double murder you were wondering about a while back?" He popped the fries in his mouth and started the swishing operation with two more. When I didn't answer he glanced up. The look on my face must have confused him. "What?"

I pointed at the fries halfway to his mouth.

"You're squeamish?" Ketchup dripped from one of the fries onto his khaki uniform shirt. "Well, if that isn't a Humdinger Dangburger."

Joe wet a napkin in Clod's water glass and handed it to him.

"Nancy Drew is squeamish," Clod said, mopping at the stain on his shirt. "So you're mothballing the trench coat? Hanging up the gumshoes?" He wadded the napkin and dropped it on the table. "I won't have to worry about you and your interfering nose again? Hallelujah. It's about dang time."

I smiled and excused myself to the ladies' room. Insufferable dolt.

On my way back to the table, I popped my head in the kitchen to wave at Mel. Mel, standing at the stove, lifted a ladle in return. Sally Ann was nearer the door.

"Sally Ann? Just to let you know, the ladies' room needs toilet paper." As I ducked back out, there was a clatter and an explosive oath from Mel. Afraid she'd burned herself, I darted back in and found her raging at Sally Ann.

"I told you twenty minutes ago to get the toilet paper!"

I'd never seen Mel acting so much like her rabid hair. She'd gone from zero to furious in less than a breath. The clatter I'd heard was the ladle hitting the wall in the corner.

"Mel?" I asked.

She closed her eyes and held her hands out, fingers splayed, fending advances.

"I'll just go get the toilet paper," Sally Ann said to no one in particular and seemingly unfazed. "Then I'm going out back for a smoke." She looked at me and tipped her head toward Mel. "She'll be all right in a minute or two. Not sure I can say the same for the wall. Or the ladle."

The evening was only made better by the arrival of the Spivey twins shortly after I sat back down.

"Cousin Kath," the first twin to the table said.

"Always a pleasure," said the second twin. "Your smiling face. It lights up our day."

My smile, I knew, couldn't be more than low-watt. I almost never thought it was a pleasure to see Shirley or Mercy. Calling me "cousin" was the only part of their greeting they got right, and that was only by the thinnest possible thread. They were Granny's cousin Alice's daughters, making them once removed from Granny and putting them at several more removes from me. They were brushing up against seventy and wore their hair in identical, dated perms with matching and unconvincing highlights. They'd married, and Shirley had even married a second time, but their identity as the Spivey twins transcended all.

"And Coleridge and Tennyson." The Spiveys nodded to the Dunbars. Just as Shirley and Mercy would always be Spiveys, to a certain generation, the brothers would always be known by their given names. Poor saps. Clod—Coleridge Blake Dunbar—could at least shorten his to something acceptable. Joe—Tennyson Yeats Dunbar—had had to fend for himself.

"We have something to show you," one or the other of the twins said to me. Without verbal clues, the only sure way to tell the two apart was to stand closer to them. Mercy wore cologne. Shirley didn't. The kindest thing I'd heard anyone say about Mercy's chosen scent was that she wore it sparingly. I think it was Shirley who said it. I inched my chair farther from them.

"It's a surprise for Angela," the other twin said, "for when she graduates from Northeast State next month. We had them made up." She passed me a business card.

Not one of us at the table had said a word to the Spiveys. Joe because he generally didn't. Clod because he was wolfing his food, the better to leave the table faster. That was the one good thing about the Spivey advent. Gulping a Humdinger Dangburger like that would probably give him indigestion. I beamed a full-watt smile at that thought.

"You haven't looked at Angie's card yet," the second twin said.

I hadn't planned to look at the card at all, but my wicked delight at Clod's imminent discomfort suckered me into it. Angie, Mercy's daughter, was only a couple of years older than I. I didn't really know her, though, and didn't remember meeting her during my childhood visits to Granny. From the few interactions we'd had since I moved to Blue Plum, and from seeing her around the edges of social functions, she seemed to be someone who struggled, someone who was never very happy. I looked at the card. Apparently she was studying for a real estate license.

"Good for Angie," I said. I meant it, too. I tried to hand the card back. I'd suddenly turned into a business card magnet.

"No, no. Keep it," said Shirley, or maybe it was Mercy.

"But strictly on the QT," the other said. "Don't talk to Angie yet."

That seemed a safe bet.

"We'll let you know when," the first twin said.

"You'll be the first to know. Count on it." That twin gave me a huge wink. Then they both smiled and left.

"What was that all about?" Joe asked.

I stared after the Spiveys, wondering the same thing. Granny had taught me to look for the good in people. *Step back and look at folks fairly,* she'd said. *Just remember, if you're able to catch sight of the good in them from that distance, it doesn't mean you have to step forward again and hug their necks.* Thinking of that now, I realized I had caught sight of something good about Shirley and Mercy. They were good at arousing suspicion.

Chapter 6

"She took the ceramic spindle. She's cheating in the knitting challenge. Now she's buying us lunch?" Ardis was either still disgusted or disgusted once again with Reva Louise. "Pffft."

Blue Plum Preserves was two days away and Ardis was showing the strain. For the umpteenth time, she was checking over what Granny had dubbed The Pattern—pages and pages of all the plans and procedures they'd devised, revised, and perfected for the Weaver's Cat demonstration booth over the ten-year history of the Preserves—and muttering darkly about ulterior motives and free lunches.

I was looking forward to the weekend with a little more bounce than Ardis. I'd never made it down to visit Granny for the festival, so this was my first Preserves experience. I was also more willing to cut Reva Louise some slack. She'd called before we opened and left me a message about the box lunches.

"Maybe it's her way of trying to make friends," I said. "Or amends. She said sandwiches, side salads, cookies, and drinks. That can't be so bad, can it?"

"Pffft." Ardis went back to poring over The Pattern, a task made more difficult by Argyle. He left the window, where he'd been dozing with Geneva, leapt up onto the counter, and folded himself into a neat loaf shape—on half the pages—for another of his many required afternoon naps. "You aren't a help, sir," Ardis told him. "But you're sweet."

"I think it would be a tremendous help to all of us if the cookies Reva Louise brings are ginger," Geneva called from the window.

"You mean gingersnaps from a Snapp?" I said. Oops.

"Sorry, hon," Ardis asked without looking up. "Did you say something?"

"I was just wondering what I can do to help you," I said.

"You can call me the Empress of Everything, hon. It'll help make all this fuss worthwhile." She added a note to one of the pages.

"New instructions, E.E.?"

She checked for customers within earshot, but it was a quiet afternoon. "A new name. This is our 'No Fly' list. Authorized eyes only. We don't want to hurt feelings, but we don't want to repeat mistakes, either."

"Like . . . ?"

"Like Charlotte Ledford demonstrating needle felting. *That* will never happen again."

Ardis shuddered and passed the page to me. I didn't know who Charlotte Ledford was, but from the way her name was underlined—twice—I was ready to back away from her if we were ever introduced. There were four names on the page. The first two were typed, part of the document from the get-go, no doubt. They were Shirley and Mercy Spivey. Ardis had just added the fourth name below Charlotte Ledford's—Reva Louise Snapp.

"And don't ask me if I think adding her name is kind or necessary. Kindness is moot because no one else will see this. And it *is* necessary because making that one small note will go a long way toward maintaining my sanity."

"Fine by me, but seeing the twins' names reminds me of something. Be right back." I dipped into the office behind the counter and found Angie's card in my purse. I went back and put the card on the counter.

"What's that?" Ardis asked.

"Hold on." I opened the drawer in the counter where I'd tossed J. Scott Prescott's cards. By then they'd slid under a notepad and assorted pens and rubber bands. "Look." I arranged Angie's card and Prescott's three on the counter in front of Ardis. "I bet I'm the first one on our block to have a whole collection of these babies."

"Have I got time for this?" she asked.

"Sure. It might give you a laugh, and you should always make time for that."

She didn't laugh at Angie, though, because she agreed with me that Angie's new career might be a good change for her. She also didn't laugh at Angie's card, because printing them up as a surprise for Angie's graduation was such an oddly touching gesture on the part of the twins. She came close to a snort when I told her about the twins' clandestine delivery of the card, but at the last minute she only lifted her eyebrows and shook her head. What finally got the laugh was telling her about my promise to J. Scott Prescott that I'd keep mum about the guns in the rewritten skit. But it wasn't a jolly laugh.

"For heaven's sake, everybody *in* the pig skit will know about the guns, and that means anyone *associated* with anyone in the skit knows."

"Did you know?"

"Knew it and forgot it. This idea of a refurbished skit isn't the big deal Mr. Prescott's making it out to be. What did he say when you told him no guns in the Cat?"

"He smiled and told me to call him J."

"Good Lord. Well, the whole weekend's a load of poppycock, anyway, but if people want to believe in the good old days, who am I to argue?"

"What's up, Ardis? You've been on edge for days. Don't you like Blue Plum Preserves?"

"It's a lot of extra bother and it doesn't really help our bottom line." She fussed with her papers, smoothing them, tapping their edges on the counter, and rearranging them again. Then she was still for a moment. "And it isn't as much fun without Ivy."

"Aw."

"Sorry, hon. Time out for a maudlin moment."

"It's okay, Ardis. You've let me have plenty of them, and being Empress of Everything probably doesn't make up for missing Granny."

"No, it doesn't. Empress of Everything is nothing at all because Ivy was High Empress of the Whole Enchilada and no one trumps that."

Argyle woke and looked at her. "Mrrph?"

"No, not even the Archduke of Napping on Important Papers," Ardis said. "But you have the right idea. Can you handle the shop this afternoon, Kath?"

"Sure. Are you—"

She stopped me with a hand. "I'll be fine. But I'm taking Argyle's advice. I'm going home for a nap. And if need be, I will take another one this evening and another one when I'm able to fit it in tomorrow. They will get my head straight so that I can participate in Blue Plum Preserves with the right attitude and a revived spirit."

"This spirit needs no reviving," Geneva hmphed from the window. "Thank you just the same."

Chapter 7

"What are you all doing here at this unghostly hour?" Geneva asked. It was six o'clock Saturday morning and we'd obviously "revived" her too early; she was grumpy. But she did have a point.

"Tell me, again, why we couldn't do this at seven thirty? Or eight?" I asked.

"It's in The Pattern," Ardis said, "and it sets the tone. If we have our tent up first, then we look calm and collected while the others are running around with last-minute emergencies."

"I feel intruded upon," Geneva sniffed.

Six wasn't Ardis' idea of an ideal hour, either, but her attitude-adjustment naps had produced results. She was present and pleasant and even had the two teenaged grandsons Ernestine had volunteered to help us smiling through their yawns. They followed her instructions, anchoring the canopy legs with sandbags in case of wind, unfolding and arranging tables, and carrying boxes and display fixtures. The morning had dawned clear and blue. We heard workmen banging the stage together at the courthouse and two teams of draft horses clopping past as we worked. When the Weaver's Cat demonstration tent was up, the grandsons yawned some more and agreed to keep an eye on it for us, and we were back in the Cat's kitchen before anyone else arrived in the parking lot.

"We made excellent time," Ardis said, "and I've just had a brainstorm." She set The Pattern on the kitchen table. "Here is *the* most brilliant editorial decision of the century." She took a pen, crossed out "Pattern," and rewrote it in large capitals—*PATTERN*. "There. Even if we make four dozen other revisions this year, you have to agree this change will be the best. See? Plan A to Terminate Errors and Random Nuttiness—PATTERN. Random and nuttiness being the key words; errors I'm not worried about. If one of the spinners doesn't show up, we'll be fine. If children run amok or drop lollipops in unspun wool, we can deal with it, and believe me we've dealt with worse. But the nuts like Reva Louise, who think sandwiches make up for shoplifting, are the ones we need to guard against. No matter how good those sandwiches are and even if they do come with chips, a side salad, cookies, and ice-cold sweet tea."

"Technically, it was more like long-term borrowing without returning," I said, "because the spindles weren't for sale. And the drink choices are bottled water or pop. Do I need to make you take another nap?"

"Pfffft."

"Your eloquence is exceeded only by your need for coffee, which is right here at number eight in The PATTERN, and I quote, 'Coffee or chocolate to be administered at regular intervals.'"

"Better yet, mix the two together," Ardis said, "and

I'll have a jumping-off point for getting into the swing of this, this . . ." She stopped, took a deep breath, let it out, and smiled. "This fun-filled family festival."

"There you go," I said. "You get a perfect ten for that jump and you did it without the caffeine."

"Ah, but," Ardis said, holding up a finger, "wait for it . . . wait for it . . . and cue the caffeine." She pointed at the back door.

The door opened and Joe Dunbar strolled in. I would have been surprised, but Ardis pointed at the schedule page of The PATTERN. There it was in twelve-point Times New Roman, *7:15 coffee and doughnuts, kitchen.* Joe's name was penciled in next to the entry. He set a pastry box from Mel's and a cardboard caddy holding three cups on the table.

"No fishing plans?" I asked, helping myself to one of my weaknesses, a chocolate-frosted chocolate cake doughnut.

"Fish wait patiently," Joe said. *"Caffeine habits not so much. Mocha with whipped cream?"*

Ardis latched onto the cup he handed her, closed her eyes, breathed in the steam, and sighed.

"Mrrph." Argyle sat in front of Joe and put a paw on his leg.

"No mocha or doughnuts for cats," I said. "You can have a little more kibble if you want. Come on." He followed me to his bowl in the corner near the fridge. Geneva materialized on top of the fridge, her knees drawn up to her chin.

"Cats wait patiently," she said, *"but not for cakes or kibbles. Argyle loves haikus."*

"Mrrrph." Ignoring the kibble I'd just tipped into his

bowl, Argyle leapt to the counter and then up to the fridge top. Geneva scooted over to make room. He gazed at her with happy cat eyes.

"'Loves' isn't really strong enough, of course," Geneva said. "He adores haikus, but 'adores' wasn't going to scan in my last line once I started it with his name. It's an interesting quirk in his personality, though, don't you think? Also interesting is how completely idiotic you look standing there catching flies with your jaw hanging open. I have told you about that before, you know, and I thought you'd broken yourself of the habit. Honestly, your inter-paranormal-personal skills are backsliding. You should work harder at that."

I closed my mouth and spun around. Ardis and Joe immediately started playing with crumbs on the table, looking suspiciously nonchalant.

"What did you say about fish and caffeine when you came in?" I asked Joe. "Were you speaking in haiku?"

"Haiku isn't a language," Ardis said. "It's a poetic form."

"I know—"

"It's highly structured," she said, "and it would be an extremely unusual person—not to say odd—who was able to compose them on the fly as part of a normal conversation. You come on back over here, hon, and drink your coffee. We have a long day ahead of us and no time for uncaffeinated poetic whims." She muttered something else that sounded like "or eccentricities."

I ignored the mutter. Geneva snickered.

Joe said, "See you later, alligator," and ambled on out the door.

Those were another couple of differences between

the Dunbar brothers. Joe was an ambler by nature, his long legs graceful and unhurried. The starch in Clod's spine made him look as though he was itching to bark orders even when he was out of uniform, slouched in a chair, raising a bottle of beer. And I doubted that he ever spouted a haiku, memorized or otherwise.

The PATTERN had Ardis and Debbie handling the tent and the spinning volunteers for the first half of the morning while I watched the shop. At noon, two TGIF members would arrive to take over the shop and I would join Ardis under the canopy for the middle part of the day, which, if Blue Plum Preserves tradition held, was far busier than the sales counter in the Cat. Debbie had farm obligations and never worked past noon on Saturdays.

"Ernestine and John are still on for noon?" I asked. They were good choices because they both felt at home in the Cat and had helped behind the counter before. In case of Errors or Random Nuttiness, we had our phones and we'd be right across the street. If nothing else, they could open a window and shout. Ardis nodded. "And lunch, courtesy of Reva Louise, at one."

I could hear the "we'll see" in her voice. "The skit's at two. Do you want to take a break then and watch?"

"Pffft."

By the time our first demonstrators arrived with their spinning wheels and whorls and baskets of fleece and roving, the rest of Blue Plum had awakened in Brigadoon-like splendor. Most of downtown was closed to motorized traffic. The sharp blasts of a steam whistle came from a "petting zoo" of antique farm machinery in the middle of

Main Street down past the library. There was a screech of feedback and then the amplified strains of an old-time fiddle tune from the stage at the courthouse. Other canopy tents had popped up in parking lots and shaded areas where people would be demonstrating, watching, or trying their hands at making butter, brooms, shingles, nails, and more.

I wondered how much of all that Geneva would recognize. Would the music catch her ear? Would the smell of chicken dinner on the church lawn tickle her nose the way Reva Louise's gingerbread did? Or the smell of fresh horse dung? I wanted to take her around with me later in the afternoon, if there was time. Maybe the sights and sounds of Blue Plum's yesteryear would jog tidbits of her memory loose.

Ten minutes before it was time to open, no public clamored on the porch to be let in or I might have unlocked the front door early. Instead I went to look for Geneva. I thought she'd be in the display window, her ghostly nose pressed to the glass as though she watched her own personal reality show on a superlarge-screen TV. But she wasn't and she wasn't curled around the ceiling fan, either. I ran quickly up the back stairs to my study in the attic. She and Argyle were there in the window seat, looking down on Main Street from that vantage.

"You can see our tent if you look out the windows on the west downstairs."

"I could see it from the window in the gable end if it weren't covered in dust and cobwebs."

"We never use that part of the attic."

"That's obvious."

She was in a snippy mood and said no when I asked if she'd like to go sightseeing with me later.

"It could be important, though," I said, playing up to her ego. "Granny thought it was important enough to make it step number twelve in her instructions." I'd brought The PATTERN with me and showed it to her. "See? It says 'Take time to admire (critique) other tents and booths.'"

"Your grandmother was an industrial spy? That must be where you get your sneaky ways."

"What sneaky ways?"

"I've heard the whispers downwind from you and I've been behind your back when people have talked there, too. 'More like Ivy all the time,' they say and 'Crazy Ivy's granddaughter.' Crazy like a fox, is what I think they must mean, if she was that sly."

I held my breath and held my tongue, with effort, then tried to speak calmly. "Walking around town is a friendly, community-minded thing to do. It also happens to be a good way to pick up ideas to try in our own tent next year, or to see what we should avoid, but there was nothing sly about my grandmother and there is nothing sneaky, at all, about walking around the festival and how do you even know about industrial spies?"

"You're getting that shrill tone in your voice that's so hard on my nerves. You should avoid that while you're out gadding. It will put people off, and that is the opposite of being friendly. See? I'm already full of good ideas. I don't need to slink around town looking for more."

"Fine. Don't. I just thought you might like to see the blacksmith or people making apple butter or any number of other things you haven't seen or thought about in—"

"A ghost's age? No. I will stay here and watch your folderol from the attic window with loyal Argyle at my side. Unless he decides he needs a nap. Then I might watch by myself or ignore everything altogether."

Why was I arguing with this contrary creature? Walking around town would be easier and much less stressful without her. Safer all the way around—oh—*safer*? "Geneva, are you afraid?"

"Are you insensitive and rude?" She flounced her back to me. "You shouldn't call your dear departed friends names."

"I didn't mean it like that. I really want to know. Is there something you're afraid of out there?"

She didn't look at me and didn't answer. She was using her fingers to count something to herself.

"Geneva, honey, what are you doing? What's the matter?"

"You go have your fun. Walk and drink pink lemonade. I cannot; I'm dead."

"Mrrrph," said Argyle

Geneva looked at him. "Inspired poetry? Why, thank you, Argyle. I thought so, too."

At quarter to twelve, John Berry opened the door and held it for Ernestine. Joe ambled up behind them and held the door for John. I was happy to see all three. Ernestine looked more like Mrs. Tiggy-Winkle, Beatrix Potter's washerwoman hedgehog, than a mole, though still gray. She wore a calf-length white apron over an ankle-length gray skirt, a lighter gray blouse, and a white mob cap. She enjoyed dressing for a part. John gave a nod to the day with a pair of suspenders and garters at his elbows. Joe had changed his shirt.

"What's that say?" I asked, nodding at the shirt.

He spread his arms so we could read it more easily. It was navy blue, bearing a picture of an old-time handbill that read *Dr. Carlin's Incredible Tent of Wonders*.

"Any relation to Aaron?" I asked. Aaron Carlin was a character I'd run into a time or two. Ardis referred to the whole family dismissively as the Smokin' Smoky Carlins, because of the delight a few of them took in setting fires in the national forest.

"It is Aaron. His tent's facing yours in the parking lot."

"Did Ardis know he was going to be there?"

"Not until this morning. She says she's glad for the chance to finally observe a Carlin up close. I told her she should step across and introduce herself, take a look around. You should, too, if you get the chance. The place is definitely full of wonders."

"He isn't really any kind of doctor, is he?"

"Snake oil, maybe, otherwise not so you'd notice. He's going to have a genuine six-foot-tall man eating chicken over there at four o'clock."

"Right. And are you planning to see that freak of nature?"

"He gave me this shirt. How could I refuse?"

And how could I argue with that? I turned to Ernestine and John. "Thanks for coming in, guys. It might be a madhouse out there, but it's been quiet in here. Lunch is coming at one. I've got my phone with me. Holler if you need anything."

"Aye-aye," Ernestine said.

Joe held the door for me. I stopped on the porch and looked up and down Main Street. In a colorful mix of historical periods, a man in buckskins rode a high-wheel bicycle down the street, a woman in crinolines with a parasol led a walking tour, and two members of the Chamber of Commerce, wearing bowler hats and sleeve garters, sold fresh-squeezed lemonade from one push-cart and coonskin caps and sunbonnets out of another. Children towing parents, parents pushing strollers, and couples and happy gaggles wandered everywhere. The sun was warm without being hot, and the air was filled with the smell of fried food, the strum of banjo and man-dolin, and the rhythmic clang of the blacksmith who'd set up outside the historical society. How could Ardis not love jolly old Blue Plum Preserves?

At the bottom of the front steps, I was knocked side-ways off my feet.

Chapter 8

Joe caught me. He held me for a moment, his arms around mine, his breath in my hair, and then he made sure I was steady and my feet were back under me. One of his hands stayed on my shoulder. I didn't mind.

"Ma'am, I am so sorry." A bearded face peered into mine. "Clearly my feet are running ahead of my brain and they about ran right over you. I do apologize. I hope you're okay."

"Is that a fake beard?" I asked. I couldn't help staring at it. Maybe I wasn't okay. I hadn't actually landed on the ground, though. Was only a little shaken up. In more ways than one. Joe's hand was still on my shoulder.

"Oh, hey, Dunbar," the man said. "Is this your little lady?"

That's when I knew I *was* okay. "Little lady" was a knee-jerk fighting phrase for me. I tried to stand taller and look this guy in the eye, wishing I could do a Geneva-like billow to show my irritation, and then I realized he really was wearing a fake beard. Part of it was peeling off along his jaw. In fact, he wore an entire getup—the pseudowhiskers, collarless shirt and suspenders, tall boots, and felt slouch hat—probably trying to look mid–

nineteenth century, right down to the rifle crooked in his arm.

"Are you in the pig skit?" I asked. Hoped. "That thing isn't loaded, is it?" Those questions and my first one about his beard were abrupt and veering toward rude. Maybe that was why he didn't answer them or even look at me after asking if I was okay.

"Dan, I'd like you to meet Kath Rutledge," Joe said. "Kath, Dan Snapp."

Well, snap my mouth shut. Reva Louise's husband. I don't know why I hadn't expected anything so present-able, but except for the fake beard Dan Snapp was good-looking in a tall, blond, floppy-haired kind of way. He looked fit and he looked . . . nervous? On edge? When Joe introduced us, he still didn't really look at me. He glanced at me, nodded, and then looked down the street toward the courthouse where he obviously longed to be going. Maybe he was late for a final pig skit practice or had opening day jitters. A phone tweedled in his pocket and he pulled it out.

"Yeah? Yeah, I know it," he said. "On my way." He dropped the phone back in the pocket. He tipped his hat to me. "Catch you later, Dunbar."

He looked toward the courthouse again, then turned and headed in the opposite direction. We watched him go. Me, Joe, and Joe's hand still on my shoulder. And an interesting, narrow-eyed look on Joe's face.

The parking lot looked like a miniature open-air market. Under a red canopy, next to our royal blue tent, was Sprinkle's Old-fashioned Woodworking. Opposite the Sprinkle's, under a white canopy, a Mennonite family from down in Greene County was selling a variety of home-made breads, pastas, snack foods, and bars of homemade soap. Our tent and Dr. Carlin's Tent of Wonders were twice the size of the other two. The length of ours, about twenty feet, ran along the street side of the parking lot.

Because the day was so fine, the woodworkers and the Mennonites had all four sides of their tents open. We had three sides open facing the other tents and a rear wall along the street. Ernestine's grandsons had hung a banner with our name on the street side. Only the Tent of Wonders was completely enclosed.

Sprinkle's Old-fashioned Woodworking was operated by a pair of teenagers in denim overalls who appeared to be brother and sister. The boy, lanky and all angles, sat astride a shaving horse using a drawknife to round and smooth what looked to be a five- or six-foot length of sapling. The girl, her long, thick hair pulled through the back of Chicago Cubs baseball hat, treadled something that looked like a three-way cross between a sewing machine, a spinning wheel, and a loom, that turned out to be a foot-powered lathe. Thin curls of wood spiraled to the ground from the tip of her sure and steady—and lethal-looking—tool.

"This here's hickory I'm working," the boy told their audience as he continued drawing his double-handled blade smoothly toward himself. "Cuts like butter. It'll be a pitchfork by the time I'm done with it."

"What's she making?" a child asked.

"A mess," the boy said, ducking as his sister winged wood shavings at him.

The Weaver's Cat might have set the tone by being first, but the Tent of Wonders was the most . . . There was no other word for it; it was *wonderful*. The four canvas sides were exactly that—canvases. Each side was painted with a different view of the same vibrant, verdant scene, making the tent a pocket of Upper East Tennessee deep woods transplanted into the parking lot—flora, fauna, trout stream, and all. A black bear peeked from behind a tree on the door flap. A pileated woodpecker perched in the branches over the bear's head. Mayapples carpeted the forest floor, rhododendrons bloomed . . .

"Jealous?" Joe asked as I stood gaping.

"Absolutely. He didn't buy it like this, did he?"

"Customized. You want to take a look inside?"

It was tempting. An old-time sandwich board with a more detailed version of the design on Joe's T-shirt stood out front. It claimed that Dr. Carlin was exhibiting *curiosities and relics from the six corners of the globe, including three identical snowflakes, vials containing famous waters of the world, and other sights the likes of which you never thought you'd pay to see*, including the six-foot-tall man eating chicken Joe mentioned. I could see it all for a dollar or attend one of Dr. Carlin's educational presentations at one o'clock, four o'clock, or seven for a mere two dollars.

"Have you seen his show?" I asked.

"Not to be missed," said Joe.

"Maybe I can catch the show at four or seven."

Debbie caught my eye then, with a wave. She'd obviously been waiting for me to show up, and I felt bad for dawdling.

"Ardis says check to see if the spinners need anything. Gotta run," she said, dashing past. "Thanks for taking over!"

"Business looks good," Joe said. "You can hardly see the spinners for their flocks."

He was right. The four spinners, demonstrating their wheels and spindles under the left half of the canopy, were each surrounded by a dozen or so rapt spectators. Two of the spinners were young women wearing long skirts and aprons, going with the Blue Plum Preserves look. They sat on modern plastic folding chairs, working the treadles of their traditional spinning wheels. One of them had mastered the art of talking while drafting from her cloud of natural brown fleece and she maintained a steady rate of treadling as she answered questions from the crowd. The other woman, working from roving dyed in wide bands of saturated red, orange, magenta, and canary yellow, was producing a beautiful variegated yarn no spinster a hundred and fifty years ago ever saw. A boy of about four, caught up in the rhythm of the treadles and the whirring purr of the wheels, rocked in time like a metronome.

The third spinner was a sixtyish woman in blue jeans and a tie-dyed T-shirt with a red bandanna worn as a kerchief to keep her graying hair back. She had a wheel to match her retro hippie look made with PVC pipe and a bicycle wheel. As Joe and I passed, a couple of men were telling her they'd been watching and they'd figured out how the whole thing worked.

"Would you like me to explain it for you?" one of them asked.

"I'd love to hear," she said, smiling and continuing to spin.

"That's Jackie," Joe told me. "She made that wheel. She teaches auto mechanics and physics at the high school, but she's too polite to let on. She can fix their chain saws or tractors. Probably their chain reactors, too, if they had them."

"Hello, you two," Ardis said when she finished ringing up a sale. She pointed at the fourth demonstrator who was mesmerizing a circle of children with a drop spindle. From her black hair to the black toes of her Doc Martens, she was Goth, but she gave a nod to the festival with a snowy white mob cap on her head. "Abby is selling more drop spindle kits for us than you can shake a spindle at. I don't know if it's her technique or her tattoos, but I'll be sorry when her shift is over. She really connects with the kids and it's those seven-, eight-, and nine-year-olds who pick it up so fast."

"We can't talk her into staying for the afternoon?"

"She's got work," Ardis said. "Serving meals at the nursing home. That's all right. Business will slack off during the pig skit, anyway. Are you sticking around, Joe? I can put you to work."

"Sorry. Need to see a man about a chicken," he said. He slipped past her and disappeared around the back wall of the tent.

"I haven't heard that excuse before," Ardis said. She watched him go, turned to shrug at me, and said something indelicate.

"Ardis!"

"Pardon my French and Indian War, but I'll bet my daddy's best teeth and the glass he keeps them in that here comes the reason Joe went."

I looked over my shoulder. Reva Louise.

"Well, hey, you two," she called, pushing her way past the people watching the spinners. "I just thought I'd stop by and see if you need anyone to take over one of the demonstrations."

"No," Ardis and I said as though we'd rehearsed for a synchronized response team.

Reva Louise didn't blink or miss a beat. "And I'm also here to take orders for those box lunches I promised. You get a choice of sandwich—beef and cheese or roasted veg; choice of side—spinach salad or slaw; Mel's triple chocolate chunk cookies for everyone; and choice of drink—soda or bottled water. How does that sound?"

"It sounds wonderful, Reva Louise," I said. "Thank you."

"The least I can do. Oh, but hey, you two. Why aren't you dressed in the spirit of Blue Plum Preserves? Come on, girls, you're letting our side down. I mean, look at me." She twirled to give us the full effect of her costume. "Doesn't my dress capture the flavor of the period? Wouldn't the customers appreciate seeing you joining in the fun? Next time, you ask me for help with a getup of your own."

It was true that neither Ardis nor I had gone "Preserves native." From my point of view, it was too bad Ardis hadn't, because I would have liked to see her six-foot frame in hoop skirts. But her usual mode of loose top and drawstring pants made more sense for the bending, stooping, and general workout of keeping shop. Especially keeping shop in a tent with a chance of variable weather.

My own reason for opting out was a classic wardrobe cliché. There we were, celebrating Blue Plum's history back to the late seventeen hundreds, with two solid centuries of fashions and accessories to choose from, and I didn't have a thing to wear. Sure, I could have tossed on a long skirt. I could have pinned a mob cap to my auburn waves. I could have tucked a bustle on my behind and made buckles for my shoes out of cardboard, covered them with foil, and stuck them on a pair of plastic clogs the way Reva Louise had. But my internal authenticity meter would have shorted and sent a jolt like lightning up and down my spine. I'd spent too many years working with historical textiles and clothing. I would want—I would *need*—to get anything I wore accurate down to the undergarments and all the hand stitching involved no matter how uncomfortable to wear or laborious to make. I looked down at my shirt and pants. No, polo shirt and khakis was the only way to go for me.

"Shall I go write down the lunch orders for you, Reva Louise?"

"No, ma'am. You take care of business here and I'll take care of everything else."

"In that case, I'll have the roasted vegetable sandwich, spinach salad, and a Coke. Ardis?"

"Beef, slaw, and Diet Dr Pepper."

"Got it," Reva Louise said. "And you'll have them in your hands within the hour."

"It really is nice of her to do this," I said to Ardis as we watched her taking orders from the spinners.

"Mm-hmm," Ardis said, that being her all-occasion word of doubt and dismissal. "We'll see."

We stayed busy after that. The drop spindle kits were the hot sellers, but our other starter projects, packaged to attract children and history buffs, sold well, too. Roving in a range of natural and dyed colors attracted serious spinners and crafters into felting, and we did a brisk trade in handspun yarn, crochet hooks, knitting needles, and other notions.

The faces of the people watching the spinners changed; the questions they asked followed a pattern: "What's your favorite fiber?" "Do you have to kill the sheep to get the wool?" "Does the dog smell like dog when it gets wet?" "Can I try?"

In addition to her PVC and bicycle wheel, Jackie had brought a traditional wheel for the brave or inspired souls who wanted to sit down and try their hand. Many of them didn't get beyond trying their *feet* because learning the rhythm of the treadles took more coordination than one might think. For those who "felt it" and then "got it"—managing to treadle, draft the fiber, feel the pull, and see a shapeless mass become yarn winding around the bobbin—the "aha moment" was a joy to witness.

"Future fiber fanatics," Ardis said, nodding with satisfaction. "Creating customers despite our lack of costume finery."

"It's nice to hear you feeling more kindly toward the Preserves, Ardis."

"There's still room for a disaster or two," she said, "but I'm willing to allow that so far we are doing an excellent day's work."

"Granny would've been happy?"

"She would."

"Good."

The Tent of Wonders was doing a steady business, too. Every time I had a chance to look, people were moving in and out. Then, as one o'clock approached, a line formed for the first show. But I hadn't caught sight of "Dr. Carlin."

"You haven't said anything about that." I nodded at the Tent of Wonders.

"Gaudy," Ardis said. She tried to make her face look sour so I would believe she meant it, probably because the tent belonged to a Carlin. She couldn't pull the sour look off, though, and admitted her defeat gracefully. "I love it."

"And here comes something else you'll love—Sally Ann with a boatload of box lunches. I guess Reva Louise came through."

"Amazing," Ardis said. "Astounding. Wonders never cease. I'd go on but I don't want to be rude in front of Sally Ann. And as much as I hate to agree with Reva Louise, a sandwich truly does taste better when someone else is buying, and I expect these will taste especially good, considering who that someone is."

Sally Ann, carrying two large canvas tote bags, threaded her way through the visitors. She wore a coonskin cap and hadn't taken her Mel's on Main apron off before leaving the café. One of the men made a joke about coon and possum burgers.

"Double yellow line special," Sally Ann said with a smile. "Mm-mm. Always fresh; always tasty." When she reached us, she hoisted the totes onto the table we were using for a sales counter. "Eight deluxe box lunches with eight bottles of water. That'll be sixty-eight dollars even."

"Um," I said, "all water and no soda?"

"Water comes with the plain box lunches," Sally Ann said. "Anything else is extra."

"And there's a 'ha-ha' tacked onto the price tag, right?"

"'Ha-ha' what?" Sally Ann asked. "Mel said to let you know she cut you a deal. I guess that's kind of a 'ha-ha' because that's something that doesn't happen too often."

Ardis looked at Sally Ann, apparently at a loss for words, something else that didn't happen too often. But when she turned to me, I swear I saw thin jets of smoke streaming from her ears.

"Ardis," I said, "dear Ardis." I took her by the elbow, pulling her toward the end of the table and then giving her a push toward the demonstrators. "Go see if the spinners need . . . something, anything, doesn't matter what. I'll take care of any errors or nuttiness occurring just now." I gave her a bigger push, which didn't really propel her but got her moving.

She stopped a few steps away and said over her shoulder, "Not happy, not happy at all," then stalked off.

"Problem?" Sally Ann asked. "Because it's a busy day, you know? I have to get back and Mel sure won't be happy if these come back with me. Sixty-eight even."

"Reva Louise didn't pay?"

"Now, that really is a 'ha-ha,'" Sally Ann said.

Ardis was talking to some of the visitors but looking toward us. I smiled and waved so she'd see that the situation was all good and wonderful. If Reva Louise had been there, I might have "good-and-wonderfulled" her upside her head.

"Will you take a check?" I asked Sally Ann.

"Cash is good," she said, glancing at the cash drawer on the table.

"I'd rather not deplete it to that extent."

"Check is good, too."

"Then if you don't mind a detour to the Cat, I'll write you one."

"Then quick would be good, too," she said, starting to unpack the totes.

All the boxes were marked HAM and all the bottles were, indeed, water. I didn't bother asking what happened to the beef and cheese or roasted veg options. Grabbing a couple of the boxes and bottles for Ernestine and John, I mouthed, "Be right back" to Ardis, and led Sally Ann around the back wall of the tent, across the street, and around the corner to the Weaver's Cat. Mel's was down on the next corner, so at least the detour wasn't taking Sally Ann in the wrong direction.

Up the steps and through the door and even though she was in a rush, Sally Ann stopped with a soft "Dang."

"Is that for all the colors?" I never got tired of people's reactions when they were hit by the rainbow blast of our yarns and embroidery threads.

"Uh-uh," Sally Ann said, drawing her shoulders up. "It's for all the warm fuzzy you've got going on here. It reminds me of the dusty, old lady crochet I used to see back home. Gives me the willies. You got that check? I've been gone way too long, and this place has set me to itching. Sorry. Nothing against you or the shop."

I added a generous tip to the check to make up for the delay and the itch.

"Poor thing," Ernestine said, tut-tutting as she opened her lunch. "Mel must be right about the fiber gene coming from her father. Oh, and what a nice surprise—not roast beef at all. I must have misheard Reva Louise when she asked what we'd like."

"Yeah, sorry about the mix-up. I hope ham is okay?"

"Of course it is," John said. "Kath, about that check you just gave Sally Ann. I'm being nosy, I know, but it wasn't for the sandwiches, was it?"

"Yeah, but don't worry about it. It's just part of the mix-up. You guys enjoy your lunch. Is everything going all right in here? Do you need anything?"

"John, didn't we already pay Reva Louise?" Ernestine asked.

"Out of the till," John said.

"I thought so," Ernestine said. "She told us you'd authorized the payment, so you might want to check with Mel about that. I'm sure she'll straighten it out. Otherwise, business is steady but nothing we can't handle."

"It looks like most of the fun is going on out there," John said, "so you'd better run along and get back to it. We'll be fine."

"Fine and happy to help," Ernestine said.

"Jackie's vegetarian," Ardis announced when I got back to the tent. "I apologized for the ham sandwich and gave her my slaw. And yours."

"Slaw?"

"Not a spinach leaf in sight."

I waited until she'd finished her sandwich and half of Jackie's, then handed her my cookie and told her about the money from the till. I regretted giving up one of Mel's double chocolate chunk masterpieces, but I knew it was for a good cause. Ardis said nothing. She ate the cookie and calmly went back to selling spindle kits and yarn without acknowledging she'd heard a single word about the double payment for the "free" lunch.

As time for "The Blue Plum Piglet War" approached,

the crowds around the tents dispersed. A souvenir festival tabloid, put out by our weekly newspaper, featured a map with piglet icons showing the main areas of action and we assumed spectators were moving to those places. As J. Scott Prescott had said, they were mostly around the courthouse, but there were also piglets on Main Street, one near the gazebo in the park, and one very near the Weaver's Cat on Depot—the street between the parking lot and the shop. I hadn't noticed that and wondered if I should be suspicious. That was uncharitable, I decided, and instead thought wistfully of Mel's double chocolate chunk cookies and how virtuous and charitable I'd been in contributing mine to Ardis' mental health. She was on the same wavelength.

"Bless you, hon. I owe you a cookie and I'll make it two and call it a wise investment. The whole thing was my fault for trusting her and I promise that I will wring her neck the next time I see her and when I buy the cookies I will tell Mel she's looking for trouble if she doesn't rid herself of that, that b . . ."

"Boll weevil?"

"Close enough."

"Take deep breaths, Ardis, and let the aggravation of that lunch and Reva Louise slide on past. You know that's what Granny would say."

"Lord, I miss that woman. If she were here today we wouldn't have a weevil problem. Shall I tell you something I miss about Ivy? What made her the High Empress of the Whole Enchilada for All Time and not just for Blue Plum Preserves? She knew how to get rid of people. Permanently."

"Um. Do I want to hear this? What are you talking about?"

"Not that kind of permanent, hon. She would simply have found a way to talk her out of ever stepping foot in the shop again. I didn't see it happen more than two or three times, because we don't generally have that kind of trouble. And I don't know what she said, except that she was gentle and calm. And she gave each of the wretches a parting gift of wool. That seemed to cement the deal—without an angry word spoken. Hon, you've gone pale. I didn't mean to upset you talking about Ivy." She patted my back and fanned my face with a Blue Plum Preserves tabloid.

"Woo—woo—" I cleared my throat. "Sorry. Wool she dyed?"

"I suppose it was. Yes, now I think about it, of course it was. That was so like her: offering a generous, personal gift to slide on past a difficult situation. I tell you, it was a secret talent she had and I wish I knew what it was."

I was pretty sure I did know and wished I didn't. But that uncomfortable inkling didn't get a chance to slink beyond the edge of my mind—the next second it fled in holy terror as gunfire erupted in downtown Blue Plum.

"Pig skit," Ardis said without blinking an eye.

Of course. It was straight-up two o'clock and time for the war.

Chapter 9

And then the whooping and hollering started.

"That must be the famous Blue Plum Piglet War yell you told me about," Ardis said, continuing to be calm and unaffected by the increasing level of noise over by the courthouse. She saw me jump with each new volley of gunfire and said, "I'm used to it, hon. Daddy loves his Westerns, but he watches with the sound cranked up."

I wondered if I should introduce Geneva to Ardis' daddy. They were two peas in a pod with their taste in television shows. Thinking of Geneva made me wonder how she was faring with the ruckus. Was she frightened? Excited? Oblivious? I stepped around the back of the tent to look for her in any of the windows on that side of the building and stopped, surprised by the transformation of our humble block of Depot Street.

People ranged up and down the street, mostly in whatever shade they could find. They lined the front porch of Jenkins' Flowers and an insurance office to the left of the Cat, with children sitting on the porch railing.

There were people in lawn chairs on both sides of the street and people crowding the end of the Cat's porch, with more children balancing on our railing.

"Piglet War!" a child next to me shouted, and children up and down the street took up the chant, "Pig-let! Pig-let! Pig-let!"

I pulled my cell phone from my pocket and called the shop. Ernestine answered.

"It sounds very exciting out there," she said.

"How are you and John doing? There are an awful lot of people on this end of the porch."

"Isn't it amazing they all fit? There's almost no one inside. I'll send John out to watch and tell me what's happening. But you'll have to let me go now, dear. I think someone came in the back door."

I slid my phone back into my pocket and looked up at the Cat's windows. I wasn't sure what I expected to see. A flicker? The silhouette of a ginger cat with his nose pressed to a pane hoping for a glimpse of a pig? There was nothing, not even in the deplorably cobwebby window at the gable end of the attic. But when I looked up and down the street, again, I did see something—Reva Louise. She turned the corner from Main Street, scanning the crowd, her phone pressed to her ear.

With the whoops and hollers of battle in my ears, I was surprised I didn't suddenly feel a surge of bloodlust and launch myself at her. But with all the happy families around, it wasn't really the time or place. And I wasn't much for public confrontations. Often, anyway. But Ardis might be. I ducked back into the tent.

"It's getting lively out there," Ardis said. "Anything worth seeing?"

"No!" I couldn't let her go out there and see Reva Louise. She might kill her and call it an act of Piglet War.

"Hon, you need to chill," Ardis said.

"I know. Sorry. The kids are excited. No pigs yet. Everything's fine. Ernestine and John are fine. Aw, and look at that." I grabbed her arm and turned her toward the front of the tent. "Jackie's got that little girl spinning on the wheel. She looks like a natural. Isn't that adorable? And there's Aaron, the Smokin' Smoky Dr. Carlin himself. First time I've seen him all day."

Ardis knew misdirection when it grabbed her sleeve and tried to hold her in place. I let go her sleeve, tried to brush away the wrinkles my fist had crushed into it, and smiled my most disarming smile.

"The action's over there on the other side of the courthouse," I said, flicking a hand in that direction.

"I'd say the action's getting closer by the minute," Ardis said, crossing her arms. She ignored Aaron Carlin and the adorable, precocious child using Jackie's spinning wheel. Instead she looked at me, one eye narrowed.

I countered with a pooh-poohing face. "Probably won't amount to much—*Yeeow!*"

Gunshots cracked through whatever vapid remark I'd been about to make—but from where? Right behind us? I'd nearly leapt into Ardis' arms. She wouldn't have caught me, though, because she'd jumped, too. Those shots were followed by others, not nearly so close, and a series of Blue Plum Piglet War yells coming around the corner from Main Street into Depot.

"Did they even think about heart conditions?" Ardis asked, obviously annoyed at her own reaction. "Or hearing loss? Why are they making an action movie out of our simple pig skit, anyway?"

"Because watching pigs wander back and forth across a disputed boundary line wouldn't be very exciting?"

"And what in heaven's name is *that*?"

"That" was a piglet. The snout of one, anyway, trying to push its way under the back of the tent.

"Behold yon trespassing piglet," an amplified voice said to laughter from the audience.

"From action movie to bad Shakespeare," Ardis said with a disgusted tsk.

The trespassing piglet obviously wasn't impressed by either genre and didn't want to continue in its starring role. It squealed and tried harder to get into the tent.

"The poor baby is terrified," Ardis said. "I have half a mind to call the SPCA. I wonder if we should help it escape and hide it." She bent down. To get a closer look? Grab its trotters and pull? The little pink thing blinked at her. It had beautiful pale eyelashes. "Help me here, Kath. You'll have to hold it firmly and soothe it once you get hold of it."

"Me?"

"Your bacon or your life, sir!" the actor's amplified voice rang out again.

Before I could do anything, the piglet was retracted with a squeal. More shots were fired and someone farther down the street yelled, "I am hit! I die! And now my bacon is cooked."

"And yet he runs!" the first voice cried. "After him!"

More laughter and more shots, but farther down the

street, and the action moved on to the next staging area. From the sound of it, most of the audience followed.

"Well." Ardis straightened. "If we'd taken the pig, it would have been a more authentic reenactment of the original wandering livestock feud than what's going on out there, but I expect it's just as well we didn't. I can only imagine what Cole Dunbar would say if he had to arrest you for stealing and harboring a pig."

"Me?"

Then two more shots cracked—as close as the first ones that had made us jump—making us jump again. Even the tent seemed to shudder.

"Now what?" Ardis said. "That's very poor staging to move the audience in one direction and then have the action spring up again behind them. I don't know about your Mr. Prescott, Kath. Very amateurish. And what on earth has happened to the back of the tent?"

Toward the left, down toward the bottom, it had a bulge. Maybe the tent actually had shuddered because something had fallen against it. Then we heard voices on the other side of the canvas.

"All that fake blood's kind of a waste," the first voice said. "I mean, some is good and I get that she's supposed to be dead, but after a point it's just eew, you know? She gets the prize for realism, though."

"Not with those shoes," a second voice said. "They take me right out of the moment."

"Yeah, well, you could see some of the others breathing plain as day. At least this one knows how to hold a pose."

"In this heat, too. Hey, you know what? I feel like ice cream."

The voices moved off and Ardis and I looked at each other. Then we were in one of those dreams, moving against a current of water, taking forever to get around the back of the tent, knowing we were going to finally get there and that finding something terrible was inevitable.

It was the worst kind of terrible. It was Reva Louise.

Chapter 10

As soon as emergency personnel and police arrived, our section of Depot Street was effectively shut down. That included the four tents in the parking lot and at the florist's. Sheriff's deputies stood at each end of the block directing tourists and gapers in other directions.

The skit was over by then and more deputies were sent to track down the actors and determine who'd fired the fatal shot. Blue Plum Preserves continued all around our small, stalled part of it. We heard strains of a jaunty old-time fiddle tune coming from the stage on the courthouse steps to prove it, but it was going to be a while before our spinners had an audience again. Ardis and I apologized to them. The two younger women in long skirts had followed us when we ran around the end of the tent and had seen Reva Louise. They were shaken and packed up to go home. Jackie picked up her PVC wheel and basket of wool and went to find shade where she could spin and hear the music better.

"Spinning is meditation," she said. "It's what I need right now to set my rhythm right again. I'll check back later to see if you're able to reopen. That poor woman. Bless her heart."

The teenaged woodworkers had stood at the edge of the parking lot and watched until the Mennonite woman came and led them to the chairs in our tent. She and her husband hadn't left their booth earlier, but he came over now and they asked us what happened. Ardis told them the little we knew—that Reva Louise had been standing behind the tent; she'd apparently been hit by live fire; it might be a while, but the deputies told us the street would reopen. The Tent of Wonders was quiet; we saw no sign of Aaron Carlin.

The teenagers called their parents, taking turns assuring first their mother, then their father that they were all right. The parents were operating a funnel cake booth on the other side of the courthouse, and it was decided the kids would stay with the tools in the red tent, either until the street reopened or until someone could come help them pack up. They looked uneasily toward the back of our tent, then returned to their own and went back to work. I hoped the rhythms of the drawknife and lathe were what they needed, too.

The Mennonites also stayed. They'd invested time, money, and travel to be there.

I called Ernestine and John. If I'd realized they didn't know what had happened, I would have gone across the street to tell them in person. But the sheriff's deputies and ambulance had arrived with a minimum of whooping sirens, avoiding the pedestrians on Main Street by coming up Depot from the other end.

"We knew something was going on," Ernestine said, "but we thought it might be a fall or . . . oh my goodness."

"Ernestine?"

She'd handed the phone to John. "She's taking a moment, but she'll be fine," he said, easing my panic. "What can we do?"

"Are you all right there in the shop? It seems almost indecent to hope they'll reopen the street soon."

"No, it's not," he said. "And we'll both be fine. Business is quiet, but we'll find things to do. Now, would you like to hear an old man's cynicism? It was a terrible accident, an avoidable tragedy, but the street won't stay blocked for long because neither the mayor and his board of aldermen nor the Chamber of Commerce would hear of it. Nor the Blue Plum Preserves steering committee. Don't worry about us. We'll see you later."

I knew John was right and I was thankful he and Ernestine were still happy to keep shop for us. Ardis and I had decided that at least one of us should stay with the tent. Even if spectators were being kept away, the authorities hadn't drawn an impermeable cordon around the area and we didn't want to leave our merchandise unattended. One of us could have gone to relieve Ernestine and John, but we didn't really want to leave each other unattended, either.

We sat on a couple of the plastic chairs we'd put out front for visitors. Neither of us wanted to be near the back wall of the tent. We were glad it was there, glad we couldn't see the EMTs and deputies performing their duties. It was awful enough hearing them. Ardis looked slightly wilted. I felt the same and realized how good it was to just sit and hold myself together . . . except that wasn't how Granny would have met trouble, so I sat up straighter and squared my shoulders.

Ardis misinterpreted my corrected posture. "You're absolutely right, hon. Hats."

"Sorry?"

"We can't sit here doing nothing. We'll get ahead on the hats." She raided our inventory for baby yarn and needles, coming back with two skeins in a weird color that was more brown than yellow but wasn't really either one. "No one will buy this stuff anyway," she said. "We'll make hats and I'll put ears on them and people will automatically think they're cute."

I sighed and cast on sixty stitches, which I could have done in my sleep by then, and stared across the parking lot at the Tent of Wonders. The very quiet Tent of Wonders. We hadn't seen Aaron Carlin since the shooting and had only caught a glimpse of him earlier. I wondered if I should step away from my ugly hat and go across to see if the doctor was even in. I glanced at Ardis. Talk about fast and furious knitting.

"Are you okay, Ardis?"

She stopped knitting and stabbed her needles through the poor, innocent, ugly skein of yarn. "*Who* mistakes live ammunition for blanks? And what kind of *idiots* did they have running around out there? And which idiot did it? For pity's sake, she wasn't even part of the play, which means those idiots were being even *more* incompetent and irresponsible because they weren't even aiming at another idiot. Hon, I want you to know that I admire your ability to keep your cool and maintain focus at a time like this. I'm feeling just that bit scattered, although I will try not to let the authorities notice my distraction. Of course it's easier for you."

"What is?"

"Murder."

I tried not to let her notice my groaning.

"Although I suppose, technically, it's manslaughter. Tell you what, if you see Coleridge and it looks like he has a free minute, why don't you ask him about that? You're used to discussing these things with him. But here's something else I've just thought of, hon, and it's horrible." She put her hand on my arm. "In my eyes, Reva Louise was a pestilence. I spoke of her with unkind words many times."

"With words like 'pestilence.'"

"Exactly, hon. 'Pestilence' and many others just as descriptive and every bit as unpleasant. And I spoke of wanting to wring that woman's neck. And I meant it and if she were still alive I would gladly follow through and do it. But think about this. There are at least three people who may actually mourn her passing. There's her husband—"

"Dan," I said. "I met him today. I don't think I liked him. Somehow that's kind of sad."

"We didn't like her, either, hon, so I'd say that's perfectly natural. But we need to think of Mel and Sally Ann. We do like them and they are good people and her sisters. This tragedy cannot help affecting them deeply."

"Oh gosh, I wonder how they're taking it."

"Hard, hon. I'm sure they're taking it hard. But here's the horrible thing I've just thought of. I don't find myself mourning Reva Louise, not even in that abrupt, regretful reversal of opinion that people experience at times like this when they suddenly stop speaking ill. No. I disliked the woman. With a passion. And I admit that. But, Kath—the horrible part—I *do* find myself worrying that Reva's passing might disrupt business at the café."

"She didn't like being called Reva."

"Whatever. But can you picture me in the morning without my coffee and bagel or a chocolate doughnut? I am a horrible, selfish person."

Ardis was babbling, but it seemed to be doing her some good. So much so that when Deputy Clod Dunbar came to speak to us, she asked him her question about manslaughter versus murder herself. He pushed his way around the back of the tent, not that anything actually needed pushing to get to us. But Clod had a way of making everything he did while on duty look as though it took a special, official effort. Ardis posed her manslaughter-murder question and he barked in return.

"What information haven't you turned over to us?" His mirrored sunglasses flashed as he looked from me to Ardis and back to me.

I put my poor ugly little hat in my lap and turned empty hands palms up, not bothering to waste my breath on the word "none."

He, in turn, didn't bother to waste *his* breath on the words "a likely story." He used condescending eyebrows and a prissy twist of his lips to communicate them just as clearly.

Ardis, her knitting needles grasped at an aggressive angle, stood up, erasing any advantage Clod had by standing over us. He was six foot and mulish, but she was also six foot and she'd been both his third- and fourth-grade teacher, back before she found her true calling at the

Weaver's Cat. *And, hon,* she'd told me once, *put me in those skirts and jackets we all wore back then, with the heels and the hose, and I inspired hero worship in little girls, absolute awe in studious boys, and the rascals and rabble-rousers sat quaking in justifiable fear.*

Clod took a step back, tucking his chin into his starched collar, and giving me an idea which type of boy he'd been.

"We have two more questions for you, Coleridge," Ardis said. "But first, you take off those sunglasses when you're speaking to a lady." She waited. He removed them. "Thank you. Now, we want to know if you have found the irresponsible man responsible for this tragedy and have you impounded his gun or whatever it is you do with weapons used for random acts of mindlessness? It seems to me you should legally be allowed to take a sledgehammer to the thing and then wrap the remains around the guilty so-and-so's idiotic neck. And when will you be reopening the street? We realize you all are doing your jobs well and thoroughly and we appreciate your competent professionalism. But, sad though we are for the reason you've had to block access for so long, we do have a business to run and I am sure the mayor and board of aldermen will be anxious for the festival to continue at full tilt."

If I had asked those long-winded questions, no doubt Clod would have interrupted. But he listened to Ardis without even looking as though he had to keep himself in check, looking . . . uncomfortable? Evasive?

"What?" I stood up, too. My height didn't prove anything, but standing up made me harder to ignore.

"There's something going on, isn't there? What information haven't *you* given *us*?"

Clod opened his mouth, shut it again, and pressed his lips together. He was a poker player, and from what I'd heard he was a good one, so he probably didn't have many tells. But that thing with the lips was something I'd seen him do a few times before. Always before he delivered bad news.

Ardis knew that mannerism, too, and possibly in a moment of panic, she grabbed him by the shoulders. "Oh, please don't tell us she was alive and we could have saved her."

Clod, almost certainly in a moment of panic, withstood her anguished plea, ramrod posture intact, and answered her in surprisingly kind tones. "No, Ms. Buchanan, there wasn't anything you could have done for her."

"Thank you for that, Coleridge." They shared a moment of silence, his somewhat wide-eyed because she still gripped his shoulders. Then she dropped her hands to her hips. "Now, answer my questions."

"Ms. Buchanan, Ms. Rutledge, on behalf of the sheriff's department I'd like to thank you for putting your civic duty ahead of personal concerns this afternoon as pertains to the disruption of your business during our investigation."

"It was the least we could do," Ardis said.

I decided not to jump in and ask for a clarification. It sounded as though he might think we'd closed the shop as well as the demonstration tent. But if Clod didn't know that Ernestine and John were over there minding the store even as we spoke, then how could it hurt to let that bit of information slide?

"Is there something you'd like to say, Ms. Rutledge?"

I shook my head, reminding myself never to play poker with him. My face tended to be nothing but tell.

"I'm going to make this official, then," he said, "so there are no misunderstandings. Ms. Rutledge, Ms. Buchanan, I regret to inform you that your business will remain closed while our investigation continues and until such time as the investigation concludes. During our investigation we will require access to the premises. We ask that you cooperate in this matter, but if you choose not to cooperate we will obtain a search warrant and gain access in that manner. If you willingly hand me the key to your building, I will give you a receipt. I will also inform you when you may reenter the premises. We will try to cause as little disruption as possible so that you may return to a normal business routine as soon as possible. However, I can make no guarantees. We will also need to know who was in your building this afternoon, working, browsing, et cetera, to the best of your knowledge and recollection or according to whatever sales transactions exist. Ms. Rutledge, it's obvious that you now *do* have something to say and I'm sure I will be thrilled to hear it."

Sarcastic oaf. But he was right. Two things had sprung immediately to mind. First and foremost was *What?* Second was *Oops*, because if they assumed we *had* closed and locked our doors when they blocked access to the street, then we might have a problem. But I was happy to put off worrying about how big that problem might be by going with that first and foremost thought. Before I vocalized it, though, my phone rang. Someone calling from the supposedly closed Weaver's Cat.

"Kath, dear, John's been quite industrious washing windows. Now he wants to know if you'd like to keep the one in the upstairs powder room open a crack overnight, or should he close it so you don't forget it later?"

I didn't remember opening it, but if we were going to be closed, the window might as well be, too. "Sure, go ahead and shut it," I said.

"Righty-o, dear. Consider it done."

And that put me right back at *Oops*.

Chapter 11

Oops was not an emotion I hid well.

"Ms. Rutledge," Clod prompted with a growl low in his throat, "*what—*"

In for an oops, in for a pound. I cut him off with my own growl. "Deputy Dunbar, *what* happened? *Why* are you closing our business? Are you saying we, or our business, had something to do with this? Are we a *crime scene*?" My growl turned into more of a yip at the end, but Ardis added a snarl to good effect.

"*This minute*, Coleridge," she said. "Tell us."

Clod sighed and asked us to sit down. We remained standing.

"At least lower your voices," he said. "I'm not authorized to speak."

"*This minute,*" Ardis repeated in a hiss.

Clod pressed his lips together again, briefly, before starting. "We believe Ms. Snapp was shot from a height and direction suggesting a second-floor window at the Weaver's Cat. It's a working theory only, but the other buildings along that side of Depot are single-story."

The open—now washed and shut—bathroom window. No, there had to be other possibilities. "Someone on the roof of Jenkins' or the insurance building could've done it," I said. "You should check for roof access. A ladder, if nothing else. And what about the warehouse?" I pointed and Clod turned to look at the old brick two-story warehouse at the end of the block, opposite the insurance office.

"Thank you for your input," he said, turning back. He didn't modify the word "input" with an audible adjective, but a few withering options showed up in the tilt of his head and lifted eyebrow. "Ms. Rutledge, Ms. Buchanan, in all likelihood this was a terrible accident. One of the actors had live ammunition and didn't know it. He's probably scared witless and afraid to come forward. Now, come here and look at your open window up there on the second floor."

Oops. Ardis stepped out from under the tent with Clod to look at the window. I didn't bother.

"John Berry likes to keep busy," I said when Clod stomped back into the tent. "In the interest of full disclosure, he and Ernestine are minding the shop for us, and during the lull after the, um, incident, John washed the windows. And closed the one he found open in the bathroom."

"In the interest of full disclosure," Clod ground between his teeth, "please tell me why those two are puttering around tidying up the crime scene. Why are they still in the building?"

"Hey, this is not my fault," I said, "and if it annoys you—"

"*Annoys* me?"

"This whole problem could have been avoided if someone had told us sooner."

"Told you what sooner?"

"That some nut with a rifle popped upstairs in the Cat and popped off a pedestrian. And if they'd told us in plain English, instead of obfuscatory officialese, we would have locked the doors, sent John and Ernestine home, and your precious crime scene would have been inviolate." I said that with a lot of spit and my finger jabbing at his chest, because by then I didn't care who saw me confronting whom in public and, in particular, confronting that *annoying* clod.

After that the Mennonites seemed leery of us, or maybe just of me. Ardis went across and commiserated with them over their lost afternoon sales, though, and they ended up smiling and giving her a loaf of rye bread. The teenagers were happy to hear from their parents that an uncle was on his way to pick them up.

I made a quick call to Ernestine and told her what was going on. "The deputies will come talk to you. Just answer their questions and don't worry about balancing the register or anything. Ardis and I will take care of the rest later."

"Maybe it will help ease the situation if I make a pot of tea."

"Mm, better not."

"And no time, anyway. Here come two of them right now. Oh yes, very gruff-looking."

She disconnected with a chirp of greeting for the lawmen and I started packing our merchandise back into boxes and plastic totes. Clod had told us that we would be escorted to the Cat with our goods when someone in authority was free from other duties. I was sure we were supposed to feel grateful that they were letting us move everything inside and allowing us to collect our purses and feed the cat. *"And touch nothing else and then leave,"* according to Clod's directive. I reflected on how grateful I felt by spitting one more annoyed word and then apologized to Ardis.

"It's all right, hon," she said, patting me on the back. "You did good. That 'obfuscatory officialese' put Coleridge right in his place. On the other hand, I think we can understand his position, don't you? It must be frustrating to be so law-abiding and upright and have to deal day in and day out with people who aren't. Or worse, with someone who doesn't have the guts to face up to it."

"You're right."

"And when John sets out to clean something, he's thorough. That must come from his sailing days."

"I should probably apologize to Deputy Dunbar."

"Oh, I don't think you need to go that far, hon."

"But I should've saved my anger for J. Scott Prescott. What part of 'No, your good old boys with guns can't shoot them out our windows, much less point them at people and kill them' didn't he understand?"

"He has much to answer for," Ardis said. "Oh my land." There was a sudden catch in her voice. "With all this going on, I didn't realize, they haven't taken her away yet." She pointed at the telltale lump distorting the back panel of the tent. She looked at me, moved to the edge of the tent for a quick look, then came back, first nodding her head and then shaking it.

"What on earth is taking them so long?" she asked.

"I don't think it's really *been* all that long. It just seems like it."

"Well, as long as they haven't moved her, I wonder if they'll let us pay our respects one more time. I'd surely like to."

"You would?"

"Absolutely. Think about it, hon. How likely is it that one of those costumed yahoos, hamming it up for all the world to take notice, actually entered the Cat without showing off so that everyone in the shop knew he was there? And could describe him? And then tell me that he just happened to pick out, target, shoot, and kill the most irritating woman on the street?"

"You're saying someone snuck in planning to kill Reva Louise?"

"Premeditated murder."

"That's . . ." I didn't like to say crazy, but I wasn't sure what else to call it.

"Kath, someone went to an awful lot of trouble to kill Reva Louise. But if you ask me—and you know you don't need to ask *only* me, because there are dozens who will agree—she *was* an awful lot of trouble."

"Trouble from beginning to end. That's a sad epitaph."

"Isn't that the truth?"

"That might be why no one *has* come forward, though," I said.

"Killers generally don't," Ardis agreed.

"If you're right, Deputy Dunbar and his buddies will probably figure it out."

"Eventually."

"Maybe." I thought for a minute. "The police are

talking to Ernestine and John. But there's no reason we can't talk to Ernestine and John, too. They were our employees for the afternoon. We need to check on their welfare after such a traumatic event."

"Maybe have them over for a nice supper to thank them," Ardis said. "And debrief them."

"Get them to tell us everything they remember. Everything they remember seeing *and* hearing."

"Every*one* they remember."

"Exactly. And if the deputies are going to look at the Cat's checks and credit card receipts, then we will, too. They're *our* records and if those bozos can find something in them like . . . like what? Are they looking for names of people who might have seen something? Then that's what we'll do, too. We'll conduct a parallel investigation. No, wait. Not parallel. Better than parallel. Better and stronger—a *two-ply* investigation."

"This is an excellent plan, hon. So, we'll ask to pay our respects, and we'll take a good, quick look around, and maybe we'll pick up on something the deputies missed."

"They might stop us. . . . I mean, shouldn't they?"

"Absolutely. But they're operating under the delusion this is an accident. They probably aren't treating it like a real crime scene. Besides, we were on the scene before the authorities even got here. We can't contaminate it any more than we already did."

"Good point. But you don't think pretending to pay our respects might be going too far? You know, kind of tacky?"

"Not when we have the good name of the Weaver's Cat to uphold," Ardis said. "We can't have people thinking we run a den of mohair and murderers."

"Knitters and knockoff artists?"

"Weavers and wasters."

"Threads and thugs. Uh-oh, better stop." I put my hand over my mouth. We'd started snickering. The Mennonites, who were still packing up their booth, were casting leery glances our way again.

"Wait, wait," Ardis said, "one more. Crochet hooks and criminal habitats." She leaned her forehead on my shoulder and sputtered with suppressed snorts, then swallowed them and straightened back up. "Okay, that's it. No more. Now it's time for somber and serious." And being the veteran Blue Plum Repertory Theater actor she was, and nothing at all like a costumed yahoo, she closed her eyes and held her breath for a moment, and immediately became the picture of serious and somber.

I had a harder time making the transformation, but catching sight of a broken-looking Dan Snapp talking to Clod as we made our way around the end of the tent helped. They were standing beside the body. I pulled Ardis to a stop.

"The guy talking to Cole. That's Dan Snapp. And the guy in the frock coat, with his hand on Dan's shoulder, that's J. Scott Prescott. Maybe we shouldn't intrude just now." Maybe I would embarrass myself by intruding in J. Scott's face.

"No. This is even better. It'll be real natural for us to offer our condolences to Dan, and we'll size the two of them up while we're at it. I'll do most of the talking. You cast your eyes around. Now, here we go. We will be solemn and we will be sincere."

And we would be snooping, but I didn't say that out

loud in case her respectable veneer should crack and
knowing that mine would. She linked her arm in mine
and as we made our decorous way toward broken-
hearted Dan and his lost Reva Louise, I scrubbed my
forehead with the fingertips of my free hand. If the
scrubbing made me look overcome, then good. But really I was trying to scrub away my annoyance with Clod
Dunbar and my urge to get in a few finger jabs at J. Scott
Prescott.

Clod saw us coming. He was still talking to Dan and J.
Scott beside the shrouded body and he made no move to
stop us. Another deputy did step forward and ask us
what we were doing and where we were going. Ardis
answered, but she looked at Clod instead of the deputy
who asked. Whether it was her stature as former teacher
or some other vibe between them that I couldn't fathom,
I don't know, but Clod nodded to the other deputy and
we were allowed to approach Reva Louise one more
time.

Thank goodness the body *had* been covered or I
couldn't have done it. Standing next to that still shape, I
had to look away, not make eye contact with anyone,
look anywhere else, look up . . . to the attic window in
the Weaver's Cat. That time I did see a flicker, a waver of
light or shadow, and then—*Holy cow*. Did she *jump*?

I thought my heart would stop. Geneva didn't exactly
plummet, but leaving the third floor of a building like
that sure didn't look safe. That didn't make sense, considering she was already dead. Neither did closing my eyes,
but I did anyway. When I opened one eye again, a figure
of fog and dust motes stood next to me looking down at
Reva Louise. I shivered. Had she *known* she could exit

an attic window like that? Maybe not. Geneva shivered, too.

"I will always remember her for the beautiful smell of her gingerbread," Geneva said, "and her lies. You have very complicated friends. Are you checking to see if she's lying about being dead, too?"

Speaking of complicated friends, I was sandwiched between two of them. On one side Ardis held Dan Snapp's hand, blessing his heart and recalling the joy Reva Louise carried with her and the gift of surprise that she brought into all our lives. On my other side, Geneva was making sure I understood—in greater detail than seemed necessary—that Reva Louise really was no longer with us. The situation was a little hard to take. I was beginning to feel claustrophobic—not quite like screaming and bolting from between them but squeezed somewhat like toothpaste—when I glanced over at Clod. He was watching us. Intently. So was J. Scott.

"It could be you're looking suspicious," Geneva said on one side.

Ardis leaned over and whispered on the other, "Sink to your knees."

They were a pair of cartoon consciences, one nattering at my left shoulder and one at my right, except they were wily conscience and weird conscience instead of good and evil. I did sink to my knees; it would have been hard not to with Ardis attached to my left arm and dragging me down beside her. And praying would have made good sense—praying that she wasn't also dragging us into trouble or praying that Clod wouldn't suddenly find a reason to charge us with tampering or obstruction and drag us off to jail. But nothing about what we were doing made good sense, and there in front of me was a fold of Reva Louise's voluminous skirt that had escaped from under the sheet covering her.

I touched it.

"I knew you couldn't resist," Geneva said.

Chapter 12

"What do you feel?" Geneva asked.

Beyond the cotton polyester blend of Reva Louise's skirt, I didn't know. The other times I'd experienced the weird effect, I'd had an immediate impression of emotions. I couldn't necessarily tell to what or to whom the emotions were directed, but they'd been clear enough that I could name them—love, fear, dishonesty, hatred. The feeling that came from Reva Louise was a confused swirl. Anticipation? Excitement? Suspicion? Cunning? Some of all of them, maybe, but they were as slippery to catch and be sure of as the shreds of a half-remembered dream. Geneva was right when she'd said I had complicated friends. Except I didn't think friendliness was part of that Reva Louise mix.

"What?" Geneva asked.

I gave a small shrug.

"Try again. I'll distract the flatfoot."

With that, Geneva flew up into Clod's face. He took half a step back. He couldn't see her, but he sensed something and he batted at what he must have thought was an insect. Geneva stayed with him, Dan Snapp, J. Scott, and

Ardis looked at him, and I slipped both hands under the sheet.

My eyes on the others, I ran my fingers over the near edge of Reva Louise's skirt, feeling the cunning and excitement again, but also something real and tangible, under the fabric, along the seam. Quickly, I felt for and found a slit in the seam—a pocket—with a card in it. Did I dare? Yes. I palmed the card, brought it out, and took a look.

So did Geneva, which meant she was no longer distracting Clod.

"You removed a personal belonging from the body." Clod sounded aggressively aghast. He'd marched us away from the body and over to his car.

"I was tucking her skirt under the tarp," I said.

"It didn't need tucking. We don't call it a tarp." He looked dangerously explosive.

"I found J. Scott Prescott's business card sticking out of a pocket," I said, sure that I looked and sounded completely reasonable. "So I did you a favor, because it might have gotten lost when you moved the body. And you'll be interested in this—his card was in a hidden pocket. More like an enlarged seam. Come to think of it, you might want to check for more of them. It isn't unusual in a nineteenth-century dress, with that kind of full skirt, to find openings in the seams or hemmed slits in the panels. They'd give access to a loose pocket worn on a tape tied around the waist or have flat bags sewn to the openings, much the way our pockets are today. But the openings for pockets in a nineteenth-century skirt, even a reproduction like this, might not be where you'd expect to find them. Usually they were on the right side or right rear. But sometimes they were all the way around in the middle of the back. Ardis, do you mind?" I showed him what I meant, using Ardis for my model. She obliged by turning her side and then her rear toward him.

"So the pocket I just found in the seam halfway *down* the skirt? There's something sneaky about its size and its placement and if I were you I'd check *all* the seams. It reminds me of an early twentieth-century morning coat I saw in a costume collection in a local history museum in Niles, California, that must have belonged to a pick-pocket. The coat did, not the museum, and it was *so* cool. It had to have been custom-made. It was a piece of art, really. And what a piece of work the guy it belonged to must have been."

Clod looked less than impressed by my rapturous knowledge of pocket placement in nineteenth- and twentieth-century costumes, standard or sneaky. And as so often happened when he and I tried to exchange information, I was less than impressed by his imagination.

"The way I see it," Ardis said, "there are two things you should be wondering. What was Reva Louise doing with a business card for a commercial real estate agent from Knoxville hidden away in her ingenious little pocket? And what bearing, if any, do the card and the pocket, or the owner of the card *in* the pocket, have on her murder?"

Clod made a low noise in his throat.

"You have only yourself to blame, Coleridge," Ardis said. "In fact, I find it hard to believe you let us traipse all over what might be more of a crime scene than you realize. If your people had done their job right to begin with, you would have had the business card sooner. But you have it now and everyone's happy."

"It will make me very happy," Clod snarled, "if you two will stay put, in my car, and stay out of trouble." He slammed the door of his car and stalked off. It was his official car, the kind where suspects and perpetrators were put in the backseat and the doors couldn't be opened from the inside. Ardis and I were in the backseat.

"I think he's just blowing off steam," Ardis said. "I don't think we're really under arrest."

"I don't think he could make the charges stick if we were."

"I wish you would try to look more desperate and dangerous," Geneva said. She'd glided into the front passenger seat. "You look irritable, but that's hardly inspiring. Try sneering."

"You were brilliant, though," Ardis said. "So, tell me, was it your textile expertise that led you to that pocket or was it your keen understanding of Reva Louise's underhanded personality?"

"Would you believe me if I said I really was just tucking her skirt under the tarp?"

"We can stick to that story if you want."

I did want.

"I just realized, though, hon, that there's a problem with your theory that someone targeted Reva Louise, in that spot, at that time."

"I thought it was your theory."

"We won't quibble over ownership. But you see the problem, don't you?"

What I saw was the ghost now sitting in the driver's

seat of Clod Dunbar's official car. I was glad she couldn't turn anything on. Like a siren.

"I can tell by your scowl that you do see the problem," Ardis said. "And you're right. It's going to be a stumper. I'm looking forward to seeing how you tackle it. Oh, look, here comes Ten."

Joe never seemed to mind that Ardis called him Ten. It slipped into her conversation as easily as "hon" and with just as much warmth. She'd been Joe's third and fourth grade teacher, too, but they'd ended up with an easier relationship than she and Clod had. Maybe being the younger brother let Joe be more relaxed. I'd noticed that Ardis never went as far as calling him Tennyson, which made me think she used Clod's full name for the same reason he would always be Clod to me.

Joe opened the squad car's back door. "Must be getting kind of warm in there. Why don't you come on out?"

"Are you allowed to do that?" I looked nervously past him to where Clod was wrapping up his talk to Dan Snapp and J. Scott Prescott. Clod shook J. Scott's hand and put a hand briefly on Dan's shoulder. Dan's head was bowed. He appeared to wipe away a tear.

"You aren't under arrest or material witnesses, are you?" Joe asked.

"*Are* we?" Geneva, her eyes huge, looked at me over the headrest.

"Nope," I said, scooting out of the car. "Not under arrest and not witnesses in any way, shape, or form."

"Good enough," Joe said.

Ardis followed me out. Judging by the sharp intake of her breath at Joe's question, she was as excited as Geneva at the prospect of being a lawbreaker. She might have opted to stay in the car, but it really had been getting warm in there. Geneva did stay. She trickled into the backseat and sat very still, looking at her wispy hands clasped in her lap.

"So, did you just happen to wander by to see who you could spring from your brother's car?" I asked.

"No." Joe shut the car door. Geneva didn't look around. "I came to tell you they're canceling the rest of the festival."

Chapter 13

"Who's closing the festival down?" Ardis asked. "The *mayor*? I cannot imagine. The very idea of it would make his head explode."

Geneva hadn't left the squad car. Joe saw me looking in and he peered in, too. At nothing he could see.

"I thought you'd be more upset about the festival," he said to me. "What are you doing? Did you leave something in there?"

Geneva continued to sit in the backseat, her hands worrying in her lap.

"Ardis is upset enough for both of us," I said. "But yeah, I ..." I tried to get Geneva's attention with a nervous patter of my fingers on the window.

"Grab it fast, then," Joe said, opening the door again. "Here comes Cole."

I thanked Joe and leaned in, pretending to grope for something that might have slipped down the back of the seat. "Come on," I whispered to Geneva. "The sheriff's deputies are going to take over the shop."

"Looking for clues? And witnesses?" Geneva asked.

"Yeah, and maybe more. I don't know, but this is re-

ally serious. They're closing the festival." I looked over
my shoulder. Joe and Ardis stood shoulder to shoulder,
stalling Clod. Clod wasn't happy. I scrabbled down the
backseat with renewed vigor. "Geneva, come on, there's
no time for this."

"I should probably stay."

"Why?"

"Why what?" the voice of Clod asked. Ardis and Joe
had parted like the Red Sea and he'd boiled on through.

"Um, why am I always losing something?"

"Out," he said.

I wished I had the nerve to imitate Miss Piggy with an
indignant *"Moi?"*

Clod, of course, had plenty of nerve. He opened the
front door of the car, stuck his head in, and looked
around with exaggerated care, ending the tour with his
eyes on me. Except that he'd put his mirrored sunglasses
back on so I couldn't see his skewering glare. "*You*," he
said, then pointed at several random spots in the car,
"and all your little friends. *Out.*"

"How rude," Geneva said. She blew a raspberry at
Clod as she swirled past him. "I will be in my room,
should anyone be interested. I want to be alone."

"Did you find it, hon?" Ardis asked.

"Find what?" I slammed the back door and watched
Geneva float through one of the Cat's first-floor windows. Could she float back up to the attic window she'd
come out of?

"Kath?"

"Hm? Oh, what I left in the car? Yeah, thanks. Hey."
I rapped on Clod's window. He'd started the car and was

probably thinking about running over my toes as he backed out instead of answering my knock, but he lowered the window anyway.

"Why are they canceling the festival?"

"No comment."

"Do your buddies still have Ernestine and John in there?"

"Ms. Odell and Mr. Berry have left the building."

"Cute. How much longer until we can move our stuff back in?"

He pointed behind me. "Ask them."

"Them" were two deputies who, after several static-obscured minutes of consultation with the radios at their shoulders, finally gave us permission to move our boxes and the tables, chairs, displays, and tent back into the Weaver's Cat. Permission but no help. The teenaged woodworkers and their uncle were kind and gave me a hand while, under the watchful eye of a third deputy, Ardis collected customer names from the day's electronic transactions and checks. All three deputies watched us with unnerving attention. As a result, we scurried, saying little. When we'd gotten everything inside and the tent and tables stowed, rather than say good–bye, the kids' uncle wished us a quiet "Good luck."

Joe had disappeared sometime earlier. That didn't surprise me.

"We need to feed the cat before we leave," I said. "And I need to run upstairs—"

Two of the deputies shifted toward me at the words "run upstairs."

"Not to the second floor," I said. "To the attic. The study. To get my purse."

"There are two pocketbooks in here," said the unnerving deputy standing in the office behind the sales counter. "A wallet with your name in it is in this one." He held my purse up, one finger through the strap.

"Thank you." I smiled. "Actually, I need to get something of a more personal nature, if you know what I mean. You can inspect it before I take it away, if that will make you feel more comfortable. I'll hand it right to you. But I really need to have it. Tonight. Or if it's better, I can tell you exactly where it is and you can run up and get it for me."

"Oh my." Perceptive Ardis did a good imitation of being aghast at the indelicacy of my bringing up the article I'd just brought up. She added a wince for good measure.

And whatever the deputy imagined that article was, it unnerved *him* to the point he didn't ask for a detailed description. That was just as well because I had nothing at all in mind. I only wanted a reason to run upstairs and pretend my phone was ringing so I could talk to Geneva. It was decided that one of the deputies would stay downstairs with Ardis while the other two accompanied me. Ardis' watchdog was in for a treat. As the other two and I left the room, she launched into a description of her latest—completely imaginary—gastritis attack.

My escort to the attic seemed like overkill, considering that people had walked around the store the whole day, going up and down the stairs and in and out the front and back doors, leaving traces and obliterating them left and right. The deputies must have been under orders, though, so up we marched, one in front and one behind and me reflecting on how handy it was, though maybe not such a good thing, that I was learning to lie so well.

Geneva wasn't in sight when we reached the study. I'd hoped to find her in the window seat, either sitting or huddled in one of her damp heaps. She'd said she was going to her room, though. Her "room" was a cupboard with a well-hidden door that Granddaddy had built for Granny. The interior was beautifully finished and painted in Granny's favorite dark blue. Geneva said she felt snug and safe in there. I couldn't tell if she'd ever thought about why that might be. I also wasn't sure it would be polite or wise to tell her the reason that seemed so obvious to me. The cupboard occupied the narrow space, floor to ceiling, between two joists. It was roughly two feet wide, maybe fifteen inches deep, and probably six feet tall. It had three shelves in it, but otherwise it wasn't far off from being the shape of a coffin standing on end. I longed to ask Geneva if she remembered having a coffin of her own.

"Hang on a tick," I said to the deputies when we crowded into the room. I put my hand on my pocket. "That's my phone." The phone hadn't made a peep or a buzz, but they didn't seem to notice. I pulled it out. "Geneva, hi! You've caught me at kind of a bad time. Geneva? Are you there?" I moved closer to the cupboard door, narrowing my eyes and leaning into the phone to show the deputies how bad the connection was. "Geneva?"

Her misty form emerged from the cupboard with a sigh and a moan—her usual behavior when I interrupted her—but her reaction when she saw the deputies was different and interesting. The moan cut off abruptly and she moved along the wall into the corner away from them, not drifting so much as slinking. She stayed there, shoulders drawn, looking at them sideways. She was like a worried cat, ready to protect herself with claws and a hiss.

"Oh, joy," she deadpanned. Appropriately enough. "I said I wanted to be alone and you brought company."

"Look, I've only got a minute and this is kind of a bad connection—"

"Have your friends come to arrest me?"

"What? No. Why would they? Not to mention *how* could they? Forget that right now. I came to tell you . . . I mean I called . . ." I cleared my throat and tried again. "Thanks for getting back to me so quickly. Ardis is having TGIF over for a get-together this evening at her house. I'm going. Would you like to come with me?"

"Will everyone be knitting?"

"Some, probably. They always do. But it's more of a supper thing. You know, talking, catching up, making plans for the inves . . . for our next interesting project."

"BYOB?"

"I guess. Would that make a difference?"

"I meant bring your own 'boo.' If I go with you, I will be the 'boo.' If there were more than one ghost, we would be 'boos.' Never mind; I do not feel much like laughing, either. Speaking of which, the jokers standing behind you do not look as if they share half a sense of humor between them. I think you should hang up and go with them quietly. They make me nervous."

"But will you come with me tonight?"

"Mmm, no, probably not. I'm fairly busy."

"Doing what?"

She slunk farther into the corner, arms crossed and shoulders drawn up to her ears.

"Sorry," I said. "I didn't mean to suggest that you don't have your own important things to do. But I wish you would come with me."

She hmphed.

"Otherwise I don't know when I'll be able to see you again. Hang on." I turned to the deputies. "Any idea how long you guys are going to keep the store closed? Do you think we can reopen tomorrow?"

"Ma'am, you need to come along with us now. Get the, er, item you came for and call your friend some other time."

"One more second. Just . . ." I turned back to Geneva, but she was gone. I finished the "call" anyway, hoping she was still listening. "I have to go now. If you don't come with me to Ardis', I'll try to stop by later. We have a lot to talk about. Keep an eye on things and watch for me, okay?"

She didn't answer. I rested my hand briefly on the hidden door. I didn't like being made to leave the shop and then being kept out of it. Even more, I didn't like leaving Geneva alone and having no way to get hold of her short of tossing pebbles at a window.

I tapped the door twice with my fingertips; then to make good on my reason for going up there, I crossed to the desk. I pulled open the middle drawer and grabbed the first thing that came to hand.

"What the heck is *that*?" one of the deputies asked.

"An orifice hook." I was feeling mean and enunciated clearly to gain the full effect of the tool's vaguely suggestive name. I wasn't disappointed. The deputy who'd asked took a step back, earning a black look from his partner. "This one belonged to my grandmother," I said. "Works like a charm. Have you ever used one?"

What I held on my outstretched palm was the most useful tool a spinner could have in addition to her wheel. It was a three- or four-inch hook with a gripping handle. That particular hook was brass and slightly flexible and the handle was a smooth, lovely-to-hold pear shape made of walnut. Granddaddy had made it for Granny. She'd used it, as spinners have used them for untold centuries, to fish the end of her finished yarn through the orifice of her wheel's flyer assembly.

I could have explained that to the deputies, but I didn't. I smiled and let them stare at it and reminded myself never to try flying with one in my carry-on luggage.

"Leave the door open when you come, will you?" I said, heading for the stairs. "The cat likes to nap up here in the window seat."

By the time the two deputies and I got back downstairs, Ardis had talked her deputy into buying a gift certificate for his wife's birthday. That one assured us, again, that they would work as quickly and neatly as they could in the shop. I gave him a spare key. He gave me a receipt for it. Ardis slipped a set of stitch markers in the bag with the gift certificate, and we left the Weaver's Cat in their hands. They weren't such bad guys, we agreed. And they were doing their jobs.

"Doing the job well," Ardis said, "with methodical minds and trained, capable hands. The kind of solid police work that will produce a useful line of information for their investigation."

"And now we start our own strand."

"Yes, we do. With more imagination and less official constraint."

Main Street didn't appear to know that Blue Plum Preserves was over. There weren't throngs of people, but there were plenty of them and the street was still closed to vehicles. The other shops were open. People laughed. A family walked past eating deep-fried pickles on sticks. It took a few minutes to realize the big difference—there wasn't any music coming from the stage at the courthouse and there were no more clangs from the blacksmith or toots from the antique farm machinery.

"Surreal," Ardis said. "For some reason, those deep-fried pickles don't look appetizing without background music."

Our first priority was checking on Mel and Sally Ann. We hadn't seen either of them at the scene of the tragedy, and we wanted to offer them our entirely genuine condolences. That wasn't something we could do in a quick call or text. Dan had told Ardis that as soon as he pulled himself together, he was going over to the café to break the news. We weren't sure, then, if we would find Mel's on Main open, but it was a good place to start.

Mel's was at the other end of our block of Main Street, close enough to the Weaver's Cat that hot coffee or soup didn't cool too much on a walk between the two on a cold winter morning. Before we reached the corner, we heard a shriek of electronic feedback and then someone testing the microphone with a finger tap. Ears perked up among the last gaggles of festivalgoers and people moved toward the courthouse in the next block, catty-corner to Mel's.

"It's the mayor," Ardis said. "And it looks like his head hasn't exploded yet, but let's go on over there and see if it will. At least then we'll have some good news for Mel in this dark time."

Sheriff Haynes joined Mayor Weems at the top of the courthouse steps and they stood together, flanked by the massive columns supporting the courthouse entablature. The sheriff looked like a column himself—tall with a solid barrel of a chest, his face grim as though he supported the weight of many woes. Mayor Weems looked strained almost to the point of hyperventilating. He was a slighter, shorter man and he was having trouble standing still. His natural, political inclination was probably to be out there in the crowd, shaking hands and slapping backs. Or standing behind the microphone, making happy news, but the sheriff held that position. Sheriff Haynes didn't look like one to budge. The "joint statement" he delivered was to the point. The gist was almost the entirety.

They felt certain the shooting was an isolated incident, he said. The public was not in danger; however, the investigation was ongoing. Evidence was being collected and leads developed. Anyone with information was asked to call the sheriff's department. Haynes asked for a moment of silence as thoughts and prayers went out to the family of Reva Louise Snapp. Then he confirmed the news that made no one happy.

"Because of the serious nature of the incident, after much discussion and with deep regret, Mayor Weems and his board of aldermen have deemed it best to cancel the rest of Blue Plum Preserves. Find your family and friends, find your cars, and go on home. We will be taking no questions at this time." With a jerk of his head at Mayor Weems, Sheriff Haynes started toward the courthouse door, obviously expecting the mayor to follow.

Mayor Weems, proving he was his own man, cast a quick glance at the sheriff's departing back. Then he leaned into the microphone and in the measured tones of someone trying to sound like an elder statesman said, "We want, and we shall have, answers."

But he was his own man only up to a point. At another look from Sheriff Haynes, he scurried after him into the courthouse.

"They know something we don't," Ardis said. "I don't like that and I don't like where this is going."

"We don't know where it's going yet," I pointed out.

"True."

"But we probably won't like it when it gets there."

"Even truer. Come on," she said. "Let's go hug a little on Mel and Sally Ann."

We didn't like what we found when we got to the café, either.

It was barely four o'clock in the afternoon, and that hardly seemed possible. The sun should have set. Blue Plum should have rolled up its streets. Shadows should be creeping in on sneaking, fur feet.

Mel's was open, though, and when I opened the door, the familiar scents of cinnamon, herbs, and coffee met us. There was a decent crowd inside. People talked and laughed. A short line waited to place orders at the counter. Half a dozen sat on the old church pew opposite the

counter waiting for tables. The sheriff might have told
people Blue Plum Preserves was over and to go home, but
it looked as though an awful lot of them had only made it
as far as Mel's.

Mel was in the kitchen chopping onions. Her staff
moved around her, calling orders, slapping burgers and
sandwiches on the spitting grill, setting up salads, carrying loaded plates out, and clattering empty ones into the
sink and dishwasher. Mel stood in her own bubble at the
butcher block table, the kitchen's swirl and hubbub sliding past. Only her spiked hair looked alert and in touch.
Maybe she needed heaps of onions for soup the next day.
Maybe they made a good cover story. She backhanded a
tear from her cheek and went on chopping.

I called her name from the doorway. The chef's knife
in her right hand stilled. Without raising her eyes from
the onions, she held her left hand up, palm out, stopping
my words, stopping hers.

"She's not talking and she won't quit chopping," a
waitress whispered.

"What do you think?" I asked as the waitress slipped
past me. "Is she okay?"

"As long as she's cooking. Don't worry. I'll stay with
her."

"Where's Sally Ann?"

"Gone home. Dan took her. She was all tore up."

"Mel, honey," Ardis said from over my shoulder,
"come by the house later. Anytime. I'll be there."

At that Mel did look up. She opened her mouth to
answer, but someone else spoke first.

"Official business," a familiar and officious voice said
behind me. "Pardon me." Clod Dunbar moved past me,

muttering not quite under his breath about nosy knitters. "You reported a theft, Mel?"

Mel stabbed her knife into the heart of a giant Vidalia. "Yesterday, Dunbar. I reported it yesterday and now you're too damn late."

Chapter 14

Ardis threw together a salad and I brought the fixings for my new favorite homemade fast food—black bean and spinach burritos—spicy, warm, and melting in thirty minutes. But only four of us sat around the trestle table in Ardis' kitchen that evening for the impromptu supper party, slash debriefing, slash planning session, with the sound of the baseball game Ardis' father was watching in the other room as background music.

Ardis and I sat on one side of the table. Ernestine and Thea Green, the town librarian, sat on the other. Ernestine had changed out of her long skirt and mob cap into her Miss Marple tweeds, the better for stimulating her little gray cells, she said, mixing her Christie characters. Thea had come straight from the library. She'd shed her jacket and a silk scarf before sitting, slipped out of pinching low heels, and settled with a small groan and then a sigh of relief. When Ardis put a glass of wine in her hand, the transformation was complete; Thea's face relaxed and she smiled.

"You'd think after twenty years in a job," Ardis said, "you'd know enough to wear shoes that let you live through the day."

Thea took a reviving sip. "You'd think after knowing me for twenty years, you'd also know my feet are happy to martyr themselves so that I look fabulous. This is an awfully small powwow," she said, taking another sip of wine. "That's good, because it leaves more for fabulous me and my feet, but why so few?"

"We're the core group," I said.

Ardis nodded. "The pith of the posse."

I'd swung by the Cat one more time, on my way over, to see if Geneva had changed her mind about coming with me. She wasn't waiting for me on the porch. I'd put my nose to the front windows and the window in the kitchen door, but didn't see her shadowy form anywhere. The crime scene tape stretched across both doors was more upsetting than I'd expected it would be.

John had given his regrets when Ardis invited him. He was the primary caregiver for his ninety-year-old brother, whom John candidly described as "meaner than snakes." He said he didn't feel right or comfortable leaving his brother most of the day and then the evening. He promised to type up everything he remembered telling the deputy who'd interviewed him and e-mail it to me.

We hadn't expected Debbie to jump at the chance to make the long trip back into town on short notice. She and her sheep lived a fair number of twisty miles up a river valley heading toward the mountains. Ardis called to invite her anyway, unfortunately forgetting that Debbie might not have heard what happened. She hadn't. Ardis didn't go into detail, but Debbie took the news hard, considering she had no particular fondness for Reva Louise. Debbie was sweet and sensitive that way, which always struck me as an odd contrast to the level-headed strength she needed to run her farm. She said she'd call first thing Monday morning, before making the trip in for work, to make sure the shop was reopened. Ardis assured her it darn well better be.

"Just in case, though, hon," Ardis said, "if you're calling *early* Monday morning, make that call to Kath, why don't you?"

Before we'd left the café, Ardis had slipped a note to one of the waitresses to give to Mel, inviting her to drop by anytime that evening. So far she hadn't. Joe Dunbar was . . . wherever Joe would go of an evening. Clod Dunbar had not been invited.

"But you've got to hand it to him," Ardis said in her retelling of Clod's arrival in the onion-filled café kitchen, "he didn't so much as flinch when Mel stuck that knife in."

"Oh my." Ernestine's wineglass stopped halfway to her mouth. "Into the Vidalia, I hope?" It was hard to tell from the look in her eyes if she really hoped it was the Vidalia or not.

"Okay, I'll admit it," I said. "Deputy Dunbar is cool in a tense situation. But how much of that tension does he create in the first place? Who approaches a woman who's just lost her sister—approaches her in her place of business when it's *busy*—and doesn't at least make reference to her loss or apologize for intruding on her business and her grief? Much less that he or someone else in a uniform should have responded to her theft report twenty-four hours earlier?"

"Who approaches Mel at *all* when she has a big knife in her hand?" Thea asked.

"Do we know what was stolen?" Ernestine asked.

"No," I said. "And it wasn't a good time to hang around and ask or listen."

"Mel didn't say boo about it when she was in the library yesterday," Thea said. "What?" She'd caught the startled look I couldn't help at the word "boo."

"Sorry," I said. "Nothing."

"It isn't nothing, though," Ardis said, misinterpreting my answer. "The theft might be another twist of yarn worth following. I wonder if that's why Cole showed up."

"Good point." I made a note in the palm-sized spiral notebook I'd brought along. "And if he thinks the theft and the shooting might be connected—"

"The ifs and mights are piling up fast," Thea said.

"It wouldn't be a good investigation without them," said Ernestine. She pushed the bottle of wine closer to Thea. "Pour yourself another glass and they won't bother you so much."

I put my hand over my own glass when Thea offered to pour more for me. "Anyway, if Deputy Dunbar thinks the theft is worth following up, then we will, too."

"You're always so *proper* when you talk about him," Thea said. "*Deputy* Dunbar. Do I detect a little deflection of elemental emotion? A subconscious squashing of flowering feelings? Now, what's *that* look for?"

"It would go with a kick to your shins if you were sitting close enough."

"Why? He's obviously got a thing for you."

"You and Coleridge, Kath?" Ardis looked at me. "Really? I thought Joe was angling to be your beau."

Thea snorted and I chewed over her comment. Over both their comments. I called him Deputy Dunbar so I wouldn't slip and call him "Clod" instead of "Cole." He, the clod, had asked me out once, but that was a complete nonstarter with me and I'd been pretty sure my response had put an end to it. Joe, on the other hand . . .

"Let's move on," Ardis said. Were her mildly disapproving look and tone of voice for me?

"Yes, let's," Ernestine said. "These 'what-ifs' and 'might bes' of murder are much more interesting than Kath's love life. Oh my. I'm sorry, Kath. I didn't mean that quite the way it sounded."

I laughed and it felt better than a second glass of wine would have. Ernestine looked pleased enough with herself that I was pretty sure she'd meant it exactly the way it sounded.

"I take it no one has come forward to admit responsibility for the shooting?" she asked.

"Not unless someone has in the last hour or so," Ardis said. "But if that happened, I wonder how soon we'd hear about it."

"The police will have to tell us something at some point," I said. "They have to let us know when we can get back in the shop and reopen. If someone comes forward, maybe that'll happen sooner."

"And if someone comes forward, Ernestine is all dressed up in her tweeds with nothing to detect," said Thea.

"But we don't have to worry about that, because no one *will* come forward," Ardis said. She crossed her arms, daring Thea to contradict her.

Thea didn't. "Fine. Good. Got it," she said, raising her hands. "We don't believe there's anyone out there who was involved in the skit, who was also stupid, is now afraid to come forward and admit just *how* stupid, but who will eventually do the right thing."

"We do not," said Ardis.

"Even though that's what the cops think happened and what sounds kind of, oh, I don't know, *reasonable*, if you think it through from *a* to *b* to *c*."

"We're working on a parallel strand," I said. "You could call it *aa* to *bb* to *cc*. We're operating on the theory that someone targeted Reva Louise specifically."

"You're kidding," Thea said. "Why would anyone do that? Pardon me for speaking ill of the dead, but who cared enough about Reva Louise Snapp to kill her? She was annoying, sure. Why do you think I quit coming to Fast and Furious? But you don't kill someone because she's as irritating as a horsefly."

"'Why' is one of the things we'll be looking into," I said.

"Hold up, there." Ardis uncrossed her arms, planted her hands on the table, and leaned toward Thea. "You said you had meetings you couldn't get out of. Do you mean to tell me you *lied* to the Fast and Furious?"

"My meetings were perfectly legitimate. They were meetings I *arranged*, but they were valid. If sparsely attended. Has Joe been showing up for Fast and Furious lately?"

"No."

"Mm-hmm," Thea said. "He probably arranged to go bother fish up some obscure creek. But that doesn't mean that either he or I or any of the rest of us killed Reva Louise so that our group could reunite and knit happily ever after." She sat forward, too, pushing her plate aside and leaning on her elbows. "Look, you know I'll help with this investigation. It doesn't matter to me if I liked the woman or not. But tell me why we're bucking the official story. Where's the motive? I'm a librarian. I want *logic*."

"We have literary logic a librarian can love," I said. "Ardis spotted it right off."

"Lay it on me."

"First, did you catch any of the pig skit?"

Thea nodded.

"What did you think of the acting?"

"Ham acting at its finest and most painful, and I'm not referring to the pig when I say ham."

"Exactly what I thought," Ardis said. She and Thea sat back and exchanged smug looks. Thea was also a member of the Blue Plum Repertory Theater.

"Glad you guys agree," I said. "So let's use Sherlockian logic and investigate 'The Curious Incident of the Ham Actor in the Weaver's Cat.'"

"Are you saying there *was* an actor in the shop?" Ernestine asked. "John and I both thought back, and neither one of us remembered anyone like that coming in. And we *would* have, wouldn't we?"

"Yes, you would," I said. "That's the curious incident. Because if there *was* an actor in the shop, as the sheriff contends, then that actor was so far out of character as to be sneaking into the shop and sneaking back out again."

"Like a ghost," Ernestine said.

I opened my mouth but caught myself before I said anything peculiar like "I don't think a ghost could actually pull the trigger of a gun." Instead I asked Thea if that answered her question about why we were bucking the official story.

"Definitively, although we're still short on motive and it leaves me with another problem."

"What?"

"I don't own a deerstalker."

"Doesn't matter," Ardis said. "We'll all play Watson to Kath's Sherlock."

"*I* don't have a deerstalker," I said.

"But you'd look good in one," Ernestine said. "That's what counts."

It was a step up from Nancy Drew, anyway, a character to whom I felt malignantly allergic. And wouldn't Clod Dunbar be pleased that I'd been promoted from Drew to Holmes? That thought put a bounce in my metaphorical step. "Anyone for more salad or another burrito or should we move on to the de—"

"Debriefing," Ardis said, thumping her hand on the table. "Sherlock, you're always one step ahead of us."

I smiled to hide my disappointment. I'd been thinking "dessert."

"Ernestine," Ardis said, "we need to know everything you told the deputy who interviewed you this afternoon. Everything you told him and everything you didn't tell him but that you *will* tell us because you know we aren't such sticklers for clear-cut evidence and proven facts."

"Excuse me," Thea said. "I have another rather large question." At an explosive sigh from Ardis, she grew defensive. "Hey, you can't hold it against me. Librarians thrive on questions and answers. The bigger, the better, okay? So tell me this, if the sheriff is so sure a yellow-bellied idiot shot Reva Louise by accident, then why did he shut down the festival? That was a huge and unpopular step to take."

"It's the times we live in." Ernestine clucked her tongue. "They probably felt they had to."

"But it does raise questions," I said, "and this is where my head begins to spin. Maybe the answer is as simple as an overabundance of caution. But if that's the case, then why did the sheriff and the mayor make their announcement on the courthouse steps, with a microphone, to dozens and dozens of people? Talk about attracting a flock of sitting ducks. Did they really think that was a smart idea? But that made me think they *aren't* worried about anything else happening. Unless it turns out they know something we don't, which they probably do, because they are, after all, the police."

"Or they only *think* they know something," Ardis said.

"Stop there," Thea said. "Please. By now we're all getting dizzy."

"What do we do, Sherlock?" Ardis asked.

The three of them looked at me. Expectantly. And the phrase "as usual" ran through my mind. When had investigating murder replaced inspecting eighteenth-century woolens for vermin as my "as usual" activity? Talk about parallel strands. I felt as though I'd jumped to an alternative and parallel strand of my life.

"Sherlock?" Ardis asked.

"I think I'd feel better if we stick with 'Kath.' "

"Why?"

"You don't want me suffering impostor syndrome, do you? Besides, every time you start to say 'Sherlock,' for just a nanosecond, I think you're going to call me 'Shirley,' and that makes my skin crawl."

"What a horrible thought."

"Mercy me," Thea said. "Surely not."

I closed my eyes and massaged the bridge of my nose.

"Would this be a good time for me to tell you what I told the deputy?" Ernestine asked.

"It would, Ernestine. Thank you. What we need—as usual—is information. We don't know enough of it about anything. So let's start with what you can tell us. Then we'll see where we can go from there."

Ernestine reached for her handbag. "Sometimes it takes my memory a few minutes to catch up with a question," she said. "But I'm a diary keeper from way back and I find the act of putting pen to paper helps. When I got home I did this." She pulled her own small notebook out of her purse. The notebook was an accessory suitable for her Miss Marple getup, something a golden age amateur sleuth would carry. It was chocolate brown and about the size of a deck of playing cards. It looked like real leather and it had an elastic band bound into the cover to snap around it and keep it closed. Half an inch of dark red ribbon bookmark hung from the bottom edge. I wanted to hold that notebook and pet it. I wanted one of my own.

While I was busy coveting the notebook, I missed the rest of what Ernestine said, but it didn't take long to catch up. She handed the notebook to me and patted it. "I thought you would like to have this, Kath. You don't mind that I wrote my notes in it, do you?"

"It's *mine*?" I sounded almost breathless. How ridiculous. But what an *excellent* notebook.

"Oh dear, you do mind that I wrote in it," she said. She reached to take the notebook back.

"No, no." I moved it out of her range, slipping the elastic band off and opening it. "I don't mind at all. Thank you, Ernestine." The first few pages were covered with precise, tiny handwriting.

"In case you're wondering, I used my magnifying loupe. I didn't really have much to report, so I wanted to make sure what I *did* report is clear and legible."

"Ernestine, you're the cat's pajamas. Thank you for the notes *and* the notebook."

"Quit mooning over it," Thea said, "and read it to us. I've got places to go. Like home and to bed."

I read Ernestine's few paragraphs out loud. She and John had taken turns running the cash register and helping customers find the yarn or fabric they were looking for, or in the case of many of them, the yarn or fabric they hadn't known they were looking for until they saw it. John did most of the stair climbing. She mentioned Reva Louise stopping in to collect money for the "free" lunch and me coming in later with Sally Ann to pay for the lunch again. Customers, as we'd expected, were mostly visitors from out of town.

"Did you know that John kept track of how many people came in who only wanted to use the bathroom?" Ernestine asked.

"That's an irritating fact of life during Blue Plum Preserves," said Ardis. "It's why God created the Porta Potti, but I don't blame people for trying to avoid them."

Ernestine went on to report the phone calls they'd had asking if we were open or asking if we carried particular brands of yarn or sizes or styles of needles or other notions. Business stopped almost completely when the skit began. The skit's opening gunshots startled both John and Ernestine. Then Ernestine was surprised at how quickly the shots stopped making her jump. She worried about the children who came and sat on the railing at the end of the porch to watch the skit when the actors and the pig moved into Depot Street.

I stopped reading and looked up. "What about my phone call? You didn't include it."

"You already know about that, dear. You made it. Would you like me to add it now?"

"No, this is fine. You did a good job." There was something about that phone call, but I couldn't think what. Drumming my fingers on my lips didn't help me remember. "Did you tell the deputy about my call?"

"At this point I can't be sure," Ernestine said. "Although I don't suppose it matters. Your movements are accounted for, aren't they?"

"Sure," I said, "plenty of witnesses all afternoon." But not for the morning. No one had asked me anything about who came in and out of the Cat before the skit and the shooting started. I wondered if anyone would ask. If Clod would think of that. Or if it mattered. Could someone have come in during the morning and stayed hidden? Or hidden a gun and come back later? Those were chilling thoughts.

"What else did you write down, Ernestine?" Thea asked. "Kath isn't sharing anymore."

"Hang on, hang on." I made a note to think back through the morning and then went back to reading Ernestine's entry.

Her brief paragraphs were followed by two lists. One was labeled WHAT I REMEMBER ABOUT PEOPLE I DIDN'T KNOW. The other was labeled PEOPLE I DID KNOW. The first list consisted of notes such as *Woman with fussy child—lime green marabou* and *Teenagers, nose rings— five skeins from sale bin.* When I read, "Young woman, large glasses—travel wheel," Ardis clapped. Anytime we sold a substantial piece of equipment was cause for celebration. There were a few more brief descriptions of customers and what they bought. Nothing about a villain with a sneer and a rifle putting oodles of handspun worsted on his or her credit card.

"What are you writing?" Thea asked. "No secrets."

"Sorry," I said. "Making a note before I forget. I just realized we don't know what kind of gun it was."

"We don't know a lot of things," she said. "That's why we're investigating."

"No, but that's *it*," Ardis said. "The gun. The police are going to find out it wasn't some reproduction antique blunderbuss or whatever. In fact, I bet that's why they got hinky and canceled the festival. They already suspect there's something funny about the firearm." She hesitated. "Did I use the word 'hinky' right? I've never liked that word, but if that doesn't describe Haynes and his 'Find your cars and go home' and Weems and his 'We shall have answers,' nothing does. Go on and finish reading, Kath. We're getting somewhere. I can feel it."

Neither of Ernestine's neatly printed lists was long, but the second was shorter than it should have been by at least three people—Reva Louise, Sally Ann, and me. She'd mentioned us in one of her paragraphs, but omitting us from the second list made me wonder how complete the list was and who else she might have left off.

The last name *on* the list bothered me.

Chapter 15

"Mel came into the shop?" I asked.

Mel's name on the list bothered Ardis and Thea, too. Ernestine didn't think there was anything to worry about.

"A quick visit," Ernestine said. "In and out. You know how busy they are at the café during the festival. She asked for you, Kath. It might have been about the mix-up over paying twice for the box lunches. I didn't like to keep her by asking. She was like a tornado, whirling through, hair on end. She said something about 'fixing it.' I assumed she meant the mix-up, not her hair."

"I'll clear it up with her tomorrow," I said.

"I did try to tell her you would, but she was moving too fast. She ran upstairs, ran back down. When she didn't find either you or Reva Louise, she said, 'Shoot fire,' and slammed out the back door. After she'd gone, John checked to make sure the window in the door hadn't cracked. That might be when he noticed the windows could use a wash."

"Shoot fire?" Thea's eyebrows couldn't have risen higher.

"It's an approximation of what she said," Ernestine

explained. "Would you like me to write down her exact words? I'd rather not say them."

I shook my head, but Thea didn't let it go.

"Under the circumstances, you might have chosen a different euphemism. Have you got something going on in your subconscious, Ernestine? You're not thinking Mel had anything to do with this, are you?"

"Oh, I don't think so," Ernestine said. She touched her hands to her head, maybe checking her subconscious for disloyal thoughts, her eyes big behind her thick lenses. "I hope not. I like Mel."

"We all like her," I said. "Don't worry, Ernestine. Mel didn't do this. But you said, 'When she didn't find Reva Louise.' Was she looking for Reva Louise in the Cat? Did she ask if Reva Louise was there?"

Ernestine shook her head. "I'm sorry. She might have asked, or maybe because I assumed she was there to fix the mix-up between you and Reva Louise, I also assumed she was looking for both of you. I'll have to think." She clucked and put her folded hands to her chin, rocking slightly with the effort to remember. She looked tired and older and grayer.

"What do we do?" Ardis asked.

"We don't jump to conclusions," I said. "We—"

"We call it a night," said Thea. She was looking at Ernestine, concern clear on her face. "We look at this all again tomorrow with fresh eyes and fresh minds." When she turned her gaze on us, Ardis and I nodded.

Thea offered me a ride home. I told her I needed the walk. She glared at her shoes, then slipped her feet back into them and gathered her jacket, her silk scarf, and Ernestine. I watched them go, wondering if between help-ing in the shop and our evening debriefing, we'd asked too much of Ernestine for one day. When I started to help with the dishes, Ardis shooed me toward the door, too.

"You go on home, hon. Get a good night's sleep. We're going to need your critical thinking skills at their best."

I told her I'd call if I heard that we could reopen the shop. "And if we can't open, we should probably meet."

"There's no probably about it. Give me time for my Sunday morning slug-a-bed fest and then I'm all yours. When and where?"

Her question bumped up against something in my head. *When and where? How could someone target Reva Louise? How did anyone know when and where she was going to be?*

"Tell you what," Ardis said. "I'll call you when I'm up and I can be sure you're properly caffeinated. We'll fig-ure out the when and where of it then, and I'll call the others to let them know. I might as well give Joe a buzz, too, although I expect he'll have an unbreakable date with some fish."

Lured.

"Hon?" Ardis put her hand on my shoulder and I looked up into her kind face.

"Someone lured her there," I said. "To that spot. At that time. It couldn't have been done any other way. Not with any certainty."

"That was the flaw in the targeting theory," Ardis said. "I knew you'd catch it, but I didn't want to stymie your cognitive processes by dwelling on it. The targeting the-ory only works if someone was truly evil."

"Someone spun a web and lured Reva Louise in. You're right. Truly evil."

"Amen."

I took the long way home, with a three-block zigzag out of my way to stop at the Weaver's Cat. On other evenings, I'd thought of the nighttime streets in Blue Plum as cozier than dark streets back in Springfield, Illinois. The streetlights were few and far between in Blue Plum, but they gave enough mellow light to keep me from tripping on uneven sidewalks. Chirping crickets and occasional voices and laughter from a front porch usually softened any worries I carried around with me. But that night I skirted the park behind the courthouse and I couldn't make myself walk down the service alley behind the Weaver's Cat to look in the back door. I passed by the mouth of the alley and then started to run. I was out of breath by the time I dashed around the corner and climbed the steps to the front porch.

As I cupped my hands to one of the front windows, trying to see into the darkened shop, a familiar trickle of cold made me shiver.

"I've been thinking it over," Geneva said. She appeared beside me, her right arm across my shoulders, her left hand cupped to the window, like mine, the better to peer inside. "I believe Reva Louise knew she was going to die. What are we looking at in there?"

"I was looking for you." I slipped out of her embrace and crossed the porch to sit on the steps. She drifted over and sat on the top step facing me, her back against the porch post, her chin on her drawn-up knees.

"Should we be seen speaking to each other on Main

Street on a Saturday night?" she asked. "Whatever will the neighbors say? Or the lamplighter?"

I dug my phone out of my purse and put it to my ear. Before speaking, I still looked to see if anyone else was out walking and might overhear. A casual conversation on a cell phone in public was one thing. Discussing murder out in the open, even quietly, made me nervous. "Why do you think she knew she was going to die?"

"She waved."

"I don't understand."

"At me. She waved at me. I'm sure there must be such a thing as a fact book of ghosts available somewhere. Maybe you can find one at the library. I never cared for reading about that kind of supernatural hogwash myself, but someone has probably done a study. Something authoritative would be best."

"Why do I want to read this hogwash?"

"I'm not sure, but I think you'll find that in the few moments before a person dies, she or he can see spirits. Ghosts. That's interesting, don't you think? Almost romantic."

"You told me that people who drink gin sometimes see ghosts."

"Well, obviously there's more than one way to see a ghost."

"I've been seeing you for several *months*. I don't drink gin and I haven't had so much as a sniffle."

Geneva shrugged. "Everyone knows you're different."

Because I was sitting on the front steps of a yarn shop that only I knew was haunted, I wasn't in a position to argue with her about being different. "Tell me what happened. What you saw when you think she waved at you."

"When she *did* wave at me. There was a terrible noise outside. People yelling and shooting. Poor Argyle had to hide under the desk. It broke my heart not to be able to cuddle and comfort him. I looked out the window in the study, but all I saw was people running around the corner, so I went to that nasty, dusty window in the gable end. People were in the street and more people, including children, lined the street, and a small, terrified animal—it might have been a puppy, but I couldn't be sure—was trying to push its way into a tent. Was that your tent?"

"Yes. That was a piglet. You were watching the play I told you about."

"It wasn't like any play *I've* ever seen. It was very loud with some people brandishing rifles and other people laughing. It was very confusing. And then most of the people moved off down the street and along came Reva Louise. She stood behind your tent and looked around. She moved a few steps to her left. She looked up and she waved at me. And then she opened her mouth like this." Geneva's mouth made a circle and her empty eyes were wide and round. "Then she fell. Dead."

"You were watching when she fell?" I tried to keep my voice steady and low, tried not to send vibes of shock or horror. "Are you okay?" She seemed okay and she'd seemed her usual self when she floated down out of the window and joined Ardis and me beside the body. But she'd started acting oddly when we sat in the squad car and later in the study. I knew that sometime in her past—in her life—she'd been traumatized by the violent deaths of a young couple named Mattie and Sam. That was the "mysterious antique double murder" Clod Dunbar had razzed me about the night he horned in on my possible date with his brother. It was a terrible memory that Geneva had asked me not to remind her of. But seeing Reva Louise shot right in front of her . . .

"Do you want to talk about what happened this afternoon?" I asked.

"I just did. Weren't you listening?"

"I was. I just wondered if you needed to—" She really *didn't* seem upset, and something else suddenly occurred to me. "Say, Geneva, when Reva Louise passed over—"

"Over what?"

"I mean when she, um, died, did she . . . is she . . . did she become—"

"A ghost? No. She is not a ghost."

That was more of a relief to hear than I expected. Talk about speaking ill of the dead, but I was pretty sure I wouldn't like Reva Louise any better dead than alive. "I know I've asked you this before, but why do you think she isn't a ghost and you are? How does that happen?"

"And I know I have answered you before and the answer has not changed. I might be dead, but that doesn't make me an expert."

"Okay, well, I want you to think about something. That gable window you were looking out of is so dusty that you couldn't tell whether the actors were chasing a piglet or a puppy, right? So maybe you couldn't tell who Reva Louise was looking at when she waved. Do you think it's possible she was waving to someone in a window below you? Someone in the bathroom window?"

"Don't you like my theory that she knew she was going to die?"

"I do like it, but I want to add a twist to it. What if someone lured Reva Louise to stand right there in that spot? What if she knew that person, saw that person in the bathroom window, and waved? To *that* person. And that's the person who shot her. What do you think of that theory?"

"I like the inescapable tragedy of mine more," she said, "but I can see where yours has a certain drama running through it. It also lets me off the hook."

"What hook?"

"You don't suppose she'd been drinking gin, do you?"

"No idea. Geneva, what hook are you talking about?"

"The hook of inescapable and tragically eternal responsibility." She actually put the back of her hand to her forehead and billowed with each lovingly added adjective and adverb. I waited without saying anything until she looked at me out of the corner of her eye.

"Is that why you acted skittish when the deputies came up to the study with me? Why did you think they'd arrest you over that?" The poor thing. No wonder she acted like a dank and dismal dishrag so much of the time. She carried an awful load around with her. Not that she didn't seem to enjoy it some of the time. "Did you have a lot of responsibilities back when, when you were alive?" I asked.

"You stutter over saying that dead-and-alive thing much less than you used to," she said. "It's a nice improvement."

"Thank you. Will you answer my question?"

"Perhaps I led a carefree and pampered life and that's why I am so quick to chain myself to the yoke of responsibility now. Remember when I thought I was responsible for Em's ghastly death?"

I did remember. And neither then nor now did she

look like the ghost of a woman without a care in the world. Then she'd looked more like a puddle of eternal sorrows. I didn't tell her that, though. She'd come a long way since then. A long, melodramatic way, but apparently we'd both improved.

"Did you go downstairs this afternoon?"

"Oh my gosh." She sat up straight, dropping her knees and slapping her thighs soundlessly with her hands. "Would I have seen the *villain*?"

"You might have." I leaned toward her, catching her excitement, hoping she *had* seen someone.

She threw her hands in the air. "What a shame, then, because I didn't go downstairs at all."

We both sighed. I took the phone from my ear and checked the time, then let it drop in my lap. It was going on ten and time to be going home. I had notes to make, questions to pull out of my head and get into my laptop. Or my new notebook. I didn't stir.

"Would it help if I told you who came *up*stairs this afternoon?" Geneva asked.

"Upstairs where? To the study? John or Ernestine might have done that, but was there someone else?"

"Oopsy."

"What do you mean, 'oopsy'? Who did you see?"

She pointed to the phone in my lap, then mimed putting it to her ear. "Oopsy," she said again. "Too late."

"Nice evening," another voice said.

Chapter 16

J. Scott Prescott must have cut across the street. He stepped up on the sidewalk, still wearing the frock coat he'd worn for the skit. Also wearing an assessing kind of look on his clean-cut Boy Scout face. He crossed his arms, head tipped to one side. Was he taking my measure? Wondering just how off-the-wall this woman talking to thin air was? But how much could he have heard? Except that, in my excitement to hear who'd been sneaking in my attic, I hadn't exactly been whispering.

"Ah." He snapped his fingers. "I get it. You can't fool a playwright. You were rehearsing something. Rehearsing what, I can't imagine, but you were good. You had me believing that old porch post there was going to answer you." He grinned and put his hand on the railing.

Geneva made a rude noise but stayed where she was with her back to the post. I palmed my phone and stood, moving up the steps so I was on the porch looking down at him. J. Scott's grin faded.

"I'm sorry we didn't have a chance to talk this afternoon, after what happened," he said. "That was a truly terrible and completely avoidable accident. I hope you can believe me when I say I did not go against your wishes. None of my actors was cleared to enter your business during the play. I am as profoundly shocked as anyone that such a mistake was made. And live ammunition." He shook his head. "Unbelievably careless and absolutely stupid. I spent most of the afternoon with the sheriff and his deputies, working with them, going over the logistics and the choreography, both of which I'd thought were impeccable. As I told them, repeatedly, I am at a loss to understand how it happened. Miscommunication? I don't know. I gave instructions and, for whatever reason, someone thought he knew better." He shook his head again, looking at the ground. "As I say, I don't know. I believe I'm still in shock. Or maybe I'm suffering from utter exhaustion."

"Has he noticed he is the only one talking?" Geneva said out of the side of her mouth.

"Seems unlikely." Oopsy.

"I beg your pardon?" J. Scott looked up.

"Either one of them seems likely," I said. "Probably both. Exhaustion *and* shock."

He and I both nodded at that wisdom. Geneva joined us for a few nods and then made another rude noise. I coughed to cover a laugh. She must have known a ten-year-old boy at some point and studied the finer points of his sense of humor. Or maybe she'd absorbed the nuances from her eternity of television watching.

J. Scott lifted his chin toward the front door with its crime scene tape. "Do you have insurance to cover loss of revenue in a situation like this?"

"Why? Do you have a card for selling insurance, too?" Judging from the reaction of his eyebrows, he didn't get my joke. "Sorry. You were saying?"

"After today's tragedy, loss of revenue is something else we have in common. Besides our love for old buildings, I mean. Do you remember that I told you I'd found a buyer for the mercantile across from the courthouse? Sad to say, but that deal might have died with Ms. Snapp."

That was interesting and that would be why Reva Louise had his card. But was the deal iffy because *someone* died or because *Reva Louise* died? While I was wondering whether or not to ask him about that, he skipped ahead of me.

"I hope you didn't mention the deal to anyone."

My mind ignored his question and thought of another interesting one of its own. Why was it that the mercantile deal only *might* have died?

Either my pondering lasted too long for his comfort or my extremely readable face was giving him an answer he thought he could interpret. He cocked his head to one side. "*Did* you mention it to someone?"

I brought my face and my lips into sync and said, "No. But why is the deal a secret?"

"You might say I'm superstitious. It must be the playwright in me."

"Are playwrights superstitious, too? I thought it was the actors."

He struck a pose, arms open, as though I might have missed his frock coat and neck handkerchief.

"Oh yeah. I guess I hadn't realized you were in the skit as well as directing it. You've got the superstition thing covered, then."

He looked disappointed. Had he expected a different reaction? Applause? I wasn't going to go that far, but the least I could do was dredge up some sympathy.

"I'm sorry your skit ended so badly today."

"The *play*," he said, emphasizing my lapse in calling it a skit. "And it actually ended well. The last scene took place in the park behind the courthouse exactly as intended. The finale appeared chaotic to the audience, but it came off without a hitch. I showed the script to the sheriff so he could see that we left almost nothing to chance except the individual actors' use of the Piglet War yell. And there was plenty of spirited yelling coming from the audience as well. The piglet himself came through unscathed. And all of that was taking place at about the same time the unscripted addition to the performance — the tragic death of Ms. Snapp — occurred."

"Or maybe after she died. I don't think she was shot too long after the action moved on from Depot Street."

He flicked a hand, indicating what? Agreement? Uncertainty? A sense of being overwhelmed by the chaos that had crashed his masterpiece? I was feeling unkind but didn't ask him that question.

"Were you able to help the sheriff figure anything out?" I asked instead. "You gave him a list of all the actors?"

"I gave them all the information I could," he said.

That didn't really answer my question, so I asked another. "Any idea how easy it'll be to figure out who used the live rounds? Will they be able talk to all the actors?"

"The sheriff gave me almost no information back, so I'm afraid we're left wondering. And looking over our shoulders." He loosened his neck handkerchief. "That I'm still wearing all this shows what kind of day it turned into." He pulled the handkerchief off and shrugged out of the long black coat. His shirt and trousers were part of the costume and looked to be reasonably accurate re-productions. His shoes, too, from the little I could see of them. "The day was too hot for linsey-woolsey," he said, "but do you know, after a point that didn't even register, because the rest of the day became too terrible." He slung the coat of his shoulder. "And now I will bid you good night. Again, I'm sorry for the trouble this has brought down on you and your business." He bowed and walked away.

I expected Geneva to clap at his performance, be-cause that's exactly what it seemed to be. A backside-covering performance of grand proportions, complete with overblown language. It had at least earned another, even louder, rude noise from Geneva, but she didn't clap or blow raspberries. When I looked at her, she hooked a thumb at his retreating back and said, "*He* crept into the study today. Uninvited and unannounced."

"*What?*"

I looked after him and saw him hesitate, head tipped as though listening. Maybe he'd caught my outburst. Then he crossed the street and disappeared around the corner. But the *nerve* of him, standing there and telling me he was in shock and suffering from utter exhaustion. Suffering from utter gall was more like it. For the brief-est nanosecond I considered running after him and wrapping his handkerchief back around his neck—tight—until he told me what he'd been up to. But I was glad when my brain stepped in and kept my feet where they were. Running after a snoop in the dark was stupid.

For an even briefer nanosecond I thought about call-ing Clod Dunbar and reporting J. Scott Snooprat. But that was even stupider. Clod would listen, ask questions, and then zero in on the ones I couldn't answer. How did I know he'd been in the study and why was I reporting it so many hours after the fact? I could tell Clod that Ernestine or John had told me and that they must have forgotten to tell him, but that would be dropping them into the middle of a lie and it wouldn't be fair. Dear, dear. It was the old conundrum: If no one else could see or hear the witness, did her evidence exist?

For lack of anything more constructive to do, I fell back on being petulant. Remembering, first, to put the phone to my ear. "Geneva, why didn't you tell me he went in the study?"

"I didn't recognize him dressed up in his frock coat. That was a very handsome style, don't you think? Men just don't dress the way they used to."

"They haven't dressed the way they used to for a long time, if you're longing for men in frock coats."

"I haven't *thought* of frock coats in a very long time. Anyway, when he took the coat off I realized who he was. Frankly, he's not my type."

"His type hasn't got anything to do with it. What did he do up there?"

"Let me think." She tapped a finger against her cheek. "Well, he didn't steal anything. I suppose that's a point in his favor."

"We aren't keeping track of points. What *did* he do?"

"Argyle and I were having a nap in the window seat. He disturbed us by opening and shutting the window."

"Did he go through the desk?"

"You'll have to ask him. Argyle and I left."

"You left while he was in there sneaking around? *Why*?"

"He isn't Argyle's type, either."

"Well, isn't that the—"

"Please don't swear at me."

"I wasn't going to. Okay, maybe I was. I'm sorry. I'm tired."

"You also have a tendency to become overwrought, but as long as you don't start overexplaining or overacting, the way he did, I don't mind."

"Gosh, thanks."

"You should stop being overly sarcastic, too."

"Got it."

"And snapping overly often—"

"Geneva? Let's go back to the part where I said I was tired. I really am. So do you mind if we wrap this up?"

"Not at all. But thank you for asking if I had an opinion on the matter."

"You're welcome. Would you like to come home with me?"

"Mm, I don't think so."

"Okay. Anyway, I am glad to know that it wasn't my imagination and that you thought. J. Scott Prescott was putting on a performance, too."

"It is possible he's always like that. It would be unfortunate for his kith and kin—do people still say kith and kin?"

"Rarely."

"Really? I'm glad I asked. I like to be up-to-date. In that case, it would be unfortunate for his nearest and dearest, but there are peculiar people in this world." Said she, who was a ghost, to the only person who ever saw or heard her.

"You're right. There are," I said. "But peculiar or not, I think we need to find out more about J. Scott and whatever his relationship was with Reva Louise. And we need to know a lot more about Reva Louise."

"Do you know if she had a butler? They're a shifty bunch."

"A butler's doubtful, but knowing more about her husband would be a good idea." I yawned in the middle of the word "idea." "And now I really do need to go. I wish you'd come home with me tonight."

"Are you afraid of the dark?"

Her question caught me off guard. Was I? And if I was, would that be a bad thing? "Maybe I am a little. But it's more that I still don't know when I'll be able to get back into the shop."

"They will have to let you back in sometime tomorrow because you left Argyle here."

"Good point."

"But I should stay here, anyway, to keep him company and to be your eyes and ears. Argyle and I will be on the alert, ready to defend the Weaver's Cat with our lives."

"Thank you, Geneva. That makes me feel better." Not much, because one of them had nine lives and the other was already dead, but it was the thought that counted.

"After all, the villain might break in tonight to retrieve incriminating evidence."

I stared at her.

"Don't you think Mr. Prescott's sudden appearance out of the dark was ominous and possibly sinister and might portend trouble in the small hours of the night? But don't worry. You go on home and get a good night's sleep. Argyle and I will be on guard, ever vigilant."

Unless they were napping or left the room because the villain wasn't their type. I swallowed panic. But, really, how likely was it that the shooter would risk leaving more evidence by breaking in to look for evidence the police would almost certainly have already found? Unless the killer knew the shop's many nooks and crannies better than the police and knew exactly where he'd left that incriminating piece of evidence behind.

Deep breaths, I told myself, deep breaths. I massaged my forehead, making large, slow circles with my fingertips. I made an effort and managed to dredge up an ounce or two of common sense and logic. If the killer left something in a nook or cranny, a place so cleverly hidden the police hadn't found it, then the killer wouldn't need to risk breaking in to retrieve it. He would wait for the shop to reopen, walk in, like any safe, smiling, ordinary customer, and get it. Whatever "it" was. Unless "it" was a complete figment of a ghost's and an overwrought woman's imagination. I really did need to go home and give my brain a rest.

"One more question. Then I'm gone," I said.

"Okay, and to demonstrate for you how fine-tuned my eyes and ears are and how I won't miss a nuance of chicanery in the Weaver's Cat until you come back, I will tell you that I've noticed it is taking you an *agonizingly* long time to actually leave."

I massaged my forehead in large, fast circles.

"I'm waiting for your question," said Miss Eyes and Ears.

"Okay, okay. You said you haven't read supernatural hogwash, right?"

"A load of drivel." She could give lessons in sniffing with derision.

"But when Reva Louise looked up and waved, just before she died, you thought she saw you. If you haven't read the hogwash, then how do you know that someone who's about to die can see ghosts?"

She drew in a—a what? A ghost of a breath? Then she drew in on herself, pulling her arms in until her elbows touched, her hands clasped tightly under her chin. "Because," she said, speaking so softly I had to lean in closer, "*I* saw one."

"You saw a—"

"*I* saw one," she repeated, starting to rock and billow. "Before I fell into darkness."

"Oh, honey, it's okay. Where were you? Where was the ghost?"

"Above. I was looking up. Like Reva Louise."

"Looking up at a window?"

"At betrayal."

"Geneva, wait—"

But she billowed and swirled and was gone and I felt almost breathless. Over the months I'd known her, she'd dropped clues about her age and I'd caught glimpses of her background, but it was hard teasing *her* memories from the tangle of story lines planted in her head during her years of endless television. Now, for the first time, she'd mentioned her own death and I had no trouble believing it *was* her memory or that she believed she'd seen a ghost.

I sat on the porch a while longer in case she came back. She didn't, so I started home, skirting the shadows, figu-

ratively and literally. The moon was high and small, far
away and far too cold to offer light or any kind of comfort. I was glad for my rubber-soled shoes—if I wasn't
making any noise padding home in the dark, it was all
the better to hear someone else sneaking along behind
me. As I passed the mercantile, sneering at it in a way it
didn't deserve, a movement across the street at the courthouse registered in my peripheral vision. The front of the
courthouse was lit from several directions by lights set
below it in the grass, but I turned in time to see someone
slip into the shadow of the columns at the top of the
steps, to the right of the double front doors. I pressed my
back against the mercantile's bricks and watched.

The person inched from behind a column, keeping an
arm around it as though hugging it for support. It was a
woman and she stayed like that, her face turned away,
turned toward the columns on the other side of the door.
She might have been looking or listening, I couldn't tell.
She peeled herself away from the column, moving slowly
so her arm still touched it, then just her hand, her fingers,
then their tips, and then she let go and walked to the
center of the top step where Sheriff Haynes and Mayor
Weems had spoken. It was Mercy Spivey's daughter, Angie Cobb.

Angie and I were a few years and a few pounds apart.
She led me in both. She led me in bravery when it came
to clothes, too. I'd seen her looking uncomfortable in
conventional, casual business wear. Uncomfortable and
unhappy. But I'd also seen her, as now, in skintight black
jeans and a formfitting camisole top. This was Angie,
tough and determined, Angie who could stand up for
herself and to her mother, Angie who, according to

Mercy, was studying for a real estate license. Her camisole top was red and it looked as if she had on red stilettos to match. She'd let her drab brown hair grow. It hung loose, brushing her shoulders.

Angie did something then that tickled me. She threw her arms out, one shoulder slightly forward, head back, and she looked for all the world as though she meant to belt out a chart-buster. But not a peep came out and I was glad she didn't seem to know I was watching. She plopped down on the top step, wrapped her arms around her knees, and rocked. In that position, if she'd been less substantial and wearing filmy gray instead of skintight black and bloodred, she would have looked like Geneva.

Someone else moved from behind one of the columns, from the direction Angie had been looking when I first spotted her. It was a man, but he didn't move far enough out of the shadows for me to see him clearly. Slim, the colors of his clothes indistinguishable in the dark, medium height to tall? I couldn't tell. He must have said something, called Angie. She jumped up and ran to him. It looked like the kind of run that should end in a hug or a kiss or an enveloping embrace. It didn't. He put his arm around her shoulders. She briefly leaned against him. They withdrew into the shadows and were gone.

I waited another minute or two, then walked the last few blocks home, wondering what that had been about. I stayed up another hour or so, making notes, getting the questions down, thinking about how to find the answers.

In the morning, I made the sleep-deprived mistake of

opening the front door to someone's knock without first checking to see who was there. It was Shirley and Mercy Spivey and it was earlier in the morning than I'd ever seen them. It was also earlier than I ever wanted to see them again, but something was obviously, terribly wrong. They weren't wearing matching outfits.

Chapter 17

"It's Angie," said one of the twins, pushing past me into the house before I could stop her.

The second twin made it in on the tail of the first. Sobbing, she still managed to echo, "It's Angie!"

I hadn't closed the door, to save the twins time when they were on their way back out. I took my eyes off them for a second and looked to see if Angie was on her way in, too. She wasn't. "What about Angie?"

"She's gone!"

"I saw her last night," I said.

"Where?" Both twins lunged at me. They probably only stepped closer, but I jumped back as if they'd lunged. They were definitely in a bad way. Both wore odd combinations of nightwear and haphazardly tossed-on daywear. One twin's hair stuck up in back; the other had combed hers but wore shoes from two different pairs. The most telling sign of their distress, though, was that neither of them, even at close range, smelled of Mercy's cologne.

I made them sit, putting them side by side on Granny's old chintz sofa. Neither of them had splashed on the wretched cologne, but they both *looked* so completely wretched that I pulled a chair over and sat directly in front of them. They leaned forward, listening, as I told them about seeing Angie at the courthouse and about seeing her leave with the man I couldn't identify. I held back the details of Angie standing with open, operatic arms and then sitting and rocking on the steps. Until I knew what was going on, her private moment of misery— or whatever it had been—would remain private.

"Has she been seeing someone?" I asked. "Maybe they—"

The twin on the right, the one who'd been sobbing and hadn't run a comb through her hair, interrupted. "She's been too busy with her coursework. Making something of herself. Making me pro-hou-hou-houd." And she dissolved back into tears. So that twin was Mercy.

Shirley, on the left, wearing mismatched shoes and what looked like a man's striped pajama top over a pair of pink capris, turned toward her sister and opened her arms. Mercy fell into them and I sat there feeling uncomfortable. When Mercy's howls quieted, I asked if one or the other would please tell me what was going on. They both did. Working in tandem, their tale was efficient, although not as dramatic as it had promised to be.

Angie wasn't home. That was the gist. I stared at them.

"We told it badly," Shirley said.

"She doesn't believe it any more than Cole Dunbar," said Mercy.

"You filed a missing person report with Deputy Dunbar?"

"Tried to," Shirley said.

"He says she hasn't been missing long enough," said Mercy. "But I know my daughter."

"But she's only been gone . . ." I looked at the mantel

clock and tried not to groan. "It's eight forty and I saw her between ten and ten thirty last night. She's been gone less than twelve hours." I thought about her red camisole and heels. "Maybe she went to a party and stayed over? Or got up early, went out for breakfast?" Surely the woman had a life of her own. I didn't say that out loud, but they read it easily enough on my face.

"Come on, Shirley." Mercy struggled to rise from the sofa.

"We'll find her ourselves." Shirley tried to pull herself up by hanging on to Mercy so that they both ended up back where they'd started. And Mercy started crying again. I quietly cursed whatever tender trait I'd inherited that attracted sobbing people and ghosts.

"Mercy, Shirley, please," I said. "I'll be happy to help. I like Angie. I'll call around. I'll look for her myself. But I need more to go on. Look at it from my point of view, from Deputy Dunbar's point of view." The thought of sharing a point of view with Clod Dunbar made me shudder. I rushed to move past it. "Angie is a grown woman. She lives in her own house. She's independent. She has her own friends." I hesitated. "She does, doesn't she? Have friends?"

Then I did something I never imagined myself doing. I patted Mercy Spivey on the knee. It was awkward, but she seemed to appreciate it.

"Let's go out to the kitchen. I'll make coffee and you think about what else you can tell me."

"We'd rather have tea," Shirley said.

"And toast," said Mercy, sniffling into a tissue she pulled from the leopard-print bra peeking around the edge of the Blue Plum High School hoodie she'd thrown on. "With low-cal spread, if you have it."

They sat at the small table in the kitchen—after I moved newspapers off one of the chairs and cleared my own breakfast dishes into the sink. While water for tea heated, I found a jar of Granny's blueberry jam in a cupboard. Every July, Granny had driven over Iron Mountain Gap to pick berries in a field outside the little community of Buladean. I wondered if she would mind if I fed her jam to the twins and decided she wouldn't.

"Do you know we've never been in this kitchen?" Shirley said.

"It looks like Ivy," said Mercy. "Lloyd, too. Must be the colors and the woodwork."

Shirley sighed. "It is one of our abiding sorrows that we weren't as close to Ivy as we might have been."

"Ivy was fey," Mercy said. "Always was." She might have noticed when I put the jam jar in front of her with more force than was called for. She blinked and added, "That's not criticism. People are what they are."

That was true enough. Shirley and Mercy certainly were whatever they were, only more so because everything was doubled. I took two plates, two knives, two teacups, four pieces of whole wheat toast, and Granny's blue teapot to the table.

"Now, tell me how you know Angie is missing."

"We talk twice a day, like clockwork," Mercy said. "I call her at seven in the morning and again at seven in the evening."

I couldn't help thinking, *Poor Angie.*

Mercy couldn't help reading that on my face. "We're very close," she said. "Sometimes she doesn't answer. She *does* have a life of her own. But then I send a text and she always gets back to me."

"Always? Even when she was married to Max Cobb?"

"Even if it's just to say, 'Back off,'" said Shirley.

Mercy glared at her. "I have always taken my role as a mother seriously and she *always* gets back to me. Angie did not answer last night, and she hasn't answered yet this morning."

"Is she working these days?"

"She's pouring her energy into her classes," Mercy said.

"Have you been by her house?" That was a silly question. Of course they'd been by her house. They'd been *in* her house, too. Mercy showed me the key.

"Her car is there," Mercy said. "Her suitcase is there."

"We don't know if she had some kind of little overnight bag, though," Shirley said.

"*Has!*" Mercy shouted. "What kind she *has*! And it doesn't matter. There's milk in the fridge and peaches sitting on the counter."

"What about her purse?" I asked.

"It's hard to say. She has several."

She hadn't had a purse with her the night before. Not unless she was able to fit it somewhere between her skin-tight clothes and her skin. "What about her wallet?"

They looked at each other, then at me.

"What about her classes at Northeast? Does she have class on Monday? Would she skip class? *Does* she have friends she hangs out with?" I'd hit a patch of head shaking, which made me think Mercy didn't have her finger on the pulse of Angie as much as she thought. And then I suddenly wished I hadn't thought of the word "pulse."

"What?" Mercy asked, searching my face. "What is it? You're worried about her, too, aren't you?"

I didn't want to answer that. I didn't know how to without upsetting the twins more than they already were, and possibly needlessly. Their whole to-do over Angie was probably needless. I couldn't believe she'd never been out of contact with Mercy for more than twelve hours.

"What were Angie's plans yesterday?" I asked. "Was she doing anything for the festival? Helping out at a booth?"

"We were busy with the historical society's booth," Shirley said.

"Giving Evangeline a hand," said Mercy.

In other words, they didn't know where Angie was during the afternoon. She'd looked upset when I saw her at the courthouse. Then she'd run to the man in the shadows. It hadn't looked like a lovers' tryst. More like she was being comforted. "Did she know Reva Louise Snapp?" I asked.

"That woman was an itch," Mercy said. "With a capital *B*."

"And Angie knew better than most," said Shirley.

"Why's that?"

Mercy pretended she wasn't making shushing motions at Shirley. Shirley pretended not to notice them.

"Angie and Dan Snapp were married," Shirley said, scraping her chair back out of range of Mercy's foot. "She needs to know it, Mercy, and there's nothing to be ashamed of in coming to your senses and cutting your losses." Shirley turned to me again. "Angie and Dan were married and divorced before she married Max and became an untimely widow. That girl has not had an easy time of it."

"How long ago did she divorce Dan?" I asked.

"Oh no, you've got it wrong," Shirley said. "It was the other way around. Dan divorced Angie. Because of that bit . . . because of what Mercy said."

A growl was building in Mercy's throat and finally exploded. "Reva Louise Snapp deserved to die!"

I should have kept the next question bottled up. "Does Angie have a gun?"

Chapter 18

"On a more positive note, the Spiveys won't be coming over for breakfast again anytime soon," I told Ardis later over the phone. I hadn't called her right away. After Shirley and Mercy left, I sat down at Granny's spinning wheel and worked the treadle for a while. I could have dug out some carded wool and started spinning, but the rhythm of the treadling was soothing enough. Sitting in a rocking chair would have worked, too. Or wrapping my arms around my knees and rocking the way Geneva and Angie had done the night before.

Shirley and Mercy hadn't left quietly. They'd screeched their way out the door like a couple of itches with a capital *W*.

"But I am kind of worried about Angie," I told Ardis.

"What are you *kind of* worried about most? Her whereabouts or her state of mind and her aim?"

"She *does* have a gun?"

"Max Cobb hunted. So, unless she sold his guns, yes. But do you really think milquetoast Angie would have the gumption to shoot someone in cold blood?"

"I think we can't rule her out. Did you know she was married to Dan Snapp once upon a time?"

"Well, well," Ardis said.

"I got the feeling it didn't last long."

"I wonder how long Dan and Reva Louise were married."

"That's something else we need to find out. I wonder if we'd get straight answers from Dan."

"I wonder if Dan ran into Angie and decided he'd finally had his fill of Reva Louise."

"I wonder—oh, here's another call and I do believe it's Deputy Dunbar. Call you back, Ardis."

"I'll call you, hon, after I wrestle Daddy in and out of a bath."

Clod's call was short and sour. The sheriff was allowing the Weaver's Cat to reopen. Clod wasn't interested in hearing anything about Angie Cobb and he cut me off almost as soon as I mentioned her.

"So that's your latest gig, is it?" he asked.

"What?"

"Kath Rutledge, Finder of Lost Persons." The smirk behind that remark came through the circuitry of my phone loud and clear, and at that point I understood Reva Louise's need for a phone-slamming app. I didn't have one, either, so I did the next most satisfying thing.

"Oh, hey, do you hear that?" I asked Clod as I walked toward the back door.

"Hear what?"

I opened the back door. "This." I took the phone from my ear, held it near the doorjamb, and gave the door an almighty slam.

My phone rang again almost immediately. Caller ID showed it was Clod. I didn't answer.

*   *   *

In my profession as a textile preservation specialist, I had always spent time researching and preparing ahead of any action I undertook so that I could move forward with confidence that I would avoid unintended consequences. Maybe, after my months in Blue Plum, my specialist chops were slipping. Slamming the back door in Clod's ear and ignoring his second call were both supremely satisfying, but that satisfaction bore unanticipated results.

After ignoring Clod's call, I jotted a few notes about Angie in my new sleuth's notebook and decided that digging into Dan Snapp's background was at least as important as finding out more about J. Scott Prescott. I'd just started doing the dishes when I heard a car pull into my gravel drive, going way too fast. It skidded to a stop, a car door opened, feet pounded up the back steps, the kitchen door burst open, and Clod Dunbar came barreling in.

"What the—" I'd been washing my chef's knife and spun around with it still in my hand, sending soap bubbles flying. A blob of suds splattered Clod's uniform shirt.

He was in an alarming tizzy. I was alarmed, too—as who wouldn't be if a large man with a gun burst into her kitchen while she was doing dishes?—but I wasn't within a hundred miles of being in the same state as Clod. Oddly enough, or maybe not so oddly, that made me happy. Happy, but not docile.

"What the heck do you think you're doing, Dunbar?" He jumped back. I might have gestured with the knife. "Put the knife down," he said. The tizzy portion of his state had evaporated, leaving behind his typical, starched cop mode.

I put the knife on the counter—more like smacked it on the counter. "What makes you think you can come barging in here? Scaring people half to death, banging doors . . ." Banging doors.

His flinty eyes looked from me, engaged in my quiet, domestic, morning chores, soap still dripping from my elbows, and then those flinty eyes glanced toward the table where my phone lay.

"Really?" I pointed at the phone. "You thought I might be—"

"You said you heard a noise. I heard a bang. You didn't answer when I called back. A woman was shot to death yesterday. Do the math."

"Huh. Does a slammed door really sound that much like a gunshot?"

"I'm paid to think the worst."

"But not about Angela Cobb, who hasn't been seen since last night?"

"I will tell you again. Please listen and see if you can follow these simple instructions. Leave the detective work to the professionals."

My question about Angie *was* pretty dumb-sounding. Three-quarters of the population of Blue Plum might not have been seen since the night before. To add immaturity to lame, I put my hands on my hips and said, "Yeah, but did you know *this*? Angie and Dan Snapp were married and she owns guns."

Clod walked to the door without answering.

"So I take it you haven't made an arrest yet?"

He turned at the door, still without answering, and

looked as well aware of the effort it was costing me not to say, "What?" He added another five or ten seconds of waiting before saying, "Thank you, Ms. Rutledge, for wasting police time." Then he nodded and walked out the door. Without closing it. Slob.

"Hey, I'm not the one who misinterpreted a cheap sound effect and I didn't ask you to come over here all macho and ready to save me, so don't tell *me* who wasted police time." I shouted that after him, but only when I heard his car backing out of the driveway and only from the safety of the kitchen.

The phone rang a few minutes later and I sidled over to the table to see who it was, feeling somewhat phone-shy. But it was Ardis, checking back in as she said she would. I told her we were good to open at our usual Sunday time—one o'clock.

"That's good," she said as though I was trying to cheer her up and not doing it well. "Yes, it's good to have work to look forward to, and also the joy of making sure they cleaned up every bit of fingerprint dust, and in the meantime I can go back to lolling in my living room."

"What gives? You don't sound happy about reopening or lolling. As if I believe you ever loll."

"I can loll with the best of them, hon, and you know I'm happy about the shop, but what about the investigation? Did we miss the boat on that? If they're allowing us to reopen, does that mean they've made an arrest? I've had one or two more thoughts about the case, and I hate to think all our efforts were a waste."

"I don't have any confirmation of this, but from all the signs . . ." I hesitated, flashing back on the "sign" of Clod bursting in the back door because he'd heard a bang.

"No, I'm pretty sure they haven't arrested anyone. And I have absolutely no confirmation of *this*, but I don't think they have any idea who they're looking for, either."

"Well," Ardis said, and I could hear the smile returning to her voice. "I know I shouldn't feel so pleased about that news, especially not if the person we're looking for is dangerous."

"But it puts a bounce in your Bargello, doesn't it?"

"I was going to say spunk back in my spinning. I'll see you at the Cat. Let's make it noon, in case we need to clean up after the deputies."

No sooner had I disconnected than the front doorbell rang again. If I'd known I was hosting a Sunday morning open house, I would have thrown on something more stylish than one of Granny's old blue chambray shirts and blue jeans. Feeling front-door-shy, too, since my surprise visit from the Spiveys, I was careful to look first. But when I saw who stood on the mat, I leapt to let her in.

"Sally Ann!"

She stood, head bowed, hugging herself as though keeping herself warm or keeping herself together. She looked up long enough to say, "Hey, Kath," then stared at her toes again.

I opened an arm, wanting to put it around her and bring her inside, wanting her to know there were people other than herself ready to give her the hug she needed. But I stopped short, turning it into an air hug and waving her inside instead. Too much had been going on in the last twenty-four hours, and I couldn't bring myself to touch her, to chance being zapped by whatever soup of emotions she was feeling.

"Come on inside, Sally Ann. Would you like some coffee?"

"Tea's good. If it's no bother." She looked as though she hadn't slept and her voice was as thin as the wisps of hair slipping loose from the knot at the back of her head. She had on a too-large Mel's on Main T-shirt and a pair of baggy cargo pants and looked altogether waifish.

She followed me to the kitchen and I didn't have the heart to sigh at the lack of coffee drinkers showing up on my doorstep. While I filled the kettle and warmed the pot again, she stood in front of the bookcase touching each of Granny's cookbooks with her forefinger.

"Do you do any of the cooking at the café?" I asked. I couldn't remember seeing her at the stove or in the prep area the times I'd stuck my head in the kitchen.

"No. I never took the time to be interested. That's what Mama said. She and Reva Louise, though . . ." Her voice trailed off as her finger slid down a book spine and she ended up with her arms wrapped tightly around herself again.

"How are you holding up?" As soon as I asked, I was irritated with myself. I'd been asked the same question countless times in the days after Granny died and I'd vowed never to ask it of anyone else. There wasn't really anything wrong with the question. Well-meaning people asked it. Good and caring people. But they were people who wanted to hear that the recently shattered weren't going to be in pieces for long. They wanted answers that would affirm what they needed to hear—that death, when it touched their own lives, would be survivable. Hearing the right answer allowed them to hold their breaths and run past or fly over that terrible black void.

Or maybe I just hadn't moved past Granny's death as well as I thought I had and could use a cup of tea myself. Or something stronger than tea *or* coffee, except it was too early.

"Sally Ann, you don't need to hold yourself together while you're here. I don't care if you're holding up or feeling hollowed out. If you need a friend to fall apart on, you go right ahead and do it, okay?"

Her face started to crumple. I grabbed the box of tissues off the counter, but when I turned back, she had the back of her hand to her mouth and she was shaking her head.

"I knew I'd come to the right person." She started to say something else but choked up. She closed her eyes and that seemed to get her past it. "Sorry. I was going to say that you're a straight shooter. Isn't that awful? Made me want to laugh and cry at the same time. I really am doing okay. Sort of. Probably because I'm in shock or something. But I'll work through it."

"Do you want to sit down?"

"Yeah. Yeah. I guess."

She didn't sit until I put a mug of tea down on the table. Then she sat and moved the tea away. I'd expected to see her put her hands around it, the way people do, gaining strength from the ceramic warmth. But the way she moved it, dismissing it and not looking at it again, jogged my brain out of its Midwestern-comfort-beverage mode.

"I wasn't even thinking, Sally Ann. Would you rather have iced tea? It won't take a second."

"That's okay. Don't bother. I don't want to take your time. I came to ask a favor."

"If I can. Sure." I sat down across from her.

"It's Mel. Will you go see her?"

"Where is she?"

"The café."

"Really? The café's open? *You're* not going in today, though, are you?" At each of my questions Sally Ann sat farther back in her chair. Geneva had told me more than once that I needed lessons in interviewing techniques. It wasn't such a bad idea; she just put it in an annoying way, insisting I could learn everything I needed to know by watching Joe Friday in old episodes of *Dragnet*. I was pretty sure I could think of better role models. But Sally Ann needed someone calm, then and there, so I told myself to relax and stop peppering her. "Sorry, Sally Ann. Tell me what's going on."

"Mel closed up early yesterday. Last night. About seven." She shook her head. "I left after . . . I left earlier, but a couple of the other waitresses came by afterward and told me. They said someone from the sheriff's department came by. And Mel was being weird before that, but then she cleared the place out. Customers, staff. Locked up. But she's still there. She never left."

"How do you know?"

"I saw her."

"I mean, how do you know she didn't go home and come back?"

"Same clothes. Same apron she had on when I left."

Or same clothes and apron put back on. But that wouldn't be like health-inspector-conscious Mel. Of course, neither was spending the night at the café.

"Any idea what she's doing in there? Have you talked to her? And what would you like me to do?" Again with

too many questions, but I kept my voice low and slow
and tried to look relaxed. It must have worked. Sally
Ann sat forward again.

"You know how you can see into that part of the
kitchen, at an angle, from the back door?"

I didn't, but I could picture it and I nodded.

"I went and knocked this morning and I could see her
standing in there. Standing. Just standing. And I'm sure
she saw me, but she didn't come to the door. Didn't wave.
Nothing."

"You don't have a key?"

"She must've turned the dead bolt. I'm worried about
her. I want you to go see her. Talk to her." Sally Ann
must have seen my reluctance and rushed on. "I'd go
again, but she won't open the door for me. Neither one
of us is touchy-feely, you know? There's not a lot of cozy
about Mel or me."

"But you're both hurting. And you're sisters."

"No. We're not. She and Reva Louise are and Reva
Louise and I are."

I'd forgotten. Reva Louise was the sister in between.
"But surely—"

"Kath, I'll remind her of Reva Louise. That isn't a
good idea right now. That's just between you and me,
though, okay? But it isn't a good idea."

I wondered about her "right now." Did she mean reminding Mel of Reva Louise would be okay in a few
days or weeks? In fact, it probably would be, time being
a healer. But what was Sally Ann worried would happen
"right now"? That didn't sound good. And Mel locking
herself in the café and not going home didn't sound
good, either.

"Aren't there already a lot of things that will remind her of Reva Louise?" I asked. "That she'll have to be the one going in early, again, to start the baking will remind her if nothing else does."

"I know." Sally Ann pulled the mug of tea toward her and moved it in circles on the table. "But it's complicated. I feel responsible. I'm the one who asked Mel to give Reva Louise the job. To give her a chance. You know what it's like. You've got sisters or brothers, don't you?"

"No, but I think I know what you mean. I've known some—"

She cut me off. "You don't really know, then. But trust me, it's complicated. Especially between sisters. And Mel didn't know she had one and now she's lost her and she hasn't got many real friends. But she likes you, Kath, and she needs someone. So could you go over there? Talk to her? Please?"

"I'll try." I cringed inside hearing myself say that. *I* didn't know what to say to Mel. Didn't know what was going on with her. Didn't want to play Dr. Kath making a horrible house call.

"Thank you." Sally Ann put her hands to her cheeks and shook her head, her eyes focused on the tea mug. "I had to call Mama and that was the hardest thing I've ever had to do. It tore her up."

And there I was, pitying myself because I didn't know what to say to a hurting friend. "Sally Ann, I'm so sorry. Does your mother still live in Gatlinburg?"

"Moved on down to Florida. She's not able to travel much."

"Poor thing. What a shock this must be. Do you know when the funeral is? Where she'll be buried?"

"Nothing firm yet. It's up to Dan."

"How's *he* doing?"

"You know how folks say so-and-so is being strong enough for two of us? That's Dan. He was more worried about me yesterday. Took me home. Stayed awhile. Taking care of people is what he knows. He took good care of Reva Louise." She blew her nose on a tissue. "But he's hurting."

"Did they have children?"

"She miscarried a few years back. Then I guess they couldn't."

"I don't even know where they lived." Why was I using past tense for *both* of them? I hurried to revive Dan with the age-old remedy. "I know some of us would like to take food around to Dan. Do you think he'll mind?"

"It'll show up on his doorstep even if he does," Sally Ann said with a sad smile.

"And some of it questionable."

"Isn't that the truth? I can't tell you the address, but it's the house at that sharp curve on Spring Street, on the way out of town, before you cross the train tracks. You know the one? Old house. Bunch of ramshackle outbuildings. Not much to look at, but Reva Louise said she liked the potential. She was all about potential."

Somehow "potential" paired with "Reva Louise" wasn't conjuring pictures of rosy hope and optimism in my head. More like sneaky possibilities. Or mayhem.

Chapter 19

"What's going on, Mel?"

I stood outside the café's back door, nose almost pressed to the window. Sally Ann had been right. Mel did look as though she'd spent the night there. She'd taken off her apron at some point, but her chef's pants, usually crisp and clean, were as tired as her eyes. At least her spiked hair looked alert. Maybe it was keeping her awake. I knew she could hear my question through the door, because I heard *her* loud and clear.

"Not buying, Red. Don't care what you're selling."

At least she'd come to the door when I knocked. Sally Ann said she hadn't even waved.

"Do I look like a door-to-door yarn peddler to you? Come on, what do you think I'm trying to sell?"

"Thoughts and prayers. Visions of a better place. As far as I'm concerned, all of that happy-happy mumbo jumbo is like alien abductions, Red. Not happening."

"I'm not peddling that, either."

"Then what do you want?"

I felt silly, but I looked left and right to make sure no one was lurking in the service alley to hear me. I gestured for her to come closer and put my mouth to the crack between the door and the frame. "Answers, Mel. We think there's more to Reva Louise's death than a trigger-happy reenactor. We're short on physical evidence, but the scenario we're putting together is the more compelling for its lack." I pulled back from the crack to gauge her response. She raised an eyebrow. I leaned toward the crack again and almost stumbled inside when she swung the door open.

"It wasn't locked," she said with a shrug.

"Sally Ann said—"

"I unlocked it after she left. I'm still not open, though. If you don't believe me, you can read the sign on the front door. It's still locked."

"A lot of good that does back here. Aren't you worried about people coming in thinking you *are* open?"

"It's mostly locals and I've been running them off all morning. Except Carl." She hooked a thumb over her shoulder. Carl, an eightysomething widower who used his morning walk to the café to jump-start his days, sat at his usual table in the back corner, nursing a cup of coffee. He lifted two fingers from the cup in greeting. "Carl needs me," Mel said. "The rest can wait until I open up again. Make up your mind, Red. In or out. You're as bad as a cat and I don't need the flies."

I went in. She closed the door and I followed her to the kitchen. The scent of onion lingered in the air from her chopping extravaganza of the day before. The onions were nowhere in sight and the place was spotless.

"Hold up," Mel said to me. She stuck her head back out the kitchen door. "Keep the riffraff out, will you, Carl? And help yourself if you want more coffee."

"Why don't you just lock the door again?" I asked.

"Nah. It'll give Carl purpose if he can run off a tourist or two. Now, what's this you're saying about my sister?" She faced me, fists on her hips, mustard spiked hair like raised hackles.

Her challenge gave me pause. How did one suggest the possibility, to a loyal and rock-hard woman—one with quick access to long knives—that her sister wasn't universally liked? And by "wasn't universally liked" one meant that her sister was disliked for several good reasons, including that she was dishonest. And that she was disliked *enough* that someone felt the need to shoot her. But Sally Ann had said that *I* was a straight shooter and that's what I'd always tried to be in my professional life. So, despite Mel's intense eyes locked on me, I could do this. I could tell her.

"Mel, Reva Louise was, was . . ." My hands flailed, trying to pull the least judgmental and the clearest, most objective words from my head as they could. "Reva Louise was a liar, a cheat, and a thief." Well, at least I was clear.

Mel's eyebrows rose. So did mine.

"Let me show you something," she said. "See what you have to say after you see it."

Everything except her spiked hair stood down and she led me to the room she used as an office. I'd never been in it, but with its high, tin ceiling and each of the four walls painted a different shade—turmeric, curry, paprika, and ground cumin—it made me feel as though we'd stepped into a spice can. The only window looked across a one-lane alley to the cinnamon-colored bricks of the next building over, but the room was large enough for an antique rolltop desk against the curry wall and a comfy chair and love seat with a narrow coffee table in between. The chair and love seat were fresh sage and dry thyme respectively. The coffee table was lacquered and could have been a bar of dark chocolate—ninety-nine percent cocoa.

"Nice, isn't it?" Mel asked, pleased with my reaction. She had, with help from her brother, taken the derelict Blue Plum Hardware and converted it into Mel's on Main. They'd carved out the dining room, kitchen, and walk-in coolers, and also this nicely proportioned space. "I don't spend a lot of time in here," she said, "but when I do, I figure I might as well be comfortable. Sit down." She pointed to the love seat.

I sat. I still wasn't entirely sure she was reacting calmly to my bald statement that her sister was a liar and a crook. While she went to the rolltop and gathered what she planned to show me, I steadied my nerves by studying the bookshelves on the turmeric wall across from me. Cookbooks were interspersed on the shelves with what were probably antique kitchen gadgets. Whisks of various designs, standing in a crock, I recognized. And a mallet, with a corrugated face, that might be a meat tenderizer. But a couple of the larger tools had cranks and hoppers that suggested grinding jaws somewhere inside their wooden boxes. Those things looked scarier, to a jumpy mind's eye, than any domestic implement had a right to.

Mel plopped into the comfy chair facing me.

"Mel."

She looked up from the papers she was spreading between us on the table. Now her eyebrows were drawn together and her mouth twisted sideways. In disgust?

Anger? She pointed a finger at me. "What you said?" She turned the accusing finger to the papers. "Yeah, she was. And I might've been slow, but I was beginning to figure it out."

Offering a "sorry" hardly covered the situation. I said it anyway.

"Thanks. Here's my summary of this episode of my life. I kind of liked the idea of having a sister. It didn't work out. Too bad."

I wondered if it was that simple and if she was that tough. She was too busy shuffling her papers to meet my eyes, which told me something. What she said next did, too.

"If someone hadn't shot her, I would've had to fire her." This time she did look at me. "Firing isn't the same as shooting her myself, Red. Okay, okay, I get it. The point your body language is making is taken. I won't talk like that in public."

"Good. And not in private to Cole Dunbar or any of his deputy buddies, either, I hope. Or to anyone who might go tell them. Why were you going to fire her? Is that what's in your papers?"

"She was cooking the café's books."

"Ooh. Sautéed by your own sister."

"Yeah." Mel jumped up and started pacing. "Not by much, though. She was smart. She wasn't greedy." She pivoted and reversed course at the end of each short statement.

"And you didn't suspect?"

"No. Because she *was* smart. She was plausible. She was an excellent liar." She stopped and held her hands out flat. Then she slapped them to her temples. *"Blinders,"* she said. "I had on blinders because I wanted to like her. I wanted to give her a chance. What a chump."

"Don't be so hard on yourself. If you didn't suspect anything, you're not a chump. And we all tried to like her."

"You tried because that's the way you are. But not everyone tried. *I* knew why Thea and Joe quit showing up at Fast and Furious, and it ticked me off."

"Really? Oh. Well, liking her and not thinking she was a—"

"Louse."

I shrugged. "Ardis called her a boll weevil. Anyway, liking her and realizing she was a louse are two separate things. I think it's fair to say we were all fooled by her, so I guess that makes us all chumps."

Mel stabbed her finger at me again. "But you don't know what I knew when I hired her." The pacing, pivoting, and short bursts of information started again, too. "I knew it up front. Sally Ann told me. I knew there was a risk. But the recidivism rate is low. I know that because I can Google with the best of them."

"Are you saying she did this before?"

Mel stopped midpace. "Didn't I say that?" She dumped herself back in the chair. "Yeah, she'd been there, done that, paid the price. You didn't know I have a bleeding heart, did you?"

"Well, yeah, Mel. Doesn't ev—"

"You did *not.*" She actually looked shocked.

"I'll admit, you hide it well. I'm sure I'm the only one who knows. Did Reva Louise serve time?"

"Two years of probation. She was still making restitution. Pffft. That's probably why she needed the money. Can you believe she stole from a church? She was the secretary and kept their books."

"You knew that and you let her keep *your* books?"

She dragged out the word "no" so that it sounded as if she was in pain. "But I should've been more careful. I let her place the orders for baking supplies. They were pretty much our regular orders. It should've been easy as pie." She made a disgusted noise. "There are a lot of bad jokes I could make about this. But I gave her a job, offered her a chance to start over, paid her well, thinking that would make a difference, and the bottom line is, I was dumb. I made the mistake of thinking, 'What could go wrong?'"

"That's a classic. It shows you're an optimist, though. Your opinion of Reva Louise was half-full. That isn't such a bad thing."

"Except to an embezzler, her bank account must always look half-empty."

"Is that what you were doing here all night? Going over accounts?"

She looked at me.

"Sally Ann told me. She was worried."

"Funny how she and I are more alike than either of us was to the real half sister."

"Except Sally Ann has an aversion to needlework of any kind."

"Everyone has a flaw or two, Red. Some of them are just more obvious than others."

"And there's my segue, Mel. We think someone's flaw, possibly Reva Louise's own, led to her death. Ardis and I do, and, you know, some of the other members of TGIF."

"Kath Rutledge and her posse riding to the rescue again?"

"Yeah, well." Ardis was the one who'd started calling our small subset of TGIF my "posse." She liked the idea of mild-mannered needle artists having alter egos. I liked the fact that we'd unraveled the clues and found the answers to a few mysteries before Clod Dunbar. Geneva, being the television Western enthusiast that she was, *loved* being a member, even if no one else knew she was. Or that we never rode horses into a sunset. But they all referred to it as *my* posse, and that made me somewhat uncomfortable.

"Hey, don't shrug it off," Mel said. "I'm giving you your due, not making fun. You've got a good track record. *We've* got a good track record. I'm part of your posse, too, so tell me what we've got."

I took out my notebook, slipped the elastic, and read. Mel listened to the points Ardis, Thea, Ernestine, and I had come up with over supper the night before, plus the questions I'd added since. I also read the list Ernestine gave us of the people she remembered coming into the shop and the list John e-mailed to me. I read Mel's name with no more or less emphasis than the rest. "We're still in the gathering stage," I said when I finished. "But what do you think?"

"That I probably scalded Ernestine's and John's ears when I made my mad dash in and out of the Cat. Did they tell you why I was there? Or do you want me to tell you so you can compare the two versions?"

I tried not to look as uncomfortable as I felt.

"Body language, again," Mel said. "You need to practice your 'I'm good, I'm cool' look in the mirror more often. It's okay, though. I was looking for Reva Louise."

"About the lunch thing?"

She threw her hands in the air. "You're not supposed to throw a line to a witness like that. I'd roll my eyes, too, Red, but the eyes are such a cliché."

"And you avoid those like the plague?"

"You're darn tootin.' What's 'the lunch thing'?"

That stopped me. She didn't know? "Um, that's what Ernestine thought you were there for, and I'll tell you about it in a minute. But then, why *were* you looking for Reva Louise?"

Mel looked at me, then looked away. "I'm not proud of my temper, Red. I figured out what she was doing with the supply orders and I needed to do something about it. It couldn't wait. Do you know what that's like? Sally Ann said she might be at your place, so I stormed over."

"You would've confronted her in the Cat?" That was an appalling thought. "Did Sally Ann know why you were looking for Reva Louise? Does she know about the orders?"

"No. She doesn't need to feel bad about bringing Reva Louise down on us."

"You don't think she's guessed something by the way you stormed out?"

"Well, she's no dummy. So tell me what the 'lunch thing' is and if I owe anyone anything to make up for it."

"Let's just say Reva Louise was a piece of work, Mel, and leave it at that."

"But that's why you think someone killed her? Pushed over the brink by a piece of work?"

"Like I said, we're still at the gathering stage."

"Clues, evidence, and no preconceived notions?" She thought for a minute. "This pig skit guy. Prescott?"

I nodded.

"He's also a real estate agent?"

"And a piano salesman. As he says, high-end."

"It'd be hard not to have preconceived notions about a guy like that," she said with a quick smile. She started tapping an index finger on the arm of her chair. "What about this? I know a real estate agent in Knoxville. You want me to give her a call? See if she can pick up any buzz about him? Discreetly."

"First, any idea why Reva Louise would have one of Prescott's realty cards?"

Mel cocked an eyebrow.

"I found one in her pocket after she, um . . ."

Mel cocked both eyebrows.

"I gave it to the police. Anyway, Prescott said he had a deal in the works for the mercantile that might be scuttled by Reva Louise's death." Which was information he'd asked me not to share. And then the skunk had snuck around in my study. "Sure, call your friend. I don't see how it can hurt."

"A dangerous phrase, Red, much like 'what could go wrong?' But I'm glad to see you haven't learned, because I probably never will, either. Make a note of that, will you?"

Instead, I wrote notes about embezzling and about Mel making inquiries in Knoxville. I got a kick out of writing *making inquiries* and thought how pleased Geneva would be if I read that to her in a plummy British accent. I was about to close the notebook with an authoritative snap of the elastic when I thought of a piece of information I hadn't gotten. "Hey, Mel, is the embezzling the theft you reported? The one Cole Dunbar asked you about yesterday?"

Mel went completely still. She could have been a bird or a rabbit, frozen in a yard when it's just realized someone is there and watching it. Talk about body language.

"No." She picked her papers up from the table. I hadn't looked at them, but I believed her when she said they showed Reva Louise had been helping herself. "No," she said again, tapping the papers into a stack. "That was something else. Entirely. Nothing to do with Reva Louise."

That I didn't believe.

Chapter 20

Mel successfully ignored my most skeptical look, one I knew I didn't need to practice in a mirror. *She* certainly didn't need to practice "studied casual." She got up and sauntered over to her desk with her papers and turned back to me and clapped her hands together. "Time for you to skedaddle, Red. I've got a café to bring back online and Lord knows I need to sell a lot of lunches to make up for the money Reva Louise took."

"Do you think you could get the money back from Dan?"

"Mm." She fluttered a hand. "Iffy. Remains to be seen."

I let her shoo me out of the office. I didn't think blocking the doorway until she coughed up the truth about the theft was likely to work. We went back through the kitchen, still rich with the ghosts of onions chopped.

"What'd you do with all your chopped onions?"

"Did you like that? Talk softly and chop with a sharp knife—that's my motto. That and a bag of onions get me out of therapy free. You should try it. The onions went in the freezer. And you want to know the best part? Reva Louise hated onions."

Carl had nodded off, but he came to with a snort and a confused look when Mel smacked the bulletin board in the hall near the back door. It made me jump, too.

"Sorry, Red." Then she called, "You awake there, Carl? You might want to get up and walk around. Did you know that when you're sitting like that you're barely burning more calories than you will be when you're dead? Come on over here and give us a consult."

"I thought I was on my way out the door so you could reopen," I said.

"We'll get to that. But the name Prescott finally ran a bell. Not too tall, right? Expensive suit and the bright eyes of a sales rep who's discovered new territory?"

"Sounds like him. Where did you run into him?"

"Where else? Here. About a week back. Midmorning. Coffee, black, and one of Reva Louise's espresso muffins. He ate and drank, didn't linger, asked if parking was ever a problem downtown, and on his way out picked up two cheese Danish and a refill on the coffee to go. I see weight gain in his future if they were both for him." Mel called her ability to describe customers by their eating habits her "mental menu and meal ticket memory." Most people who stopped in town for any length of time found their way to Mel's, and if they stopped in often enough or during a lull, there was a good chance she would re-member more about them than they might imagine.

"Did he offer you any business cards?"

"That's what rang the bell." She smacked the bulletin board again. Half of it was covered in business cards from all over the map, a low-tech but colorful form of business information exchange. People were welcome to pin and unpin as they liked. There were hundreds of cards and cards covering cards. "I saw him adding to the collection," she said.

"This might be where Reva Louise got the card she had, then." I hadn't realized how prejudiced I was toward J. Scott Prescott until there was a logical and uninteresting reason for Reva Louise to have the card in her hidey-hole pocket. Or how disappointed I would be. I started scanning the board for Prescott's pasteboard trio.

"You can leave that for Carl," Mel said.

"Really?" I looked at Carl. He stood beside Mel and smiled sweetly with a set of too-white dentures.

"Nothing wrong with my eyes," he said. "And I've got all day. Tell me which card you want."

I described Prescott's realty card, offering to run down to the Cat and get the one we had if that would help.

"No need. If it's here, I'll find it."

"While you're at it, Carl, look for Snappy Small Engine Repair, too, will you?" Mel asked. "No idea what it looks like. Or if it exists, for that matter. What do you think? Are you up for the challenge?"

"My doctor tells me a challenge is good for an aging brain."

"And what do you tell your doctor?" Mel asked.

"An aging brain *is* a challenge." He carefully interlaced his arthritic fingers and stretched his arms in a slow-motion limbering-up exercise. "Cards might fade, but they can't hide," he said. "Stand back, gals." He creaked toward the bulletin board and Mel patted him on the back. But not too hard.

"Snappy?" I asked.

"Dan Snapp's dream, according to Reva Louise. His own small business."

"Yeah? And what are you thinking?"

"Wondering if it was his dream or hers or whether that matters. It would take a certain amount of money to get even a smallish small business off the ground."

I ticked expenses off on my fingers. "Rent, inventory, supplies. He might need tools or some kind of equipment, advertising. Maybe *that's* why she took Prescott's card. And why she needed money. But was her ..." I glanced at Carl's back. "Was her self-help program going to bring in enough to start a business?"

"I think that program was healthy and starting to grow," Mel said. "But even if it wasn't, I'm sure every little bit helped. And rent wouldn't have been a problem. She liked the idea of Dan setting up shop in one of the outbuildings at their place."

"Sally Ann said Reva Louise was all about potential. If I'm thinking of the right place, potential is about the only thing going for it. At the curve on Spring Street, right? Wasn't there some guy back twenty or thirty years ago who thought he could make a living raising ostriches out there? I remember Granny taking me to see them."

"You're talking about Pokey Weems," Carl said, trying to look over his shoulder at us. That didn't work out. He teetered and Mel latched onto his elbow to help him turn around. "Pokey always has an eye out for something new. I remember away back when he thought he was one of them, what were they? Beatniks. This was away, way back. He sent off for a bongo drum and wrote bad poetry. Pokey's mama was what we called 'artistic' back then, and he picked it up from her."

"Carl, are you wandering here?" Mel asked. "Why do we care what Pokey Weems was doing fifty years ago?"

"Who's Pokey Weems?" I asked.

"Are you going to listen or not?" Carl asked. "You're talking about this fellow Snapp's place, and so am I. That was Pokey's family home place. His granny still lived there, and he took it into his head to turn one of the buildings into a coffeehouse or roadhouse or some such. She wouldn't let him use the barn because she still kept a few pigs. And the loom house was the only other out-building near big enough. And *it's* none too big. And I'll tell you what else was wrong with that harebrained idea. The place wasn't plumbed and no one liked Pokey's booze, his bongos, his coffee, or his poetry. He had his girlfriend knit him a black sweater with a neck to it. Except she didn't knit any better than he wrote poetry and the thing looked like hell. He lost a bit of money on that place. Lost the girl, too. I could've told you back then Pokey Weems wouldn't amount to much. But if you're interested in where this fellow Snapp's setting up business, look in Pokey's old roadhouse."

Mel nudged me with her elbow. "Mayor Palmer 'Pokey' Weems."

"What'd I tell you?" Carl had an old man's raspy cackle. "He's finally reached bottom. He's a politician."

I laughed long enough to be polite, then asked, "Did you call it a loom house?"

Carl's laugh sputtered to a stop. "Say what?"

"It sounded like you said Pokey turned the 'loom house' into his roadhouse."

"It's what they used to call it," Carl said.

"Do you know why?"

"One of those old names. I doubt anyone calls it that anymore. I haven't heard anyone mention the place in years except when they want to get a rise out of Pokey."

"What are you thinking, Red?" Mel asked.

"That I have a reason to go poking around Pokey's granny's place. Identifying an authentic antique loom house in Upper East Tennessee is right up my alley."

There were a number of thoughts and questions from that visit to Mel's that I needed to get down in my notebook before they flew out of my head. Or before they were covered over by new thoughts and questions the way the business cards were on Mel's bulletin board. In fact, there was a whole string of questions about business cards. What would it mean if Carl *did* find one of Prescott's real estate cards? That Reva Louise got hers directly from Prescott? That she was a client? Or had she helped herself to a card from somewhere else? Or had he simply pinned more than one card to Mel's board? And what would any of that mean or matter?

My toe found a stone and I kicked it down the service alley, thinking and trying to keep the new strands from snarling before I reached the Cat's back door. Ardis wouldn't be in for another hour. That would give me time to jot away, barring unforeseen Geneva dramas. But maybe Geneva would be up for acting as a sounding board if I filled her in while I made my notes. Arriving at the Cat ahead of Ardis would also give me some meditative lap time with Argyle, not to mention time to fill his bowl with crunchy, fishy brunch and clean his pan.

The only signs in the alley that there'd been a festival in town the day before were a couple of abandoned cardboard cores from spun cotton candy. Not bad, I thought, picking them up and carrying them to the Dumpster we shared with the florist across the alley. I lifted the bin's heavy lid and made myself peek under my arm across Depot Street to where Reva Louise had been standing. Had fallen. I was surprised to see the Tent of Wonders still in the parking lot. The Dumpster lid slipped from my fingers and clanged shut. I was glad it hadn't slammed on my other hand. By reflex, I flapped that hand anyway, shaking off the near miss and glad it was alive, attached, and able to look silly flapping around my ear.

"You all right?" a voice called.

The clanging lid had disoriented my ears.

"Ms. Rutledge, isn't it? Didn't catch your hand there, did you?"

The voice came from across Depot Street. I looked. Aaron Carlin stood in front of his tent. He could only waggle a couple of fingers in greeting. His arms were otherwise occupied, balancing a gigantic, curved antler.

"Are you sure they don't exist?" Geneva asked. "After all, you were quite rude about my existence when you first met me."

"That's true, and I'm sorry I was rude." We were in the study and I'd told Geneva about the antler Aaron Carlin told me came from the world's largest jackalope. "But jackalopes are different, Geneva. They're imaginary. They're tall tales."

"And tall antlers, too, unless you are exaggerating."

"Exaggerating is kind of the point. That's what Aaron was doing. I'm pretty sure what he's got is an elk antler and the whole Incredible Tent of Wonders is an elaborate joke."

"I don't understand his joke," Geneva said. "Why don't we go see his elaborate wonders together and you can explain everything so I can laugh, too?"

"He packed up the exhibits and he's taking the tent down. We'll have to go see it the next time it comes around." It was easier telling her that than trying to explain why explaining jokes made them no longer funny.

"Write that down, then," Geneva said. "So you don't forget. Put it in your notebook. That will make it serious and official."

I hadn't even dropped my purse on the desk yet, or myself into the chair, but she came to hover over my shoulder, so I pulled out the notebook and flipped to a blank page. I wrote *ITW w/G* so she'd be happy and go sit with Argyle in the window seat and I could stop shivering from her cold touch. But she didn't move away. She reached her arm around me and pointed at the note.

"You'd better spell it out or you might forget and think it means Imaginary Textile Workshop, and I'm not interested in attending one of those."

"It's my own shorthand. I'll remember. Besides, I only got to see the antler. I wanted to see the other wonders, too, but he didn't invite me in."

"How rude."

"That's okay. I would've slowed him down. Technically he should've packed up and left yesterday like the rest of us. He said a deputy already came by once this morning and told him to clear out or he'd get a ticket."

"How rude."

"You seem particularly sensitive to all things rude this morning."

"I believe it is important to have a sense of propriety."

"Ah."

Propriety, yes; personal space, not so much. She was still hanging over my shoulder. I slipped sideways and turned to face her. Argyle, in the window seat, gazed at her wispy form, too. Now she was the center of attention, in the center of the room. She straightened and struck a pose. It was difficult to see the expression on her face, but she clasped her hands in the middle of her chest, and although I couldn't see her feet, I felt certain her toes were turned out.

"Rudeness is an interesting topic," she said, instructing her audience of two. "Shall we now consider the Case of the Rude Deputy and the Ticket for Loitering with a Tent?"

"Well, rude might not be exactly the right word for threatening someone with a ticket, but I do think it's interesting that the police let him keep the tent up overnight in the first place. Of course, that might be because they couldn't find him last night, or maybe they talked to him last night but gave him a grace period because the guys helping him weren't available yesterday. Except he didn't seem to have anyone helping this morning."

"Did you offer to help him?"

"I did. He said he was fine."

"It's too bad you did not insist. Then you could have looked through his marvels as you packed them up and then you could have told me about them. Now I will have to wait."

"Sorry."

"How long will I have to wait?"

I was beginning to lose track of why I'd thought using her as a sounding board was going to be a good idea.

"How long will I have to wait?" the Maven of Good Manners repeated.

"Aaron said if the folks over in Jonesborough will let him, he might set up during the Storytelling Festival in October. I'll let you know if I hear anything. In the meantime the tent is packed up, so let's focus on something else."

"Good. Here is something else rude that we should discuss. Murders. Murders are extremely rude, and murderers are people who have lost all sense of propriety, either in the heat of a moment or somewhere else along their wicked way. There." She pointed at me. "I caught your attention with that, didn't I?"

"I hadn't thought of murder and murderers as being rude, but I can see your point. Don't you think some murderers have a veneer of propriety, though?"

"Yes, they do. I see your point as well." She acknowledged the point with a bow. "They come into our lives with velvet in their voices and silken manners. They catch our eyes and bid us to follow them when it is hardest to resist." She was really getting into her description. Her hands remained clasped in front of her, but she spoke with such animation that she was having a hard time keeping them still. "And then," she said, "and *then* he draws us farther and farther along, using all his pretty ways and wiles."

"His?"

"And it is such a *slender* path to tread," she said, not answering my question, if she even heard it. "That slender path between what might be and what should not *ever* be. You spoke of propriety? He wore that veneer of propriety just as he wore his fine frock coat. And that meant he was sneaky and slithering. Sneaky and slithering are also rude. Rude and evil."

"Geneva, honey," I asked softly. "Who are you talking about?"

"The murderer, of course."

She continued standing in the middle of the room, hands clasped, but she didn't billow and didn't sound particularly agitated. I, on the other hand, was feeling plenty agitated. Hadn't she told me the evening before that she *hadn't* seen the murderer? Did this mean she *had*? Or that I just hadn't asked the right questions? She could be so literal. And touchy. But if she could identify this shooter in a frock coat . . . I had visions of a lineup and Geneva hovering in front of each person as she inspected his or her veneer. No need for a two-way mirror with her. She could hover nose to nose and no one the wiser. I tried not to sound ruffled or too eager.

"Geneva, did you see him? Was he wearing a fine frock coat?"

"They both were. And we were wearing our dotted lawn."

Dotted lawn? Oh no. Her memory had slipped. She wasn't talking about yesterday's murder at all. But when she'd described that long-ago double murder, she'd said the young woman—Mattie—was wearing pale, dotted lawn. Was this another part of that traumatic memory? And how would she react if I tried to dig further into that memory? If I dared, then I would need to go with care—to use my silken manners and put velvet in my voice.

"I wish I could see you in your dotted lawn, Geneva. You must look very pretty."

"I will never be as pretty as Mattie with her chestnut hair. And never be as loved." Her voice started to rise. "But neither shall I ever be as horrified or covered in blood. . . ."

Argyle, who never usually minded her moans and groans, drew back into the corner of the window seat, his ears flat.

"Geneva, Argyle and I are here—"

She wasn't listening. Her wispy figure pulsed and swelled. "He shot them. I know he did. On his evil, sneaking feet he followed Mattie and Sam with his shotgun." She swirled at me, surrounding me. "We need to find them," she wailed. "We need to get there first to warn them and I *didn't*. We need to find them and stop him!"

"Geneva, we will, we *will*. We'll try."

She swirled around me and I sank to the floor, my arms reflexively protecting my head. But another movement caught the corner of my eye. Argyle. Poor guy. I expected to see him streak for the door and down the stairs. But he crept toward me. Toward us. By then, I felt engulfed, as though Geneva was wrapped around my head along with my arms, as though I was wearing a cold, clinging shroud. Her sobs tore at me. But Argyle nudged my knee with his forehead until I made a lap for him and when he climbed in, it went through my head that if he could lend comfort with his fur and his purrs, then I could use something softer than the shriek rising in my throat.

Sitting there on the floor, I started to rock, too fast at first, then more slowly, and tried to remember the lullaby Geneva liked to sing. It was one of those lullabies with an oddly melancholy lilt that she'd sung to me once under other fraught circumstances. I couldn't recapture the tune, though, so I gave up and slipped into something old I'd learned in Granny's lap. I sang and rocked on the floor and Argyle purred and eventually Geneva calmed and quieted and finally was still. I stopped singing but continued rocking gently.

Through a small sniffle Geneva said, "You probably should not try to become a professional singer."

"I was a little off-key, wasn't I?"

"That's okay. Argyle liked it." She unfurled from my head and shoulders and I experienced an odd sensation that made me think she was attempting to pat my hair into place. Then she floated over to the window seat and sat in as small a space as possible, hugging her knees. "My singing is no prettier than yours, but Mattie sings like an angel."

I watched and waited, but she remained calm. I chanced a question. "What made you think of Mattie today?" I was wondering if I would, or even could, disband the posse if talking about and investigating yesterday's murder was too upsetting for her. Or would I be able to keep my involvement and any discussions away from her? But it would be impossible to keep talk out of the shop altogether. Customers would naturally bring it up and people would be curious about where it had happened. "Were you remembering Mattie because we've been talking about Reva Louise?"

She shook her head.

"Then what was it?"

"I heard her singing last night."

Chapter 21

Geneva couldn't be shaken from her belief that she'd heard Mattie singing. Not that I tried all that hard. There wasn't much point. She said she heard the singing only faintly and couldn't tell where it came from. When I suggested it might have been someone listening to a radio or a recording somewhere outside, she scoffed, making a good point about hearing no announcer, no commercials, no static or skips, only the one sweet voice singing a verse over and over. I didn't try to explain digital recordings. I did ask if she recognized the song and knew its name, but by then she was getting restless again. She said I was confusing her. She said that Mattie's singing had confused her, too. At first she'd been delighted and excited, but then the singing scared her and she'd hidden in the safety of the cupboard that she called her room.

"You mean you were afraid of Mattie? Didn't you want to go find her?"

"I didn't know what it meant, to suddenly hear her like that."

I didn't know what it meant, either, but it was time to distract Geneva. To distract us both. I wasn't about to admit it, but somewhere in the back of my mind was a tiny worry—no, to be honest, it was more than a tiny worry; it was a fear—that somehow Geneva was right and she *had* heard Mattie singing. To dispel thoughts of a ghost who scared *my* ghost, I scooped the sleeping Argyle from my lap into my arms and stood up.

"Do you feel up to helping me think a few things through before Ardis comes in? We probably don't have a lot of time."

"Why wouldn't I be up to it?"

Was she serious? Of course she was serious. She was sitting up straight, on the edge of the window seat, looking as though she'd been ready and waiting—with hard-won patience, possibly for hours—while I frittered our valuable time away. My mercurial mirage. It was a wonder I didn't have a migraine.

"I just wanted to make sure you're feeling okay, that you're fully recovered. I see that you are, but you *were* having kind of an intense few minutes there, reliving—"

She held up a hand to stop me. "Please be aware that using a word like 'reliving' when speaking to someone at my stage of afterlife is insensitive. Your insensitivity does, however, remind me that we were talking about rude people."

Argyle was still in my arms. I might have held him a little too tightly at that point. He kindly didn't tell me I was either rude or insensitive, but he did decide it was time to jump down. He chose the desk as a good landing spot and promptly started a bath. I counted to ten.

"Don't you remember?" she asked. "Because I do quite perfectly. You were talking about the Immeasurable Tent of Wonders. You said a deputy was going to give the man, Aaron whatever-his-name-is, a ticket if he didn't pack up and get out of town and I helped by saying how rude that deputy was. Although overstaying one's welcome is also rude. Does that put us back on track?"

"Nicely, thank you."

"You're welcome. Are you going to contribute anything to this conversation?"

"I'm thinking, Geneva."

"You should try thinking faster. All the best detectives and Western sheriffs are able to solve crimes in under an hour. Would you like to know their names?"

"No, that's okay."

"They know all the most likely motives, too. Would you like me to list those?"

"No—oh, wait. That might actually be helpful."

"I will overlook your use of the word 'actually.' You sit at the desk while I dictate." She put her hands behind her back and floated back and forth in front of the desk, head down as though studying the floor.

I opened my notebook and clicked my pen. "Ready when you are."

"Right. I expect this will take quite a lot of ink. First, cattle rustling. Second, avenging a father's death. Third . . ." She looked up. "Why aren't you writing?"

"Why don't we go for a more generalized list? For instance, cattle rustling could go in a larger category called 'greed' and the next category can be 'revenge.'"

"You would rather have a summary?"

"Short and sweet, yes."

"Greed, jealousy, revenge, passion, political gain, mob hit, insanity, thrill-seeking, and just plain mean. There, does that tell you why someone aimed a gun out the bathroom window of our shop and shot Reva Louise?"

"No." I dropped my pen in frustration.

She stopped her floating pace or pacing float or whatever it was and hovered in front of the desk. "Short might well be sweet," she said, "but a story is spun with details. The story is *in* the details."

Being a detail-oriented person, I liked what Geneva said about needing them, even if the way she'd said it sounded suspiciously like one of her haikus. She looked serious, though, rather than sly or smug, and Argyle didn't chirrup his two haiku cents, so I let it go. I also tried to let go the sudden realization that I was taking poetry cues from a ghost and a cat. I might like details, but there were certain details of my reality since moving to Blue Plum that didn't bear close inspection.

"You're very philosophical this morning," I told her.

"Thank you for noticing. Cats are philosophical by nature, I believe, and I think Argyle is rubbing off on me. In fact, we enjoyed being philosophical together while we kept watch last night."

I'd forgotten she was going to be my alert eyes and ears. I was surprised *she* remembered. "I take it there weren't any problems?"

"Only the philosophical one. Try as we might, we could not decide that chicken and egg problem."

"You mean which came first? You're in good company, then. That's been stumping overnight philosophers since the first chicken hatched. I was talking about problems *here*, though, in the shop."

"So was I. When we thought about it afterward, we could not decide which came first, the breaking glass or the creeping about with flashlights."

*   *   *

Ardis arrived as I was examining and remarking over the broken window.

"Good *Lord*," she said, "with all the noise you're making I thought you'd severed an artery at the very least."

She might have exaggerated how loud my remarks were, but I meant every decibel of them. Someone had thrown a big rock through one of our windows along Depot Street. Judging by the lack of jagged shards sticking out of the frame, Geneva was right; someone had climbed through and been creeping in our store. A horrible feeling crept down my spine to think that person could have still been in the building while I was up in the study.

Geneva pooh-poohed that notion. So did Clod. When Ardis called 911, he arrived suspiciously fast and out of uniform. Geneva took one look at his T-shirt and running shorts and turned her back with a scandalized "Eep."

"Can this possibly be considered an official police response," she whispered to me, "if the officer involved is wearing so few clothes? I have never been this close to a man with such long, exposed, and *hairy* legs." She held a hand up to shield her eyes in case he moved into her view.

Clod was surveying the window frame, the glass on the floor, and the rock. "You know what's interesting about this is that, from out on the street, you don't realize the window is broken; it looks open. No," he said, scratching at the T-shirt stretched across his chest, "your perp would've climbed out again as soon as he finished what he came for. If he came in at all." He looked around at the innocent baskets and bins of yarn that always seemed to make him jumpy; then he squatted down for a closer look at the rock. Geneva "eeped" again and moved behind me. "This is a good-looking chunk of granite," he said. "*It* might tell you a few things. One, it's not local. Two, no one walks around with a rock the size of his own head, so where'd he pick it up?"

"Farm and Home," Ardis said immediately. "Landscaping materials around the back. Anyone could have helped themselves. But what I find interesting is how you're able to determine this was a male. And what do you suppose he was after?"

She stood closer to Clod than he probably liked, trying to see what he was seeing. He wasn't seeing much, as far as I could tell, because he hadn't spent enough time looking around.

"He's using the generic 'he,' Ardis."

"Would you like me to cite the statewide statistics on burglary arrests broken down by gender?" Clod asked.

"No. But I would like you to do two other things. *One*, while you're down there, look for evidence that will identify the person who did this. Fingerprints would be good. Blood on a sliver of glass, preferably with a lot of juicy DNA, would be great. *Two*, let me know when you're finished collecting it so I can sweep up and we can open our business."

"She's a trifle overwrought," Ardis told him. "With good reason, I think you'll have to agree. Kath, hon, why don't you go call Ten and see if he can come fix the window? Coleridge and I will walk through the shop and see if we find any other damage or discover anything missing."

"Wait. Joe has a key, right?" I asked.

Ardis nodded.

"Okay, good." That meant if he wanted to *get* in he had no reason to *break* in. Not that I had any hard evidence, as he would be the first to tell me, that he'd ever broken anything to get in anywhere.

"Don't bother calling Joe," Clod said. "I tried all morning, finally went running without him."

"Oh yeah? Watch this." I pulled my phone out, pressed buttons, and put it to my ear. "Oh, hey, Joe ... Yeah, me, too. Thanks ... Well, we've got kind of a situation at the Cat. We found a broken window ... No, it's okay, we're all right. Thanks for thinking to ask ... Ardis is going to walk through with your brother to check and we're wondering if you can come see about the window ... Oh, that's great. Thanks! Bye."

I probably could have been smarmier if I'd tried. It's also possible that Joe *wasn't* answering his phone. I wouldn't know; I hadn't called him, because I saw no reason to give Clod the satisfaction of being right.

Clod did actually look more closely at the glass shards before he and Ardis went on their tour of inspection. He didn't find any blood, but he put some of the more wicked-looking pieces in a paper bag to take with him and said he'd send someone over to dust the frame for fingerprints. I refrained from thanking him because I couldn't have done so without dripping insincerity and I was trying to cut back on negative emotions.

Geneva recovered from seeing Clod in his running gear after he left the room and she told me that whoever came in through the window hadn't stayed long. Her sense of time wasn't the most reliable, but she remembered hearing footsteps go up the stairs to the second floor, move along the hall, then almost immediately turn around and go back down. She said she heard nothing further. That didn't quite jibe, because it must have been at some point after the break-in that she thought she'd heard Mattie and she'd gone to hide in her room. Rather than risk upsetting her by bringing that up, I didn't mention Mattie or the singing. I did have more questions for her, though.

"You *heard* all this? Didn't you go look to see who came in? I thought you said that you and Argyle were going to be my eyes and ears."

"Half is better than nothing, don't you think? We were your ears. But the breaking glass upset Argyle and he did not want to come with me to be your eyes. I did the friendly and caring thing by staying to comfort him."

"But I thought you said you saw a flashlight."

"One of the things I like about you is that you think a lot. That is something we have in common. Here is what I think. I think I must have assumed there was a flashlight because that would be the best way to sneak around in a dark building. Do you own a good flashlight? Because we can use it if you and I ever go out as a sneaking team."

My friend the ghost; poster child for the unreliable witness.

Ardis' walk-through with Clod didn't take long. They found no other damage. Nothing obvious was missing. Except for the smashed window and the rock, one might not believe anything had happened. Except for the ghost, whom no one else knew existed, one might conclude that no one had climbed through the window and up the stairs. And if one were Clod, that was exactly what one did conclude.

"What about the jagged shards of glass left in the window frame?" I asked.

"You swept up all the glass, right? What's your point?"

"That is my point. I swept up the glass. You said it yourself; the window looks open. There was no glass left in the frame. That's because someone removed the jagged shards so as not to get cut when climbing through the window before walking upstairs." I probably shouldn't have added the part about the stairs.

Clod looked at the window. He looked at the stairs. He looked at me. He held up the bag he'd put some of the shards in. "I'll ask the lab to run these for fingerprints, DNA, RNA, curare, explosives, and dust from a passing asteroid. If you think of any other tests that might be helpful, give me a call." He looked pleased with his sarcasm, but then he turned thoughtful. "Upstairs, huh? As I said, give me a call."

Ardis let him out the front door and relocked it. Then she demonstrated her own love of sarcasm by dusting her hands. "And that's what he thinks about that. Tempest in a teapot. And he completely missed your reference to the curious incident of the dog in the nighttime, so I don't hold out much hope that he'd get it if you tell him about the 'Curious Incident of the Ham Actor in the Weaver's Cat,' either. Never mind, hon. Come on; time's a-wastin'. Tell me how the investigation is going."

"In a nutshell out on a limb, J. Scott Prescott is the number-one suspect. That is, if we could pin a motive on him and figure out how he had the opportunity. But he's sneaky and somehow he and Reva Louise are connected. After leaving your place last night, I came and sat on the porch here. And he just happened to walk by. Planning to snoop, is what I think, and I think he threw the rock through the window. Except no motive. No proof."

"That's a big nutshell. You didn't tell Cole you think Prescott threw the rock."

"It's a pretty flimsy limb. Let me run up and get my notebook. Meet you in the kitchen."

Geneva floated up to the attic with me, complaining the whole way about Ardis. She'd never really warmed up to Ardis. She would watch her and often followed her around, but I got the feeling Geneva was jealous of her, of her position in the shop, and of her friendship with me. It was too bad and I wished there was something I could do about it. I was pretty sure Ardis would be delighted to know a ghost and to call that ghost her friend. But Geneva received the eternal cold shoulder from her, and that had to be tough.

"You were going to go over things with me before she arrived," Geneva said. "I think my contributions to the investigation will be more important than hers. Why don't we make her wait in the kitchen while I contribute now?"

"Because that would be rude. Besides, three heads are better than one. You can sit next to me and read my notes and make suggestions." That was taking a chance. "Also, I'm going to need you to watch the shop again tonight."

"Are you expecting skulduggery?"

I doubted it. "It's possible." Argyle had helped himself to a nap on the notebook I'd left open on the desk. I carefully and successfully extracted the notebook with only a minor flicking of cat ears and tail.

"What if Mattie comes back?" Geneva asked.

"Did you hear her any more last night, after you went to your room? Or have you heard her at all today?"

She shook her head.

"If you're worried, you can come home with me."

She wavered—literally and figuratively. Then she floated over to hover in front of me. "No. You are counting on me and I will not let you down."

"Thank you."

"So instead you can spend the night here with Argyle and me. It will be like in the old movies and quite a lot of fun. A pajama fiesta."

Bizarre pictures went through my head. "Gosh, *doesn't* that sound like fun? I think it's going to have to wait until the investigation is over, though. We both have important work to do and we should stay focused." And maybe she would have forgotten about a pajama fiesta by the time it was all over.

The cat roused himself and followed us down to the kitchen. Ardis wasn't there, but I heard her moving around out front. Argyle trotted over to his bowl and waited for me to tip kibble into it. I gave him fresh water, too. As he rubbed another layer of cat fur around my ankles in thanks, Ardis came back.

"That rock is heavy as the dickens," she said. "I put it on the counter next to the cash register. I'm counting it as a war trophy."

"A Piglet War trophy?"

"That's something to consider, anyway, even if we don't think the culprit was an idiotic, overzealous actor.

Unfortunately, the rock gouged the bejeebers out of the floor. When Ten comes to take care of the window, let's get him to look at that, too. Did he say when he'd get here? We don't want Argyle jumping out."

"Oh, heck, I hadn't thought of that. Hang on." I pulled my phone out again. Sure enough, Joe wasn't answering. I left a message, with a touch of urgency, and disconnected.

Ardis, head atilt, regarded me. "You want to be careful with subterfuge, hon. You don't want to get one brother in trouble with another."

"Yeah, I know. I feel kind of bad about doing that."

"You don't have to go that far. But do remember what goes around comes around. I don't want to see you or anyone else hurt."

"Are you referring to either anyone else in particular?"

"Hon," she said, "I've just remembered we have some old adjustable window screens down in the basement. They're simple, but they're useful. I've always liked them for their reliability and flexibility. Why don't you keep track of Argyle while I go find one?"

"How rude," Geneva said to Ardis' departing back. "She didn't answer your question."

"Yes, she did. I think. Anyway, let's not start all that 'rude' business again."

"Aye-aye," Geneva said, saluting, just as Ardis came back up from the basement with a screen, saying, "Exactly what we need to batten our hatch."

"We're all very nautical this morning," I said, trying to lighten the mood. Oops.

Ardis looked around the apparently empty kitchen. "Are you including the cat?"

"Anyone who's listening. After you put the screen in, let's sit down and work out our plans for the investigation."

"Aye-aye," Ardis said, saluting.

Geneva groused about people stealing her best lines. I distracted Argyle with a piece of crumpled paper and myself from Geneva's continued fussing. She floated in the middle of the room, muttering, "Aye-aye, honey," and saluting with either hand indiscriminately and then with both hands at once. I'd finally had enough and planted myself in front of her, hands on my hips, and a stern cease-and-desist look on my face. Ardis caught me in midlook when she came back.

"Hon?"

"Sorry. Don't mind me. Just thinking about all the questions we need to look at. There are so many directions the investigation can go and there's been nothing but interruptions all morning. Most of them adding more questions and sending us in more directions."

"Even with Prescott as suspect number one?"

"But so far there's nothing pointing a big red arrow and saying, 'Here's the proof. He's the bad guy.' It's frustrating."

"It's okay, hon. We'll do what we can, as we can, and we'll be happy that we don't have to wrap everything up in less than sixty minutes. So let's breathe and be calm and go forward."

I nodded, dropped my hands from my hips, and relaxed my shoulders. Geneva harrumphed.

"And now to test your newfound calm," Ardis said, "here's another interruption. Before we can work on the investigation, we need to make plans for the day, because if I'm right, we aren't just going to be busy—we are going to be *swamped*."

She pulled a chair out and sat down at the table. I knew she was right, so I sat down opposite her. Geneva sat in the chair next to her without pulling it out, which was somewhat disturbing. Argyle, being the gentleman he was, leapt up to join us, politely sprawling on a copy of the tabloid rather than the bare table.

"The town is still crawling with tourists," Ardis said. "They're looking for things to do, and that includes sightseeing. Not that most of the folks who traipse through here will actually buy anything." While she talked, Geneva mimicked her, first putting her hands on the table and then leaning forward with her arms crossed and her elbows on the table. "Oh, they'll pretend they're interested in buttons or bouclé," Ardis said, "but all they'll really want to see is the scene of the crime—the bulletridden bathroom."

"It *isn't*, is it?"

"Of course not, but you know how these things get distorted. Spreading stories and going to gape at the scene of a tragedy are ghoulish, but it's human nature to do both. I say we take advantage of it while we can and try to make up for closing early yesterday. Let's call a couple of the spinners. See if one of them will sit and spin on the front porch and another in one of the front rooms upstairs. And it might behoove us to call some TGIFs. They can park themselves around the shop and answer questions."

"And keep an eye on things?"

"That, too, but it'll save us running back and forth and up and down and leaving the counter unattended. I won-

der if we should ask one of them to monitor that dad-
blamed bathroom. There's no telling what might happen
if folks take it into their heads they want some kind of
macabre memento."

"We could charge a dollar a head to see the head."

"Not bad," Ardis said.

"Really?"

"No, hon. Too crass. It is tempting to lock it for the
day, though."

"But wouldn't it be a shame to . . ."

"A shame to what, hon?" Ardis asked.

I'd trailed off because Geneva suddenly stopped mim-
icking Ardis. Her hollow eyes opened wider, she squeaked,
and then she zipped up the back stairs. Argyle watched
her go and chirruped. He continued to loll in the middle
of the tabloid in the middle of the table, though, and I
didn't hear anything else. Such as singing . . .

Ardis' gaze followed mine toward the stairs. "Hon?
Everything all right?"

"Yeah, sorry. I guess I'm kind of spooked after everything that's happened." Spooked since Granny died, to
be exact.

"Well, I'm not surprised and this old building is full of
noises. But do you know what Ivy used to say? A cat
makes the best watchdog. All you have to do is look at
Argyle and you'll see there's nothing to worry about.
He's perfectly calm. He's making his happy cat eyes and
his ears aren't doing their radar swivel. See? He doesn't
hear anything out of the ordinary. So what were you going to say, wouldn't it be a shame to what?"

"To lock the bathroom if that's what people are coming to see." I rubbed Argyle's chin in thanks for being

such a good alarm. He purred that all continued to be well. "No one is really going to take anything, are they?"

"Never underestimate the public, hon. I tell you what, though, we'll ask John if he can come in and watch the john. He'll get a kick out of that and it'll give him a chance to feel like he's making up for wiping away all the fingerprints and whatnot yesterday. Now, on to plans for the investigation."

I glanced at the clock. "If we're calling in reinforcements, we'd better get on the phone, and that doesn't leave time to go over much. But as long as we're calling in John, let's start our TGIF calling with the others from Fast and Furious."

Ardis rubbed her hands. "The posse. Excellent plan."

"If they can't come, no big deal. Mel won't make it, with her hands full at the café. But maybe we can have a meeting afterward and any who can't come this afternoon can join us then."

"With *supper* from the café. An even *more* excellent plan." She rubbed her hands again and then rubbed Argyle between his ears. "All right, I'll go get on the phone and you, my fine reclining cat, shall be Lord of the Kitchen Table, watching over your kingdom and those who come and go through the back door."

That brought up an issue I'd been wrestling with. "Um, Ardis, do you think we ought to start locking *that* door?"

"I hate to think of doing that. We'd lose something that's very much a part of Blue Plum if we do."

"But maybe Reva Louise lost her life because we didn't."

Ardis slammed both hands on the table. Argyle

jumped to his feet, tail puffed. "The very thought affronts the Lord of the Kitchen Table *and* the Empress of Everything." The Empress of Everything leaned close and made little kissing noises at the Lord of the Kitchen Table. He head-butted her chin. That goo-goo interval was at odds with his tail and her vehemence.

"Know this, Kath Rutledge," the E of E said, "whoever killed Reva Louise was intent on killing her. That villain—or villains unknown—would have killed her in another place at another time if the deed hadn't been accomplished from our bathroom window yesterday. That woman was nothing but trouble all the way around. We will not allow her death to change the friendly way we've always conducted business and we will not let anyone tell us that Reva Louise would be alive today if we had kept that back door locked."

And no one did. Until a couple of hours and a steady stream of "customers" later.

Chapter 22

Ardis was right; most of the people coming into the Weaver's Cat that afternoon were only pretending they were interested in spinning or knitting or weaving. But enough of them were helpless to resist the lure of the colors and textures of our fibers and fabrics, and left with bags small and large, that we were happy. Jackie (of the PVC and bicycle parts spinning wheel) and Abby (the Goth teenager so adept with a drop spindle) were on the porch, spinning and inviting people to step inside. Jackie was using a smaller, travel wheel and Abby was wearing a pirate hat instead of the white mob cap of the day before, but between the two of them, they attracted plenty of attention.

We had no lack of volunteers from the membership of TGIF. Needlework and chat were pleasant enough ways to spend a Sunday afternoon, but when Ardis threw in the request that they keep an eye on nosy visitors, we ended up with two or three pairs of needles flashing in the comfy chairs in each of the rooms upstairs and down. Ernestine, Thea, and John came to help, too. Debbie couldn't, being involved with sheep, and another call to

Joe went to voice mail. Ardis left a message, adding her urgent plea to my earlier one, throwing in an invitation to supper at the Cat after we closed, and asking for a consultation on another matter.

"We need your skills and your input," she told his inbox. "We need that window fixed and we want you to rig something better than a tiny tinkle bell on the kitchen door so we know when someone comes in. Plus, Mel wants your opinion. She's bringing a new sweet potato salad."

Ernestine must have come from teaching Sunday school. She wore a touch of lipstick and a flowered shirtwaist that she might have owned for fifty years. It was hard to think where she would have bought a new one like it recently. She sat in the kitchen, knitting baby hats for her weekly Fast and Furious quota and handing out flyers advertising the classes we offered for the rest of the summer and into the fall. John said he was delighted to monitor the second-floor john. But as much as he liked the joke, and though his white beard and moustache were well brushed and his khakis pressed, his old blue eyes looked troubled or tired.

"Both," he said when I asked. He hadn't had an easy night with his brother. I'd never met Ambrose, but the difficulties he caused for John didn't endear him to me.

"I did get an old sailor's laugh on my way in," he said. "Some landlubber with an indecently iridescent, spanking-new bass boat had both lanes blocked at the curve on Spring Street. The fool was boat-proud and had no clue how to back a trailer."

"Ooh, that's a bad spot."

"I told him he'd better learn fast or his glittery beauty

would be broadsided and scuttled before her maiden voyage or even before she'd been christened. He was close to tears. It was mean of me to laugh and it made me realize I'm more like Ambrose than I care to think."

"You're not, John."

"I ended up moving it for him, so maybe I'm not as bad as all that."

I assured him he wasn't and went to find Thea. She'd agreed to sit in the study with my laptop instead of knitting needles.

"Do you mind?" I asked her as we climbed the stairs to the attic.

"Nah, threads are all the same to me," she said. "In my hands or on a screen, doesn't matter. It's the process that I like. Log me in, sister, and stand back. If you're looking for info on Prescott and the Snapps, I will find it. Although, I have to say, I could've stayed home, and stayed in my pajamas, and done the same thing."

"Seriously? It's past one and you weren't dressed?"

"I'm an off-duty librarian. My dress code is none of your business."

I glanced over my shoulder at her. She might be off-duty, but she was as stylish as ever, wearing a burnt orange, sleeveless tunic and chocolate brown slacks a shade darker than she was. No heels, though. Maybe her flats were her concession to having the day off.

"Say no more," I said. "You're kind to give up your personal time like this. To tell you the truth, though, I'll feel better if someone's up here today."

"You think the rock through the window is connected to the shooting?"

"I think it's connected to Prescott." I gave her my nut-shell suspicions of him.

"But except for the rock and the business card, you have no corroborating evidence?"

"No, but . . ."

"What?"

"I think Prescott might've been snooping around in here yesterday afternoon."

"Really?" That piqued her interest. "What makes you think so? How did you know? Was something out of place?" She asked her questions rapid-fire, darting a glance in a different direction with each one, eyes narrowed. "Was something disturbed?"

Of course, the answer to the last question was *Yes, my friend the ghost was disturbed; but only disturbed because Prescott wasn't her type, so she left the room and didn't watch to see what he was up to.* I shrugged instead of saying that, but I glanced around, too, looking for Geneva. I hadn't seen her since she squeaked and flew off. I still didn't see her, but maybe she was in her "room." I also didn't read any skepticism in Thea's tone or face, but her questions made me glad I hadn't called Clod and told *him* about Prescott's intrusion.

"There isn't anything I can put my finger on," I said. "But haven't you ever gotten the feeling someone's been around when you didn't know it? Forget it; it's lame."

"No, hey, you don't have to convince me. I know exactly what you're talking about. I know when someone's been in my office, in my kitchen, in my *anywhere*. I can tell. And you know what I think it is? Smell. This pretty brown nose isn't just for decoration." She tapped her nose, then looked around the study again, taking a few sniffs. "I bet you smelled aftershave or a shampoo you aren't used to smelling. The trouble is, you're right; that isn't anything you can put your finger on and how do you prove or preserve that kind of evidence? Catch it in a jar like a firefly? Not to worry, though." She smiled a wicked smile and played her fingers along an imaginary keyboard. "Dr. Thea the Infomagician is here. If J. Scott Prescott has left threads of any type out there in the World Wide Web, I will find them, I will follow them, and if I can I will twist them into a rope with which we can hang him high."

"Um—"

"What? You don't like my dramatics? Because they're part of the package."

"No, you're fine, just don't forget to look for Dan, too. Did you know he was married before? To Angela Cobb?"

"To Baby Mercy? I did not. What other useful information are you hiding in that head of yours?"

"I didn't want to prejudice your search."

"You know better than that. Tidbits of information, including rumors and scandals, are called access points. Give."

"Reva Louise had a record. She embezzled money from the church she worked for."

I counted and Thea was actually quiet for four and a half seconds.

"Yee-*ow*," she finally said. "I did not see that coming. Where'd you hear it?"

"Mel told me this morning."

"Did she know it ahead of time? Before hiring her?"

"Sally Ann told her."

"My, my, *my*, my, my. I knew Reva Louise was no good, but I did not realize she was so low, she would steal from a church. *My*. Okay, I am on this like a cat on catnip. Like I said, log me in and stand back. You are in the hands of a professional. And if Mr. Prescott shows his nose up here today, I will show his nose right back out the door. And anyone else's nose, too."

"You were right, hon," Ardis whispered to me as the string of camel bells at the door jingled yet again. "A dollar a head to see the head would have been a great idea. And after the stress of being polite to that last bozo, when she told me she loved what she saw and was writing everything down so she could find it cheaper online, I find myself a whole lot less worried about being crass."

"You are the consummate purveyor of customer service, Ardis."

"I smile until it hurts," she said. "And I go home at night and have a little nip."

"You sound like Granny."

"I learned at her feet," said Ardis.

Sally Ann came in an hour or so after we opened. I was at the counter ringing up another spindle whorl kit, thanks to Abby's spinning skills out on the porch. The next woman in line had what Ardis called a "guilt offering." She handed me a skein of cotton embroidery floss and a dollar bill. I smiled and handed her the floss and change.

"Can I have a bag for that?"

I took the floss back, put it and one of our class flyers in a bag, smiled, and handed it back.

"You might as well save this." She took the flyer back

out of the bag and dropped it on the counter. "Oh, but hey," she said, sounding unconvincingly casual. "Mind if I use your restroom? It's upstairs, right?"

My smiles were becoming progressively more plastic, so I was glad when the next person up to the counter was Sally Ann.

"Thank you," Sally Ann said.

"For what?" I looked around on the counter but didn't see anything.

"Talking to Mel. I don't know what you said. It worked, though. The café's open and she isn't spitting nails. She isn't exactly Miss Sunshine, but that's Mel. She'll be okay. So thanks."

Ardis slid down the counter. "What about you, hon?"

"I'll be okay, too," Sally Ann said.

"Mm-hmm."

"Oh boy," I said. "When Ardis starts in with her 'mm-hmms,' nobody's safe."

"There are only two things you can do at a time like this," Ardis said, sliding over more so that I had to move and she ended up in front of Sally Ann. "Throw yourself into your work or take yourself out of it altogether. My recommendation is that you take some time for yourself."

"Like that ever happens," Sally Ann said.

"Make it happen, hon."

"Yeah?"

"Mm-hmm."

Sally Ann picked up the flyer the floss woman had dropped.

"Pick out a class," I said. "Come to the fiber side."

Ardis nudged me with her elbow. "That's a great idea. That's exactly what I'm talking about."

"Work might get in the way," Sally Ann said. "Seems like something always does."

"The first class is on the house," I said.

Ardis immediately agreed. I was glad. The offer was pure impulse, but I wanted to see something other than "glum" show up on Sally Ann's face. As if learning to crochet was going to make her beam. Or replace her sister. What was I thinking?

"Ardis and I are kind of nutty over things like knitting," I said. "You don't need to take the flyer."

She hung on to it, though, when I tried to take it back from her. "But maybe I could give something a try? But I don't want to look like an idiot," she quickly added.

"You come by one day," Ardis said, "and we'll make it a private lesson."

"I might. Anyway, thanks."

We watched her go.

"I didn't like to tell her to straighten her spine and look life in the eye," Ardis said. "She's got too much weighing her down right now."

I made periodic swings through the kitchen, up to the study, through the second and first floors, and out onto the porch to see if any of our volunteers needed anything and to see how things were going. Ernestine was happy in the kitchen because she could make tea. Thea told me to hush and leave her alone. John's rough night caught up with him and he'd fallen asleep in his chair. I let him doze. The various TGIFs waved and said they were fine. They'd brought what they wanted with them. The spinners, Jackie and Abby, asked for water.

"How are our spinners and spies faring?" Ardis asked after I delivered two glasses of ice water and returned to the counter.

"All's well," I said.

I was immediately proved a liar.

Chapter 23

As soon as I'd spoken, a commotion erupted over our heads. The commotion was that immediate for me, anyway, because Geneva flew into the room and swirled around and over the counter, looking as though she'd seen a, well, a ghost. My knee-jerk reaction was to jump and look around wildly for Mattie. That surprised Ardis, who wasn't aware of anything except a slight chill wafting overhead. I was saved from looking too peculiar or inviting comment, though, when the shouting began upstairs.

"What on earth?" Ardis asked.

"I hope it *is* something on earth," I said, though not very loudly, as I tried to catch Geneva's attention.

The yelling overhead was too frantic and garbled at first to pick out individual words. Then, just as I realized that Geneva was giddy with excitement and not scared out of her wits, one word came through the hubbub clearly.

"Gun!"

Geneva yelled it, too, increasing the excitement by adding an *s* to the word. "Guns!" she shrieked in my face.

"It's the sniper!" someone running down the stairs shouted. "He's got guns!"

By then people throughout the store were screaming and running, some for the door, others in confusion. It was my nightmare vision come true—people panicked by guns in the streets of Blue Plum—except this was worse because they were panicked by a man with guns in the Weaver's Cat.

Ardis did the smart thing. She dropped to the floor behind the counter and then reached up and dragged me down, too. Geneva followed me, still in my face.

"Are we playing hide-and-seek?" she asked.

"No!" I mouthed as hard as I could.

"Because John is looking for you and it would not be nice to make an old man like him get down here on the floor to show you the guns he found in the linen closet."

Ardis was already speaking urgently into her phone, to the 911 operator, no doubt. I snatched my phone out of my pocket.

"Tell me," I said to Geneva

"John found several guns—"

I cut her off. "No one else?"

"There were all those silly screaming people, but—"

I didn't wait for her to finish that sentence, either. The screaming people might have left the building, but screaming sirens were fast approaching. I jumped up. Ardis made another grab for me. I pulled away and dashed for the stairs. Ardis shouted after me, and Geneva came whooping on my heels, but all I cared about was getting up the stairs to John before someone mistook him for a sniper and shot him.

In going over it in my mind afterward, I'd have to say I didn't think through my assault on the stairs with guns at the top and the near certainty of more guns coming through the front door behind me as thoroughly as I might have. Not that I was about to admit that to Clod Dunbar. He was the first responder through the front door.

I was halfway up the stairs, quietly telling an aghast John Berry he probably ought to put the guns down and move away from them. He was asking me, in his extraordinarily polite way, if Ardis and I really thought the linen closet was a safe place to keep guns. That's when Clod and his cavalry showed up.

"Down!" Clod yelled as he came through the door. "Get down on the floor! Everyone down on the floor! Now!"

"Hey!" That was Thea, disturbed from her research in the study and annoyed by the continuing ruckus below. She obviously didn't know what was going on and didn't know to whom she was issuing orders. She came down the attic stairs bellowing, "Librarian at *work*, so *shut* the floss *up*!"

John and I sat down next to each other on the stairs, hands in our laps, and waited for things to calm down.

Ernestine came from the kitchen about then, with a smile and the teapot, her myopic lenses flashing as she searched faces. "Which one of you just ran through the kitchen?" she asked. "I didn't catch your answer. Did you want tea?"

Geneva squeezed onto the stair between me and the wall, making me shiver.

"Well, Ollie," she whispered in my ear. "This is another fine mess you've gotten us into."

Two or three deputies did a sweep of the shop, rounding up the few customers and TGIFs who hadn't made it out the door, and bringing the wide-eyed spinners in off the porch. Stragglers and spinners were questioned briefly and then allowed to leave. I wondered if Jackie and Abby would ever volunteer to spin for us again.

On her way out, the woman who'd irked Ardis by telling her she would shop online later stopped to ask her own question. "So, is there some kind of gang operating out of this place? Hiding their guns and ammo? Because I don't think that's a safe situation. Especially for a small-town yarn shop."

It's possible the sheriff's department had a standard, scripted, authoritative answer for a question like that. If so, one of the deputies should have spit that answer out faster. Before Thea gave her unscripted answer.

"Are you implying that it isn't so bad for yarn shops in medium-sized or large towns to be taken over by gangs?" she asked. "Because I'd be interested in knowing exactly what population figure tips a town from the safety of 'especially' into the abyss of 'whatever.'"

It was easy to tell that Thea was still annoyed at having her research interrupted and then being told she couldn't go back up to the study to continue. Even one of the deputies picked up on her cranky mood. He escorted the now pop-eyed woman with the question past her and out the door. Ardis grabbed the nearest crochet hook and skein of yarn and put them in Thea's hands to calm her.

John's crisp, naval bearing was taxed, but it held up well, when he had to explain several times to three armed and hyped-up deputies why he'd been rooting around in the linen closet in the first place. (A child had opened the door and started pulling things out onto the floor. John found the guns when he was refolding and putting things back.) He continued to hold his own while explaining *more* than several times why he'd felt compelled to do anything other than leave the guns under the tablecloth where he'd found them. (He didn't think that under a tablecloth, in a linen closet with no lock on the door, was the safest place for two semiautomatic handguns that might be loaded.)

"Calling *us* is the *first* thing you should have done," Clod said, hammering at John. "And running up the stairs toward a suspected gunman is the *last* thing *you* should have done," he said, rounding on me. "Unless you knew those guns were there and knew they weren't loaded, but even if you did, you could not possibly have known who was up there waving them or some other guns around. That was a *stunningly* stupid thing to do."

"Stunningly," Ardis said, shoulder to shoulder with Clod. "Hon, I thought you'd lost your mind. You scared the sheep dip out of me. What on earth possessed you?"

I couldn't disagree with them or think of a reasonable-sounding explanation.

Geneva could. "I am affronted," she said. "Please explain that being haunted is not at all the same as being possessed and then tell them you were acting for God and country. And thank *him* for putting on his uniform."

I went with looking at the floor, a hand to my brow, and shaking my head.

When John's repeated answers had finally satisfied the deputies, he came out to the kitchen where Ardis, Ernestine, Thea, and I were.

"That's twice I've been grilled by police in two days," he said, sitting down at the table with the rest of us.

"John, I am so sorry," I said.

"Nonsense. Everyone needs a bit of fun. A good lawyer probably helps, too. No, don't worry," he rushed to assure us. "I won't need one, but did you know that's what Ambrose is? Was. He didn't make many friends during his career—that's how very good he was. But, no, answering the phrased and rephrased questions of these good old boys is a piece of cake compared to dealing with Ambrose when he gets obstinate or querulous. These boys wouldn't know querulous if it bit them in the . . ." He coughed. "Bit them in the alpaca."

Clod came out to the kitchen. Ardis stood up, glowering at him eye to eye. Ernestine, rapt, peered from Clod's face to Ardis' as though watching a Ping-Pong match. Thea sat and ignored everyone else, crocheting something oddly narrow and rapidly getting longer. John waited until Clod broke eye contact with Ardis and looked toward him. With Clod's eyes on him, John yawned and flicked something off his sleeve.

"What is the loud one making?" Geneva asked as she watched Thea's blazing hook.

"I don't know."

"You don't know *what*?" Clod snapped.

"I don't know what we're all still doing here," I said.

"Well, you want to know what *I* don't know?"

"It isn't a competition, but sure."

"I don't know why this door is still open to anyone who wanders into town and down the alley." He thumped the kitchen door with his fist. "Did it even occur to you that Reva Louise Snapp would be alive today if you'd kept the door locked?"

"Oh no, you don't." I was on my feet and as eye to eye with him as I could get without developing a neck cramp. "No, sir. Don't you put that on us. Her death wasn't a mistake. And it wasn't random." Out of the corner of my eye I saw Ardis give a sharp nod and a fist pump.

Clod surely saw them, too; he had the most infuriating not quite half smile. "You're saying the rumors are true? You and your shop are the unwitting hosts of a sniper's nest?"

"Vipers?" Geneva asked. "Where?"

"We are no more a *sniper's* nest," I enunciated, "than the sheriff's department is a haven for redneck yahoos. Okay, okay, I tell you what, why don't we all calm down? We"—I gestured with open, nonthreatening hands to Ardis and myself—"We will tell you that you should be considering other possibilities for the solution to this crime. You should open yourself to the idea that someone targeted Reva Louise. You should wonder about J. Scott Prescott and his real estate deals in town. You might even look for Angie Cobb. You haven't, have you?"

He didn't answer.

"You haven't thought about her as a suspect, have you? And you haven't looked for her?"

No answer other than lips pursed.

"Despite the fact that, until Reva Louise came along, Angie was married to Dan. And despite the fact that she owns guns. I saw her last night. She and some guy met up at the courthouse and went off together. What if it was Dan?"

No reaction.

"And now it's your turn, Deputy Dunbar. You tell us if you've located and spoken to all the actors. Tell us if you've accounted for and verified all their movements during that free-form street play, including Dan Snapp's and J. Scott Prescott's. You tell us that you're even *close* to finding the nut who's making everyone believe that we *are* a sniper's nest."

"Ask him if any of that gives him grist for his mill," Geneva said, studying Clod's starched, nonreactive face. "On second thought, maybe you should hush. You might be giving away our best clues and leads and I should warn you; that is never done by professionals like Sheriff Andy Taylor."

Once again, the Weaver's Cat was forced to close early. Deputies were poised to crawl all over the shop, waiting while we closed up and gathered out belongings. Geneva and Argyle followed me to the attic. Before I could invite her home with me, she reiterated her commitment to being my eyes and ears.

"Unless we hear Mattie."

"Okay."

"Or an entire gang of cutthroats breaks in. We couldn't possibly keep track of more than two or three. But we will be on duty, just as we were this afternoon."

"Where?" I hadn't seen her any of the times I'd walked through.

"I was worried at first that my lookout post would be indelicate and I would have to cover my eyes and ears, defeating the purpose of being there. If I'd had to do that, I wouldn't have seen what I saw."

"What did you see?"

"Nothing."

"How is that helpful?"

"Because it is like your pet dog theory. Isn't it helpful to know that nobody did anything but gawk? A few also gasped, but nobody tried to make off with the macabre mementoes you worried about."

"You were in the *bathroom*?"

"Yes. Wasn't that clever? Would you like to know how clever?"

I wasn't sure. Indelicate hardly seemed to cover the situation.

"I know that nobody put those guns in the linen closet this afternoon. No one but the young rascals John was cleaning up after opened that door. I believe that is important information."

I did, too, and I thanked her.

"Do you know what you can do to reward me?" she asked. "I shall tell you because you will not ever guess. You can bring me a piece of gingerbread so that I can sit quietly and breathe it in."

I thanked her again and told her I would do that. What a sweet, simple request. I grabbed my purse and Thea's, my notebook and laptop, and promised to be back in the morning, if I could. When I got down to the kitchen, John and Ernestine were gone. Thea stopped crocheting long enough to tell me she'd saved her searches to a file.

"It's called 'Spinning in Her Grave,'" she said. "I put it in a cloud, too, just in case."

"What file?" Clod asked.

"Sorry, Dunbar. Need-to-know basis only." She put her hook down, snapped the yarn with her hands as though she were breaking someone's neck, and started doing something else with the crocheted length she'd made.

"Here's what *we* need to know," Ardis said. "When can Joe get in to fix our window?"

"When did he say he'd get here?" Clod asked.

"He didn't," I said reluctantly.

"Kind of what I thought. Tell you what; *if* he shows up, we'll let him put a board over it for the night."

"After the fingerprint guys go over the frame inside and out?" I asked. "Because they haven't been here yet, but when they do, they should dust both sides of the frame. And maybe examine the wall inside and out, too."

Clod's response to my helpful suggestions was a second or two of silence and an infinitesimal twitch at the corner of his left eye. Then he said, "If Joe doesn't show, I'll cover the window for you."

And we'd be beholden to him. Blast Joe for not getting back to us. Ardis must have felt the same way. The "thank you" she strained through her clenched teeth sounded painful.

"Coleridge, that is what we needed to know," she said, "but here is what I cannot believe. I cannot believe that you dismissed our broken window as petty vandalism. It was not petty vandalism. It wasn't someone coming in to take something. It was not bored teenagers. Any questions so far?" She'd reverted to her glory days as Clod's fourth-grade teacher, pausing to make sure she had his full attention. "Either your people missed those guns yesterday, or that window was broken by someone who came in to plant them last night, going up the stairs, as Kath so presciently suggested when we first called you. Which scenario do you like best? I can go with either, but neither is flattering to your colleagues or your department."

"Ms. Buchanan," Clod said. He again waited a second or two, and I realized he might just as easily have learned that trick in fourth grade as at deputy school. His sense of timing was good, too. He waited until Ardis was about to spit but not quite boil over. "My apologies," he said calmly. "Mistakes were made."

"I thought I made a mistake once," Thea said, "but it turned out I was wrong." She held up her crocheted creation. It was a flamingo pink noose.

Chapter 24

The posse's supper and planning session at the Weaver's Cat was scrubbed along with the rest of our business day. In not the friendliest of moods, I called to leave a message for Joe to let him know that if he hadn't bothered to listen to his messages yet he didn't need to bother at all. When he picked up, instead of his machine, I had trouble thinking of something more intelligent to say than "wha."

"Hey," he said in his pleasant, soft voice. He'd not only recognized me by my single, mangled syllable, but also managed to give the impression that I'd sounded pleasant and friendly, too. "I got your message and I heard what happened."

"The window *and* the guns?"

"Would you like to hear what else is burning up the grapevine?"

"I don't know. Do I?"

"It'll keep. I'm over here at Mel's. She says why doesn't the posse meet at the café? It's Sunday. She says she'll have folks cleared out by seven."

"You'll stay for the meeting?"

"You should see the Moroccan sweet potato salad."

*   *   *

There was an advantage to being turned out of our business several hours before closing time. Again. It gave us more time to stick our noses into police business. Whether Clod had the imagination to wonder about that, I couldn't say, but as Ardis, Thea, and I went down the Cat's front steps, I looked over my shoulder. Clod stood at the door watching us go.

Ardis stopped me at the bottom of the steps with a hand on my shoulder. "Hon, did you tell me about seeing Angie last night?"

I glanced back. Clod watched. "Big Brother's got his eye on us. Keep walking."

"It'd be more fun to stand here and make him nervous," Thea said.

"But a waste of time," said Ardis. "We can still confuse him by crossing the street and heading in the wrong direction for any of us. But the sooner we're out of sight, the sooner he'll get to work in there. We need our shop— and its good, safe name—back."

We could have gone to the corner to cross at the crosswalk. But with unspoken coordination, we looked back at Clod, turned back to Main Street and its sedate twenty-five-mile-per-hour traffic. With Thea holding up her noose like a crossing guard's stop sign, we sauntered between cars to the other side and turned a direction none of us needed to go.

"Nicely done," Ardis said. "Now, hon, you told me you were worried about Angie, and asked if she has a gun, but what's this about Angie and a man?"

"Sorry. I forgot to tell you that part. After I saw Prescott, I saw Angie on the courthouse steps."

"It was getting late by then," Ardis said.

"And it was odd. She stood at the top of the steps and spread her arms like she was going to burst into song. She didn't, though. Then she sat down and looked like she was alone in the world. And then the guy—I couldn't see him well enough to recognize him—he called to her from the shadows between the columns. She went to him, he put his arm around her, and they went off together. It's not much of a story, but where is she and who's the guy?"

"You're right, hon. We have lots of questions and lots of directions to go in. What's the next step?"

I patted the laptop and notebook under my arm. "The sooner I get home, the sooner I can figure out what we know and what else we need to find out."

"She's got more threads spinning in her head than went into the yarn in my pretty pink noose." Thea swung the noose in front of her eyes. "I love this thing. I'm going to go hang it from the overhead fan in my office right now. And then I'll get back to trolling for information so we can hang someone."

"What can I do to help the cause this afternoon?" Ardis asked.

"There's an important piece of information we need. Knowing it might eliminate one of our dangling threads."

"I'm on it like cat fur on black pants. Where do I look?"

"Can you make a phone call?"

"Tell me who. What, where, and when would be good, too. And if you don't know the number, I'll ferret that out and do you proud."

After we'd crossed the street, I'd made sure Thea was

walking between Ardis and me. Call me chicken, call me prudent.

"Find out if Angie is still AWOL. Call her. And if she doesn't answer, call one of the twins."

I called Shirley when I got home. Ardis had demurred. She'd called it demurring and I let her, because it wasn't worth arguing over. To make up for it, she'd offered to go over the sales, receipts, and Ernestine's and John's lists again. Neither of us really thought poring over them would produce results, but it was another task that might eliminate a dangling thread, and if she wanted to spend her afternoon doing it . . .

"You set her up for that," Thea said after Ardis left us at the next corner and headed home.

"Worked like a charm, too."

"And you're stuck with calling a twin."

"Which at least won't be boring."

And it wasn't, because the twins might be many things, but boring wasn't in their oeuvre. Mercy answered Shirley's phone. She didn't say as much, but I knew it was Mercy when I asked if they'd heard from Angie.

"My baby!" Mercy shrieked, drilling the words straight into my ear. She said more, but I didn't hear it clearly. I was holding my phone at a safer distance and Shirley was wrestling her phone from Mercy.

"Is that you, Kath?"

"I'm right here, in your phone, Shirley. Please stop shouting."

"Sorry. Caught up in the drama. What do you want? Hold on a sec, Mercy's trying to tell me something."

There were noises in the background that sounded

like the honking and hissing of an angry goose followed by someone swinging a rusty gate. Then Shirley came back on.

"Mercy wants to know what you want and haven't you done enough with your innuendos and she hopes to hel— to high heaven you didn't tell the police that you think her angel Angela shot that woman. She said all that before she fell apart. Now she's crying. And now she's crying even harder. And now she's stopped crying—"

A shaky-sounding Mercy had the phone again. *"Kath Rutledge . . ."* She paused, drawing in a long, raspy breath. Before she could let it out in another shriek, I cut in.

"Mercy, listen to me. I'm taking Angie's disappearance seriously. I don't know if I can find her, but I'll try, if you can give me some information. Can you do that?" I heard the rusty gate swinging again and Shirley was back on.

"She's crying again. You don't know what it's like to lose your only baby like this. Let me tell you, it's rough. On all of us."

I believed it. The baby was a twice-married woman of more than forty, but Shirley sounded ragged herself and I was beginning to question my sanity in calling them. Still, it seemed like the right thing to do, so I asked Shirley if they knew about any places where Angie liked to go, places where she might meet friends, where I could go and see if anyone had seen her or knew who the guy I saw might be.

"You know," I said, "does she have any usual hangouts?"

"She wants to know where Angie hangs out and

meets strange men." Shirley helpfully shouted that to Mercy while still holding the phone near her mouth.

I hung up before the answer exploded my eardrum, turned my phone off, and locked the doors.

Joe acted as doorman at Mel's that evening, letting us in at the back, and letting anyone else who happened by know that the café was closed for the evening but would open again at its usual hour of six the next morning. I got there first, half expecting to see Carl, still drinking coffee, at his table in the corner. Thea arrived with Ernestine on her arm. John came next, then Ardis. She'd changed into dark slacks and a black-on-black embroidered tunic.

"The better to sneak down dark alleyways," she said when Joe complimented her, ignoring the fact that the sun hadn't set.

We sat in the kitchen, not the most comfortable place for a meeting because there were only counter-height worktables, but doing so meant our meeting was safe from prying eyes.

"Your elders get the best seats," Mel said when Thea complained about sitting with her chin nearly even with the butcher block prep table. Ernestine and John were perched on two tall stools so they could use the tabletop easily. "And I can't have you getting too comfortable. I'm providing a room out of view, board, and solid information, but someone's got to get up and bake for the morning before the bats fly home to roost, and I don't think it's going to be you."

"Did you hear anything about Prescott from your real estate friend in Knoxville?" I asked.

"Let's get the chow line started first," Mel said. "Chop-chop."

Mel's invitation to hold our meeting at the café came with strings attached—delicious strings if looks and smells could be trusted. We were guinea pigs for three new recipes, the Moroccan sweet potato salad and two others. One was a crispy, thin-crust white pizza with ham, baby green peas, mozzarella, a smattering of Parmesan, and a scattering of fresh mint. The other was dessert—sourdough rhubarb bread pudding with orange zest, pecans, and crystallized ginger. There probably wasn't enough scent from the crystallized ginger to satisfy Geneva's aroma request, but oh my goodness, that pudding looked good.

"What do you think of the salad?" I asked Joe. He was eating with concentration, tipping his head every so often as though listening to the food as well as tasting it.

"It's simple," he said. "Yet the spices and lemon, mixed with the parsley and cilantro, are bright and bold. It's pretty and it's delicious."

"The toasted almonds absolutely make it."

He'd just taken another bite, but he nodded and swallowed. "It'd be great at any potluck."

"Heaped in that black stoneware casserole dish you've got."

"Or Ivy's big round stoneware bowl. Perfect." Joe was a connoisseur of Blue Plum potlucks and known for his photographic memory of which dishes to make a beeline for or which ones to avoid. "What do you think of the pizza?"

"Do you see any left on my plate?"

"More?"

"Saving room." I gave an exaggerated and longing look toward the bread pudding. Mel noticed.

"Not yet, Red." She made us vote for or against adding the salad and pizza to her menu. The salad received unanimous raves. The pizza only lacked Thea's approval. She hadn't cared for the mint.

"But peas and mint are a classic combination," John said.

"Mouthwash," Thea retorted.

"You don't think the saltiness of the ham and cheese works with the mint?" Joe asked. "That they're balanced and made more complicated by it?"

"No. What I think is toothpaste."

"Don't order it, then," Mel said. "Majority rules. The salad and pizza are both going on the menu. Now, you're welcome to tell me what you think of *this*," she said as she handed around plates of the gorgeous bread pudding, "but I'm already in love, so we won't vote. Until my dying day and as long as I have a source for good rhubarb, I will serve this bread pudding. It is that good."

I looked at the plate she handed me. It had a very *dainty* portion of the pudding on it. All the plates were the same and everyone looked as surprised. All the plates were emptied in two or three bites. Two or three dainty but *superb* bites.

"What do you think?" Mel asked. "Good enough for seconds?"

"Or thirds or fourths, hon," Ardis said, eyeing the acres of pudding left in the pan with a barely disguised drool.

"Good. Anyone who stays to help with the dishes gets more. Red, let's get down to business."

I stood up and looked at each of them. Six good, earnest faces looking back at me. The basic setup, a meeting and expectant faces, reminded me of the many planning sessions I'd led back at the museum in Illinois. Then we would have been gathered in the conservation lab ready to discuss pest eradication or textile stabilization. How different this room, this group, the purpose . . .

"Treadle to the metal, Red, so we can spin on out of here."

"Don't be nervous, hon."

"I'm not nervous. I'm looking for the right words to begin. But there aren't any right words for what happened. And so far the words we're coming up with for who or why aren't so good, either."

"She needs a push," said Thea. "This'll get her going. One word. Stinkin' embezzler."

She sat back, looking pleased with herself and the stir she'd created. It was as good a place as any to start, too.

"All righty," I said. "We've got a lot of strands going — probably too many for some people to count — and it's time to spread them out, look them over, see if we can toss any of them, and see which ones we can spin together." I pulled a sheaf of papers from a file folder I'd brought. "On one side of these sheets is a summary of what we know — what I *think* we know. Below the summary are some of the questions we still have. It's a lot of questions. More questions than summary. Take a minute to read the summary and the questions. Then we'll go around the room, and if you have information to add or more questions, that'll be the time to do it." I handed the papers to Joe. "Pass them around, please? And, Thea, if

Ernestine trades places with you, will you take notes on my laptop? That'll be more efficient."

Also, Ernestine was beginning to look tottery on her high perch. Mel helped her down and she plopped onto Thea's vacated chair with a sigh. Not only did she look mole-ish, but like a mole, she seemed happier closer to the ground. The stool worked better for Thea, too, putting her at a better height for typing at the butcher block. She pulled a pair of zebra-striped glasses from her purse.

"Librarian Spyware model 007," she said, settling them on her nose.

"I take it we are to keep these papers out of the public eye?" John asked, scanning the front and back of his sheet. "What with names and nosy questions . . . Ah, no, I see. Initials only."

"But they're still nosy questions and the initials aren't much of a safeguard," I said, "so yes, let's keep them private."

"More of a safeguard than you might think," John said. "I can see that R.L.S. is Reva Louise and D.S. is probably her husband, Dan, but who are J.S.P. and A.S.C.?"

"And which A.C. is Angie Cobb and which one is Aaron Carlin?" Ardis asked. "Context isn't helping."

"But R.L.S. could be Robert Louis Stevenson," Thea said. "It always is in crossword puzzles. But he's long dead and I don't think there are any ghosts involved."

It might have been better if I'd run the initials past the ghost who *was* involved. She would have been happy to tell me the idea was a miserable failure right off the bat. Why did they keep insisting I be in charge?

"Have you got half a dozen pencils, Mel? Forget the

initials. Dumb idea. I'll tell you who they are and you can write them down."

"I like the initials," said Joe. "A.S.C. is Angie, right? Angie Cobb with *S* for her Spiveyness."

"You also do the Sunday crossword in ink," said Mel.

"It's good to have the copies here now so we're all on the same page," Joe said. "But before we leave, why don't we give them back to you and you can e-mail updated versions after the evening's meeting? That way, we can write on them, but if you take them home with you, we'll know they're safe."

"Thank you. That's a great idea."

Mel handed around pencils. When she came past me she whispered, "You're doing great, Red, and the initials were a nice touch. We all needed a laugh."

I told them who each set of initials stood for. Everyone but Joe and Ernestine wrote them down. Ernestine caught my eye with a wiggle of her fingertip toward her temple.

"No need to write them down. I've been practicing memory-building skills," she said. "Plus . . ." She held the finger up and then dipped into her purse. She brought out a large, ornate magnifying glass and held it to her eye. "No more need to use my needlework magnifier. My grandson gave me this. He says my new name is Grammy Gumshoe."

As they read over each side of the paper, Ernestine reading hers through the magnifying glass, I wondered what else I'd left off or garbled or twisted. The summary was three short paragraphs containing what I hoped were basic facts and not opinions.

The first shouldn't have contained anything anyone

didn't already know: Reva Louise Snapp, wife of Dan Snapp, half sister of Mel Gresham, half sister of Sally Ann Jilton, baker at Mel's on Main, was killed with a shot fired from the window of the second-floor bathroom at the Weaver's Cat.

The second paragraph was meant to catch people up to events after the shooting: my suspicion that J. Scott Prescott had snooped through the study at the Weaver's Cat; Prescott's stopping by while I sat on the porch in the dark the night before; Angie's meeting up with someone at the courthouse and subsequent disappearance; the rock through the window and with probable entry by a person unknown; John's discovery of the guns; the bombshell for some of them—Reva Louise's record for embezzling. I could tell when Ardis read that. She sucked in a breath and shot a look at Mel.

The third paragraph was where I might have slipped into the realm of subjective reporting. It was my catalog of out-of-the-ordinary things I'd noticed since the shooting or remembered from just before it. Things that might have nothing to do with the shooting, but details it seemed important to include, especially since Geneva had pointed out that the story is in the details. It was the shortest paragraph, mentioning the Tent of Wonders staying up overnight, Dan Snapp's dream to run a small engine repair shop, and Cole Dunbar's statement that mistakes were made. That last was where I really did slip into subjective mode, but for all the work I'd put into this, I felt entitled. What mistakes were made, I wanted to know, and when and by whom?

Appropriately enough, there were a baker's dozen of questions:

- Can the police be right and was it just a careless actor?
- Are all the actors and their movements accounted for?
- Have the police located any witnesses?
- Motive? Why did someone kill Reva Louise?
- Was Reva Louise lured to that spot at that time and, if so, how?
- Why did Reva Louise have J. Scott Prescott's realty card?
- Who planted the guns in the linen closet and when?
- Was Reva Louise back to her old tricks— embezzling?
- How can we find out about an insurance policy and who the beneficiary is?
- Why didn't J. Scott Prescott want anyone to know about the mercantile deal?
- Why would Reva Louise's death cause the deal to fall through?
- Was it Dan who met Angie Cobb at the courthouse?
- Where is Angie?

There were a few more questions than that, but they were questions I needed to ask individuals in private. Keeping them from the group might make a difference in how the investigation played out, but asking them in front of everybody else might make a difference, too, and the wrong kind of difference.

People were reading at different rates, as people do. Mel and Thea were each making use of their pencils, scribbling in the margins as they read. John had tucked his pencil behind his ear the way I remembered Grand-daddy doing when he was working in his wood shop. Joe's page was covered with doodles. Ardis stared at hers with pursed lips. Ernestine tapped her forehead as she read, maybe tamping the information in so it would stay. They were each concentrating in their own way.

They each startled in their own way when someone knocked on the back door.

Chapter 25

The knock, a sharp rap on the door's glass, sounded more like a shot to my oversensitized nerves. I jumped, then froze. Ardis and Thea froze, too. Ernestine and John didn't seem to think it was anything out of the ordinary. Cool Joe dabbed his mouth with his napkin and went to see who was there. It wasn't until I saw him put his napkin down that I realized he'd been eating another piece of the bread pudding. Mel caught my aggrieved look.

"Special circumstance," she said. "He's the one who made it. And the salad and the pizza. He's been here all day."

All day. Cooking with Mel. I knew they were good friends. She was the one who'd taught him to knit. What had she said about the bread pudding? No voting because she was in love? But had she meant in love with the pudding?

"All day, huh?"

"It's what the good guys do, Red. I'm suddenly down two staff. You know what that's like for a busy small business. Joe's helping out while Sally Ann's on compassionate leave."

She was right. And there was no need to be jealous. After all, Joe and I hadn't even decided if we were dating and they'd known each other a lot longer.

Joe came back then, with Sally Ann.

"Oh, hey," Mel said. "Come on in."

Sally Ann hesitated at the door until Joe touched her elbow and repeated Mel's invitation. She still wore the cargo pants, but she'd put on a light flannel shirt over the T-shirt. She stood with her hands sunk in her pockets, arms close to her body. John hopped off his stool and offered it to her. She didn't take it.

"I saw the light," she said. "I just wanted to make sure you were okay, Mel." She turned to Joe. "When you said 'some people,' I thought you meant two or three. I don't want to crash."

"Not a bit," Mel said. "Have you eaten?"

Sally Ann waved a plate away. "I promised Dan I'd stop by."

"How is he doing, Sally Ann?" Ardis asked. "I've been meaning to get over there with a casserole. Come on and sit down, hon, and tell us."

"Tell you what?" She looked and sounded uneasy.

"If there's anything we can do to help," Ernestine said.

"Arrangements we can help with?" John offered.

Neither suggestion made her look any easier, and I was glad when Mel came to her rescue by bringing her a piece of the bread pudding.

"It'll do you good," Mel said. "It'll only fix things for about five minutes, but for those five you won't have a care in the world."

"Like that ever happens," Sally Ann said. But she

took the plate and hitched up onto John's stool. "Sorry about missing work."

"Not a problem."

While Sally Ann picked at the edges of the pudding, Mel stood behind her and did her best to mime pretty much what I'd been thinking: Tell Sally Ann what we were doing. I glanced at the others, and although Ernestine hadn't followed Mel's subtleties, the rest nodded. But while it was handy that we were able to communicate without words, our silence didn't help Sally Ann feel any more welcome.

"Gosh, don't everyone talk at once," she said with an uncomfortable laugh. "Ya'll look like you're at a prayer meeting. Trust me to create an awkward moment."

"It's not you, Sally Ann," I said. "It's just that we're doing kind of a crazy thing." I paused to think how best to say what it was that we *were* doing. Pausing after the phrase "crazy thing" wasn't helping, though, so I plowed on. "We're looking into Reva Louise's death. And we could use your help."

Trust me to make someone who's already feeling awkward feel even more so. But was there really a gentler way of telling a bereaved woman a bunch of us were being nosy about her sister's death? Besides, Sally Ann worked for Mel; she had to be used to brusque and blunt. And I was getting the feeling Sally Ann was the kind of person who accepted what came along. That she didn't get too excited about anything one way or the other and she was always ready for the next splat of rain to hit her in the eye. Even that beautiful rhubarb bread pudding didn't seem to be doing anything for her. She ate it, but I could see the disappointment on Joe's face when she took the last bite with no show of emotion and put her empty plate on the butcher block without comment. The important thing was, she stayed and talked to us.

"You're taking notes?" she asked, nodding at Thea's fingers poised over my laptop.

"We're serious," I said, and held up my notebook.

"And we have a track record," Ardis said.

"We might look like kooks and quack like kooks," Thea said, "but we aren't without skills."

"I guess I heard something about that," Sally Ann said, a note of skepticism or wariness in her voice. "About a group showing up the sheriff sometime back. That was you?"

"That depends on what you heard," Mel said. "No time to rehash past glories, though. Red, let's kick this shindig into gear so I can make someone do the dishes and kick you out. Sooner, not later."

"Do you mind answering some questions, Sally Ann?" I asked.

"Depends on what I hear," she said with a quick smile. "No. It's okay. My answers might not be worth much, but I don't see how it can hurt."

Blunt, brusque Mel jumped in with the first one-two punch of a multipart question, proving that it could hurt. "Were Reva Louise and Dan getting along and did you know he was married before, to a currently unattached woman who lives here?"

"Is that what you're doing?" Sally Ann asked. "Pinning this on Dan?"

"Mel, honey," said Ardis. "Hush. Let Kath ask the questions. At least she hems and haws enough to soften them. And, Sally Ann, you need to understand that we're fact-finding only at this point in the investigation. We aren't attaching any more significance to one question or another, and you shouldn't, either." Sally Ann nodded and Ardis looked around at the rest. "Are we all agreed? Kath asks the questions. She does not mean to pry. Well, yes, she does, but not any more than necessary, and we are here to absorb and cogitate."

"I love that word," Thea said. "I'm bolding it in the notes."

"Um," I said, deciding I liked Ardis' description of that as "softening."

Sally Ann must have liked it, too. "Because, you know," she said, "I don't want you to think he did it, and I don't want you to take this the wrong way, but they fought like frickin' cats and dogs."

That statement was what we needed to finally break the ice with Sally Ann. It was warm in the kitchen, and cozy in a way I wouldn't have expected in a roomful of sharp knives and tools for whipping and beating and roasting ingredients into submission. It was Sally Ann's workplace, too, though, and that probably helped. She relaxed enough to shrug out of the flannel shirt. Mel hung it on a peg beside the door. Sally Ann started by saying she appreciated what we were doing and ended by telling us that if she'd been asked to place odds, she would have bet on Reva Louise killing Dan before Dan would have gotten around to killing Reva Louise.

"I told you how she was all about potential, didn't I?" she asked. "She saw a lot of it in Dan because he's a dreamer. But dreamers don't always live up to their potential. Doesn't mean they're worthless. But for someone like Reva Louise, with stars in her eyes—"

"And no compunctions," Thea said. "Ooh, another good word."

"Here's another loaded question," I said, "and I don't know if you have any way of knowing this, but do you think there's an insurance policy? And if there is one, is Dan the beneficiary? Or wait. How about this—with Reva Louise gone, is Dan in any way liable for what she still owed in restitution? Or is he free of that?"

"I don't know about insurance," Sally Ann said. "The way Reva Louise talked about him, it's hard to believe he had the forethought for something like an insurance policy. But if she could've afforded it, I bet she would've insured him."

"But what *she* would have done doesn't get us anywhere," Mel said. "She didn't kill him."

"Unless what she *would* have done would have sunk his potential even further," Ernestine said. "What if she was planning to leave him? Or what if she threatened to? I'm remembering several angry phone calls during our last Fast and Furious. She certainly sounded threatening, and from what she said, I assume she was talking to her husband."

"But does that make any sense?" Thea asked. "He didn't want her to leave, so instead he killed her? Is he that twisted? Or that energetic? He sounds more like a lazy good old so-and-so. If he did anything, you'd think he'd wave good-bye and say good riddance. I read the reports and court documents online this afternoon. I dropped them in a subfile for you, Kath. It's called 'She was an Embezzler, for cripes' sake.' This woman might have been a sister of the fiberhood, but she had an impressive lack of *moral* fiber."

"She also cheated at knitting hats for hospitalized babies," Ernestine said with about as much censure as I'd ever heard her muster.

Ardis gave Mel a hard look. Tough Mel didn't flinch. Sally Ann heard, saw, and began to crumple.

"I thought she'd straighten herself out," she said. "You know, why shouldn't she? She was lucky she didn't do time. She had a chance to make good. I thought I was doing her a favor getting her a job. But that wasn't enough for her, I guess."

"It might help if we knew why she was doing these things," I said. "You know her better than any of us, Sally Ann. Was she like this as a child?"

"Like what?" Sally Ann asked. "The center of the universe? Seems like she still is. You all are paying more attention to her now than you did when she was alive."

John broke an uncomfortable silence. "Does Dan work?"

"Farm and Home," said Joe. "Part-time."

"What else does he do?"

"Fish," Joe said. "Bait and bass. I tried to interest him in flies and trout a time or two." And if Joe couldn't raise a spark of interest for either in Dan Snapp, not a fly fisherman alive could.

"He isn't such a bad guy." Sally Ann said that so quietly I think only Mel and I, who were closest to her, heard. "You don't know him."

"I like the idea that he's a dreamer, Sally Ann," I said as quietly. "Did I hear right, that he wants to open a small engine repair business?"

"*She* wanted him to. Not that he's against the idea.

Just that, like she said, he needs a kick in the behind every now and then."

"Do you think she'd given him a kick to get the business going? She had a real estate agent's card in her pocket. Did she talk about renting or buying?"

Sally Ann didn't answer. I wanted to know why she didn't as much as I wanted to know what her answer would be, but her body language suggested she'd reached her limit, either of questions or emotional stamina. Her limit looked more believable than J. Scott Prescott's limit of shock and utter exhaustion had. Or just more pitiful.

Mel rescued her again, jumping up and announcing it was time to wrap things up. She walked Sally Ann to the back door. Joe went with them, his hand at the small of Sally Ann's back. I wondered what he was feeling. And for whom. And couldn't help myself—I went to the kitchen door and watched as Mel, uncharacteristically demonstrative, gave Sally Ann a hug. Joe hung back watching, too.

"But we aren't done yet, are we?" John asked.

I turned back to answer him and caught sight of Sally Ann's flannel shirt hanging on the peg. "Sally Ann, wait. Your shirt." Without thinking, I grabbed it and headed for the back door. Almost immediately the floor seemed to tip and I went with it, stumbling and smacking my shoulder against the bulletin board. I stayed there, leaned there, feeling out of breath. Feeling . . . the same confusion I'd felt after touching Reva Louise's skirt . . . something sly, furtive . . .

"Hey." Joe's soft voice cut through the fog. "Are you all right? You're looking puny, there. I hope it wasn't something you ate."

I blinked. How long had the café been out of focus? Not long. Mel and Sally Ann were still at the back door, only just turning toward me. Not long enough for anyone in the kitchen to notice. When had Joe noticed?

"Kath?" Joe touched my cheek. "I want to see your eyes. Look at me."

I did look at him, not sure what he would see in them. The same confusion I'd felt? Something furtive? I'd been fine until I picked up the flannel shirt. My hands were empty. The shirt lay on the floor. I bent to pick it up but stopped.

"I'll get it," Joe said. "Sally Ann's, right? Stay here. I'll be right back."

But by then I was fine and I needed to try something, to take a chance. Mel and Sally Ann had only just started back toward us. I followed Joe and heard them ask if I was okay.

"Sorry," I said, trying to sound strong and confident. "Stood up too fast, I think. Sally Ann, thanks for coming." I hesitated and then made myself put my hand on her shoulder. And hoped my face reflected the friendly words coming out of my mouth and not the little voice in my head screaming, "Aieeeeeee."

Nothing. I felt nothing when I touched Sally Ann's T-shirt. What *was* this? Why did it happen and what did any of it mean? Mel said something to me I didn't catch. She shook her head and unlocked the door for Sally Ann.

"It's her brain," I heard her say. "It works overtime but seems to have intermittent communication with the rest of her."

"I don't suppose that matters much," Sally Ann said. "Not if it'll help her figure out who did that to Reva Louise. Thanks for the time off. I won't stay gone long." She slipped the flannel shirt on and was on her way down the back steps into the alley when I called after her.

"Does that shirt belong to Reva Louise?"

Sally Ann stopped and looked down at herself and then up at me, puzzled. "No."

"Oh." I shrugged. Didn't even consider explaining why I'd asked. Didn't like the questions her answer raised. Were the "feelings" from Sally Ann and Reva Louise so much alike because they were sister? Or was Sally Ann really not such a straight shooter herself?

I ignored the two sets of eyes studying me as I headed back to the kitchen. If Mel and Joe came to any conclusions that would explain the last few minutes of my life, it was fine with me. I wanted to know, too.

Ardis looked up when I returned. She, Thea, and John were gathered around Ernestine and the laptop. Ernestine was perched on the stool again so she could peer directly at the screen.

"Mug shots," Ardis said. "Thea's brilliant idea."

"Did you all hear?" Thea asked. "I'm brilliant. All of you please remember that."

She'd done an image search that afternoon for the people on Ernestine's and John's lists, TGIF members, Blue Plum citizens in general, and people in "The Blue Plum Piglet War" specifically. Working from names mentioned in the tabloid, which led her to more names, Web sites, and social media sites, she was able to put together a slide show of people who were in town for the festival. Like a book of mug shots, there were numbers with each face or full-length photo, but no names. She'd included more than one picture of a person if it showed different angles or expressions, but these people didn't necessarily appear in the slide show one after the other. They were writing down numbers when they recognized someone they'd seen around the time of the shooting.

"Of course, I might be fingering the woman who was in front of me in the grocery store last week with twenty-seven items over the limit in the express lane," Ardis said.

"Or someone else entirely," said Ernestine.

"How long is this going to take?" Mel asked.

"No time at all," Thea said. "I can send the link or Kath can when she sends her updated info sheet."

"Good," said Mel. "I'm fading. Do that. Do the dishes. Then go."

"No." I said that loudly enough that, although no one jumped, everyone but John looked surprised. He was still engrossed in Thea's mug shots. "Sorry," I said, "but we need to get more done tonight. We have to."

"You're a little touchy since the shirt incident back there, Red. What was that about?"

But Ardis was more than a little hot under the collar and she didn't leave me room to answer. "I'll tell you what *I'm* a little touchy about, since I *finally* heard tell." She stood, arms crossed, staring hard at Mel. "I'm touchy about the fact that you knew up front Reva Louise was an embezzler and a liar and a cheat and yet you saw fit to let her loose in this town without a single neighborly 'Oh, by the way' to warn your friends and business associates. At least Sally Ann had the grace to apologize for bringing that—that *infestation* here."

While they had a static-filled stare-down, I wondered when Sally Ann had apologized. Maybe I hadn't heard.

"Ardis," Mel finally said. "I want you to be the first to know. I am not the best judge of character. True fact."

Ardis stood scowling one moment longer, then relaxed enough to drop her arms and sit down on the other high stool. "When it comes down to it," she said, "who among us really is? And giving Reva Louise a job when she needed one speaks more to your true nature than poisoning the well against her by telling her story. It's over. She's gone. And I believe I've talked myself out of voluntarily exiling myself from the café, which would have proved precisely nothing. We are all tired after a frightful two days. Kath, what more can we do tonight? Ms. Crotchety Pants needs to go home."

"I won't ask which of you is Ms. Crotchety Pants. Before we tackle the dishes—and take our seconds of the bodacious bread pudding with us—let's have progress reports from Mel and Thea. You all know Carl? Old guy, one of Mel's regular coffee hounds? She had him look for Prescott's business cards on the bulletin board by the back door. Any luck?"

"He looked for Snappy Small Engine Repair, too," Mel said. "That's what Reva Louise said Dan was going to call his business. Carl found Prescott's real estate card. Nothing else."

"So Reva Louise might have gotten her card straight from Prescott."

"Or not," Ardis said. "From what you said, he handed out various and sundry by the deck-full. She could've taken it from the bulletin board and he put up five more. We still don't know what her having the card means. If anything."

I made a note. "Next report, also from you, Mel. Did you say you heard from your real estate source in Knoxville?"

"Nothing firm in terms of real estate," Mel said. "Except that Prescott—"

"Was there a hole in it?" Ernestine asked. "Oh, I'm sorry. You go ahead, Mel. It just occurred to me that a hole might tell us something."

"A hole in what?" Mel asked.

"In her pocket," Ernestine said. "No, I mean in the card Kath *found* in her pocket. Not in her *own* pocket; in Reva Louise's pocket. If there wasn't a hole in the card, then Reva Louise didn't take it from the bulletin board."

"Very good, Ernestine," said Ardis. "The curious incident of the hole in the business card."

"Exactly what I thought," Ernestine said, so delighted with herself that she'd turned as pink as the flowers in her dress.

"I don't think it had a hole in it," I said, "but I can't swear to it."

"And that only tells us where she didn't get the card," said Mel.

"Eliminating possibilities is a big help, though. Good work, Ernestine. Any more thoughts on the business card? Back to you, then, Mel. You said there wasn't anything firm about Prescott's real estate business, but?"

"He's been hyper and secretive, which she says fits with working on a big deal, and rumor has it that he lost the piano sales job. That was easy enough to check. I did. He did."

"That must've been a blow." I knew something about that kind of blow, and it was almost enough to make me feel sympathetic toward Prescott. But not quite. "Do you know how recently? He was still handing out piano cards less than two weeks ago."

"I didn't ask, but Paula—she's my source—she thought he might be feeling a pinch."

"That could explain the amount of spare time he has on his hands for dabbling in plays," Ardis said. "But if he lost a real estate deal because of Reva Louise's death, unless he's dumber than a box of rocks, doesn't it seem unlikely that he went to the trouble of killing her on purpose?"

"What if he lost the deal because of *her*, but not because of her death?" Thea asked.

"Murder by absolute fury as a result of sliding another step toward financial ruin?" Mel asked. "That's not a bad theory. I'd love to know what that deal was. You'd think someone here in town would've heard something. I'll check back with Paula and see if she can pick up anything else." Mel was involved enough in the discussion by then that she took a seat, ran her fingers through her spikes to make sure they were upright, and knitted her brow in concentration. "He's working at three chancy professions in a tough economy," she said. "I don't imagine boatloads of expensive pianos are selling when people are struggling just to stay in their houses. And the ones trying to sell their houses aren't having a lot of luck, either. Moving commercial properties can't be much easier. And the mercantile? That thing's been empty for donkey's years. Plus, look how far he's ranging from home looking to make a buck."

"Like a predator expanding its territory when prey is scarce," Joe said.

It wasn't until I heard his voice across the room that I realized he'd gotten up and was doing the dishes. Such quiet ways he had about him, and such keen observation skills had I. I would've gone to give him a hand, but I didn't want to interrupt the energetic flow of our discussion. I told myself.

"What if her death is something else?" Thea said. "What if her death is misdirection, diverting everyone's attention from some other plan or scheme?"

"Killed for a sneaky reason, instead of for obvious gain? That would fit with . . ."

"Fit with what, Red?"

I'd almost said, *With what I felt from touching her skirt and Sally Ann's shirt.* "It fits with hiding more guns in the Cat, trying to make it look as though some nut set up housekeeping and is planning who knows what. But how would we figure out what that plot or scheme is? The hard part of figuring this out is that we're starting from the end. We've got a solution—Reva Louise is dead. And now we're looking for the problem her death solved, whether it's sneaky or straightforward."

"And whose problem it was," said John, surfacing from the mug shot slide show.

"Well, yes. That's kind of the point of the investigation," Mel said. "I recognize an evil smile when I see one, John Berry. What are you up to?"

"Reliving my evil past." He told them about his encounter with the man and his bass boat earlier in the afternoon. "I had way too much fun watching him make his problem worse with each maneuver, and I just found him here in one of Thea's pictures. I was going to show you so we could all have a laugh. But he doesn't deserve my piece of meanness. He's only a flatland landlubber with a new toy."

Joe was finished with the dishes and drying his hands. He looked over John's shoulder at the flatland landlubber pictured on the laptop.

"Heh," came Joe's abrupt and stifled laugh, "he's also Dan Snapp."

Chapter 26

Finding out that Dan Snapp suddenly had enough money, or the promise of enough money, to afford an expensive bass boat and trailer to haul it, combined with the sensitivity of an earthworm for running out and buying them within twenty-four hours of his wife's murder, gave new energy to the posse that Sunday evening. Mel was absolutely nuclear. Ardis and Joe cooled her down before she reached critical mass.

"Walk it off, hon," Ardis said. "We'll walk it off together." She marched Mel back and forth across the kitchen until Mel quit spitting and could stand still and listen to Thea's good sense.

"No one's so stupid in this day and age," Thea said, "that he would kill his wife for the money and immediately start spending it. That kind of behavior just raises so many red flags."

"But he might be that smart," Mel said, "that he'd know no one would be that stupid, so he'd make himself *look* that stupid to throw off the stupid sheriff's deputies. No offense intended, Joe."

"None taken."

The energy so quickly gathered, as quickly dispersed.

Before we dispersed, too, I told them I would e-mail the updated summary to them and a link to the mug shot slide show. I asked them to look again at the questions below the summary.

"I especially want to know more about that mercantile deal and where Angie is. If we don't find her, Shirley and Mercy will hound me for the rest of my life."

"Goodness," Ernestine murmured.

"And really quick, if you don't mind, I have one more question that probably hasn't got anything to do with what happened, but . . ."

"Spit it out, Red. Then let's drag ourselves home," said Mel.

"Did any of you hear a loud stereo or hear a woman singing downtown late last night? Oh, and wait, one more. Have you ever heard an old story, a hundred, hundred fifty years old, about a young couple shot and killed walking home through a grassy field somewhere around here? Their names might have been Mattie and Sam."

"Red, go home and get some sleep."

Judging by the looks from the others, Mel was right; time to go home. Joe handed us each a bakery bag at the back door. Mine had a double portion of the rhubarb bread pudding.

Home and sleep would have been nice. I wanted to stop by the Weaver's Cat again, though, to see if Geneva would come out and sit with me on the porch. And to see if everything was quiet and not more paranormal than normal. And to make sure she wasn't afraid to spend the night alone in the dark shop with only Argyle the sleepy watch cat for company.

Joe caught up with me before I reached the Cat. "Hey."

"Oh, hey."

"You're feeling all right now? Are you sure you were just light-headed?"

"Yeah, it happens sometimes. Low blood pressure, standing up too fast. I'm fine. Thanks for checking." It was hard to say whether his deep blue eyes were concerned or unconvinced. Time to move on. "I've got a couple of questions for you, if you don't mind."

"One of the things I like about you, Kath, is that you don't mind if people *do* mind your questions, so go ahead. If I mind, I'll go fishing."

"But with flies, not bait."

"Damn right."

"The other morning, yesterday morning . . ." When I'd enjoyed the feeling of his hand at the small of *my* back. And this evening he'd treated Sally Ann the same way. Had his touch only been a gesture of courtesy?

"Kath?"

"Sorry, thinking things through. I got the feeling yesterday, and again tonight, that you don't care for Dan Snapp. Is that only the bait-versus-tied-fly thing, or is there more to it?"

He didn't answer right away, which pretty much gave me my answer, but I pressed for more anyway.

"The reason I'm asking is that, although Mel says she *isn't* a good judge of character, I think you are."

"So you want to know if I think he could shoot his wife in public."

"That's a . . . brutal way to put it and completely accurate. It's horrible, isn't it?"

I slowed our pace as we came to the Cat. The lights

were on, so Clod was still there. There was no glimmer of
Geneva on the porch or in a window looking for me. Just
as well; she would've made comments or questioned my
judgment for walking in the dark with Joe. As we crossed
Depot, I looked along the side of the building and saw
the boarded window, the boards like a bright scab on the
mellow, old bricks. Joe saw me looking.

"Cole covered it?" he asked.

"You recognize his work from that distance?"

"He called. He said you asked him to do it if I didn't
have time."

"Oh. That's not exactly how I remember it, but as long
as it's covered."

"I'm sure he did a fine job and I've got an idea for a
new kind of bell for the Cat's back door. Anyway, about
Snapp. I don't like the guy. He's lazy and there's a lot that
goes with being lazy, including the possibility of being
brutal if that's the easiest path. But I'm not going to in-
dict a man on my gut instincts."

"Yeah, that could be the downfall of the lazy detective. So, on a different subject, any idea what Mel reported stolen the other day?"

"Recipe file."

"What?" My "what" covered incredulity at the item
stolen, at the fact that Mel reported that peculiar loss,
and at Joe's insider knowledge. I'd asked, but more as a
way to put a bug in his ear. I hadn't expected an answer.
He knew but Mel hadn't told *me* when I asked?

"I probably shouldn't have said anything."

"Then we won't talk about it." *So there.* "Really,
though? She reported a missing recipe file to the police?"

"It was more of a box than a file."

"A valuable box? Valuable recipes?"

He looked uncomfortable.

"Never mind. If you weren't supposed to say anything, then we won't talk about it." *It or anything else. Hmph.* I should have respected him for keeping his word, but he'd only kept it up to a point, and that point was at the brink of my inveterate nosiness. My nosiness wasn't as miffed as the rest of me, though, and Joe was a man with many streams of interesting information. "Any idea why Aaron Carlin didn't take down his Tent of Wonders yesterday?"

"You're wondering about that, too? Huh. If we both are, maybe it's worth finding out. I'll see what I can do."

By then we were at Granny's little yellow house—now mine—on Lavender Street. I was bone tired and must have looked it.

"I won't keep you," Joe said when I stepped up onto the porch. "You should try to get a good night's sleep, Kath."

He waited until I unlocked the door and opened it. Then he waved and he was gone. The story of Joe.

A good night's sleep had a nice ring to it. While I brushed my teeth, planning on no further detours before diving headfirst into my comfortable bed, three more questions bubbled up. I rinsed, spit, and went to find my notebook. Suddenly not liking the idea of giving them bullet points, I wrote them one after the other in paragraph form:

> *How smart or dumb is Dan Snapp? If he needs a kick in the pants to do something, and if he killed Reva Louise, who gave him the kick? Angie? Or, if J. Scott Prescott, a near-*

desperate real estate agent, is a suspect in the death of Reva Louise, shouldn't he also be a suspect in the disappearance of Angie the fledgling agent and potential rival? And what about Sally Ann? What do we know about her? How bitter or jealous is she of "the center of the universe"? But are bitterness or jealousy motives for murder?

I closed the notebook and slipped the elastic around it, hoping the questions would stay there inside and not come knocking for answers in the early hours.

"What are you planning to do?" Ardis snarled into the phone the next morning. "Rouse the entire town before the first mockingbird is up or just your soon-to-be-lost friends?" She never woke well when wakened early.

"It's not all that early, but I apologize anyway. Deputy Dunbar gave us the all-clear to open this morning, and there's a lot I want to get done today, starting with checking—again—to see if we need to clean up after him."

I heard movement and flapping noises and pictured her throwing back covers and swinging her legs over the edge of the bed.

"If you have important agenda items," she said, sounding more upright, "Debbie and I will handle whatever needs attention at the Cat."

I'd hoped she would say that. "That's fantastic, Ardis. I'll go by and feed Argyle, but I'd like to run a casserole over to Dan Snapp, and do you know what else I thought might be interesting? I thought I'd make an appointment to see the mercantile. Maybe it'll tell us something. Maybe I can even get J. Scott Prescott to show me around."

"I don't think it's a good idea to go poking that Prescott to see what happens. And the same goes for Dan Snapp. Remember our motto, hon, safety in numbers."

"We don't have a motto, Ardis, but if we adopt one, I'll vote for that."

"I don't want you going alone to ask Snapp or Prescott questions. Do you understand? And not just because I'll feel left out."

"Message received."

"Come to think, the obvious ones to call Prescott about the mercantile are Ernestine and John. He won't know them. Their snooping—excuse me—their interest in looking around will appear innocent. What do you think of that?"

"I like it. John can take mean-as-snakes Ambrose along for protection. I'm getting a low battery beep. I'd better go."

"Then I'll call to see if Ernestine and John are game for the mercantile ploy. You charge your phone so you have it when you need it."

"Yes, ma'am."

Before she let me go she also made me promise no solo interviews with Dan Snapp or J. Scott Prescott. There was nothing in her extracted promise, however, about snoop— excuse me—about looking at and showing professional interest in Dan Snapp's loom house.

Geneva was oddly bright and chipper when I went by the Cat. She'd felt safe having the sheriff's deputies there much of the evening. She said it was like having her own armed security force.

"An amusing armed security force. You should have heard their wonderful jokes about yarn and knitters."

"Any singing last night?"

"No, and wouldn't that have been a hoot? I would have liked to hear a deputies' chorus singing songs about weaving around and spinning and dyeing."

"I'm sure you would, but I meant did you hear Mattie?"

She hadn't and she hadn't liked being reminded. I'd popped her lonely bubble of joy, she said, and now she would spend the rest of the day in gloom. I fed Argyle and left.

The loom houses I'd heard of in the Southeast dated to the early nineteenth century. They were built at a time when estates consisted of a main house and several separate buildings, usually log structures, such as a kitchen and an office and sometimes a loom house where the women sat to weave and spin. I was surprised, if there was a loom house worth its name anywhere near Blue Plum, that Granny hadn't ever mentioned it. That probably meant the structure at the Snapps' wasn't worth the name, but that didn't mean it wasn't worth my professional—and amateur—attention.

No one appeared to be home when I arrived. That suited me fine. I parked in the drive and knocked anyway, on a front door in sore need of a lick of paint. The house was a tall, narrow, two up, two down with another set of two and two built onto the back. At one time the place might have been full of happy voices. My knock was answered by silence.

Around the back, out of view of the street, which was more of a country road this far from the bustling center of Blue Plum, I knocked on the kitchen door. I also peered through a window, pressed my ear to the door, counted dirty dishes on the table, and decided there were too many for them to be a useful clue. Except—if Angie was staying there, would she put up with that mess? I didn't know. And if I saw signs of female habitation, they were as likely, or more likely, to be signs of Reva Louise.

The fancy new boat and trailer weren't there. Just as well. I knew next to nothing about boats and didn't need to spend precious time gawking at one. Boat and trailer might be in the ramshackle barn, but the barn looked so unstable I didn't think the new owner of an expensive boat would risk it. Besides, my skill at reading tire tracks and flattened grass, coupled with my knowledge of Dan's backing abilities, told me he'd spent a deal of time maneuvering the thing in the open area between the house and the barn and then driven away. It helped that the grass hadn't been mowed in recent weeks.

What I took to be the loom house stood across the gravel drive from the house, snuggling up against the woods surrounding the place. It looked as though it had the right proportions for a log building of the right age. It was hard to tell; ivy covered one side and the roof and someone had covered at least the front, and probably the whole thing, in tar paper shingles. The shingles could be removed, though, and wouldn't it be sweet to find out what was underneath? Or inside?

I'd brought my camera as part of my cover story. I took a few pictures to "document" my search for a candidate for the National Register of Historic Buildings. I didn't walk all the way around the building, because the weeds around the back were thick and more than waist-high. I wasn't that invested in my cover story. I took pictures of the ivy, though, pretending I was doing before and after shots.

The door was my first clue that this really was an old log building. It was also covered in shingles, but only on the outside. I knew because, conveniently, the door was unlocked. That probably meant there wasn't anything inside worth stealing. But the door itself was massive by modern standards. The timbers were solid and thick. No signs of termites or borers. I closed the door behind me, for privacy's sake, and set to my real work of snooping.

The place needed a new roof. There were two or three walnut-sized holes overhead, and after a few minutes I was able to see well enough in the deep twilight to navigate without tripping or bumping into something. I had a small flashlight with me, too, good for closer inspections. Three of the walls were covered with cheap paneling, so cheap someone had been able to pull it away in places and break pieces off. All of the paneling had been removed from the fourth wall. Sections of more, newer paneling were stacked against that wall. A shy little tendril of ivy peaked around the edge of the paneling and there, in the corner, my flashlight showed the original logs. Wow, good-sized logs. I wondered if they were American chestnut. The building definitely had potential—poor Reva Louise.

There was actually quite a lot of stuff in the loom

house worth stealing, including yard and lawn tools Dan
wasn't wearing out with overuse. I looked through the
tools and equipment, half hoping to find a rifle casually
hiding next to a weed trimmer. No such luck. It did look
as though someone had dreams of repairing small engines. As far as I could tell, anyway, but what did I know?
There was a workbench and a newish-looking set of
socket wrenches. Cans of various weights of oil. Cans of
gasoline along the back wall. Seven of them. For running
small engines, I guessed. Oddly enough, there was also a
restaurant steam table and a collection of industrial-
sized kettles and roasting pans. A meat slicer. I might
have thought they were left over from Pokey's roadhouse, but they weren't dusty.

There was also a two-drawer filing cabinet. The top
drawer had a few folders containing parts catalogs full of
exciting things like gauges and gaskets. Maybe Dan
found them as exciting as I did. They were all addressed
to Reva Louise. Behind the folders was a sturdy metal
box, about the size of a large shoe box, with a lock. No
key. I put the flashlight between my teeth and lifted the
box to get a sense of what was in it. Nothing too heavy,
nothing that clanked. I reminded me of a cashbox, although it didn't look like any cashbox I'd seen. I set it
back in its nest behind the file folders.

The bottom drawer had a mouse nest in it. Geneva
would have hated that. I did, too, and slammed the
drawer shut. Although, speaking of mice, I heard noises
at the back wall. Yeek. Mice? Rats? Raccoons? Bats?
The sounds from the back wall didn't come any closer,
and the hair on my head was beginning to lie back down,
when someone rattled the door latch.

I didn't panic and I didn't hide. But I was crouched next to the bottom drawer of the filing cabinet, behind the steam table, which was almost as good as hiding. I flicked off my flashlight and I stayed there, quieter than the bears or whatever they were at the back wall.

Whoever came in seemed to know I was there. I wasn't afraid, but I didn't breathe and willed my heart to stop crashing against the walls of my chest. Whoever came in closed the door so that we were there together in the dark.

And then whoever it was held his flashlight under his chin and turned it on.

"Boo, Ms. Rutledge." Stupid Clod.

"You are without a doubt the biggest cl— What do you think you're doing coming in here like that? Women suffer silent heart attacks, you know. How do you know I'm not having one right now?"

"Well, not a silent one, anyway."

He had a point.

"And while we're on the subject," he said, "what are you doing in here? In the dark. Hiding."

"Research." I'd never heard myself say that word in such a squeaky voice before. It was pitiful. I coughed and tried again. "I'm developing documentation to prove that this fine log building is an early nineteenth-century—"

"Quiet."

"I beg your pardon?"

"Do you smell that?" he asked.

"You don't need to be quiet to smell smoke."

"Did you hear *that*?" He pivoted to the door where it sounded as though something bigger than a mouse was doing something outside.

Then the word "smoke" and the smell registered in my brain. I didn't panic right off the bat, though. I waited until it made good sense.

"The door?" I asked with admirable calm.

"Something's blocking it."

"Your phone?"

"Front seat of my car. Stupid. What about yours?"

"At home, plugged in, so it'll be fully charged when I need it."

Chapter 27

"What do you mean you won't use your gun?" The incredulity in my voice should have scathed the ears off any self-respecting sheriff's deputy. But Deputy Clod Dunbar did nothing more than momentarily stop staring at the heavy wooden door behind which we were trapped and give me some kind of look over his shoulder. There wasn't time to decipher Clod's look, though. The smoke was getting thicker and I heard an ominous crackling—that most definitely was not mice—in the far corner. Scratch that. None of the corners in this misbegotten, soon-to-be-flaming loom house were far enough. National Register–worthy status be hanged. "Take your stupid gun *out* and shoot the stupid door *down!*"

"You're getting hysterical," Clod said.

"I'm trying hard not to. I am also trying not to be critical or sarcastic, but I'd like very much not to become a smoked ham in here, so *please use your gun!*"

"Look at me, Kath. Look at me." He shone his flashlight up and down his length. "Am I wearing my holster?" He was using the infuriating tone of voice of someone who doesn't know how to calm a two-year-old, let alone the woman with whom he's about to become seared tuna. "Do you see my gun, Kath? I did not say I *won't* use my gun. I said I *can't*. I *can't* use my gun because my gun is not *here*. No gun. Besides, you obviously watch too much TV or not enough of the right kind of TV. Shooting a door, especially a thick oak-plank door with iron hardware, isn't the best way to get out of a building. Especially a burning building. Especially a burning building that also contains seven cans of gasoline."

He had to mention the gasoline again. I spun around to see how close we were to blowing sky-high and following the seven cans, the roof, and the rest of the building to either North Carolina or Kingdom Come, Kentucky. I'd already dragged the cans from the back wall into the middle of the structure, but that wasn't going to help much. The whole place was only fifteen feet by twenty. The middle of it wasn't a safe distance from any other part of it, smoking, smoldering, crackling, or otherwise.

"We'd better finish coming up with an alternative exit plan fast, then," I said, turning back. "*Now* what are you doing?"

He'd put the palms of his hands on the door. He held them there for a few seconds, and then moved them to another spot, and then another lower down.

"Testing for heat," he said.

"Even the *door's* on fire?"

He didn't answer. Instead he straightened, reared back, and rammed his shoulder into the door. He made a good thump when he hit, and he let out a muffled "oof," but nothing else happened. The whole sweet little loom-house-turned-storage-shed might be starting to smolder, but you couldn't fault its stout materials and construction. Deputy Dunbar rubbed his shoulder and clamped his lips on anything further.

"Ouch," I said for him. "Okay, now I *am* going to be critical. Why *don't* you have your gun? What were you going to do if I hadn't been *me* you found snooping around in here? Did you think of that? What if I'd been someone else, who *did* have a gun?"

"You want to know why I don't have my gun with me? It's because I was afraid I'd want to shoot *you*. And you know what the difference is between you and me?" He turned from the door to scrabble through the motley collection of yard tools I'd already searched. "It's the difference between talk and action. You can't shut up about the gun." He swept aside leaf rakes and a snow shovel. "And I'm trying to get us out of here."

"With that?"

He held the weed trimmer in his white-knuckled fist.

"No." He tossed the trimmer aside and lunged past me. *"This!"* With a look of triumph, he grabbed a three-foot length of black pipe from the shadows against the wall behind me. He weighed it in both hands like a trophy fish. Then he moved his hands apart and I saw, as though he'd performed sleight of hand, there were actually two pipes, one sliding in and out of the other, and the inner piece ended in a wicked-looking wedged tip, like a giant screwdriver.

"What is it?" I asked.

"Solid-steel salvation!"

"Hang on a second, though—"

"No time."

We were both coughing from the acrid smoke by then, and flames licked the back wall, but there was something there in the shadows. . . .

"But there's—"

"No buts. Wish me luck, little sweetheart, and then stand back." Before I realized what was happening, he swept me into a one-armed embrace, planted a kiss on my lips, and pushed me behind him.

And then Deputy Cole Dunbar, man of action but not so many listening skills, holding the whatever-it-was like a medieval pole-arm or miniature battering ram, charged full tilt at the door. And in the split second before he smashed our way out of that fiery death trap, I knew I should be impressed, grateful, and possibly in starry-eyed love with a true hero.

Instead I felt like a complete heel. There I was, surrounded by smoke, threatened by flames and exploding gasoline cans, being rescued by a tall, fit, gung ho deputy sheriff, and the only thoughts sputtering in my head were *A kiss? Little sweetheart? Well, this is a disturbing turn of events.*

Almost as disturbing as Clod's unforewarned endearments was the tremendous slamming clang of one metal pipe sliding into the other and, judging from the tremendous explosion of cursing, the massive pinching of fingers between those pipes when they all met that really sturdy early-nineteenth-century door. But it was exactly that commotion that convinced me I wasn't even on the outskirts of the neighborhood of being in love with Clod Dunbar. Because if I were in love, or even in strong like, then I probably would have turned around to see if he was bleeding or in one piece.

Instead I groped for the edge of the paneling stacked against the wall where Clod had discovered his implement of self-destruction. That shy tendril of ivy I'd seen earlier—that tendril of *green* ivy—was sneaking in from behind those panels and it must be coming from somewhere with sunlight and fresh air. Maybe, just maybe . . .

I pushed and pried and coughed, shifting the panels . . .

Clod clanged and banged and cursed away at the door and then he was coughing and retching. I looked over. He'd dropped his battering ram and had his hands on his knees, trying to get a breath.

"It's no use," he gasped. "I'm sorry. I'm sorry. I thought that would work."

"That's okay. Maybe this will. But now we really do need to hurry."

By the time we'd wrenched the long-unused window open, and clawed our way through the thick curtain of ivy hiding it from the outside world, and tumbled through, and stumbled to a safe distance to collapse in the bright sun and the sweet, sweet green, unmowed grass and gulp clean, fresh air, we heard the sirens of the Blue Plum Volunteer Fire Department.

And Clod looked over at me and said, "So, you wanna grab a beer sometime?"

I started to think that I couldn't believe this guy. That he had some nerve and that nerve was blind or unobservant. Did he never catch my aggression? Aggression that ranged from quiet sarcasm to a fist breaking his nose? *That* didn't tell him this was a no-go? That I was not interested?

But maybe sharing a near-death experience does more than make one's life flash before one's eyes. It had certainly added another layer of confusion to my life. I looked at him. He sat up and cradled the fingers he'd creamed with the log splitter, an expectant, clueless look on his face, waiting for my answer.

"Make it a whiskey," I said, "and you're on."

Chapter 28

We didn't get around to setting a day or time. The commotion of the fire trucks arriving took over the moment and Clod dragged himself to his feet to go be in his element.

"Stay over here," he said. "Stay out of the way."

No strings attached. That was the first thing I needed to tell him when we met for our drink. No strings attached or I really would stay out of his way.

Someone had wedged a length of two-by-four between the ground and the antique door latch so that the more Clod had tried to crash our way out, the tighter the two-by-four became wedged. One of the volunteer firemen told me that. There was also evidence of an accelerant, possibly gasoline.

"I guess we're lucky to be alive." I'd turned my back to the loom house. Fiery death trap aside, it was a piece of history and it hurt to watch it burn.

"You are lucky to be alive!" Ardis stormed when I walked through the front door of the Cat. Debbie stood beside her at the counter, fists on her hips. I got the impression

Ardis had coached her. The look of relief on her face didn't match the posture, and when I smiled at her she raised one hand in a little wave. Ardis grabbed the hand and put it back on Debbie's hip.

"Shh, Ardis, the firemen said they would've gotten us out in plenty of time because old buildings like that take a while to really catch. I'm fine. I've been home, took a shower, smell as good as new. It's okay."

"Except for the small matter that someone tried to kill you."

"Which is great, because it proves our point that someone *meant* to kill Reva Louise. I'm looking at this as a win-win situation. I'm alive. The police believe us."

Ardis still didn't look happy, but her eyes weren't focused like lasers on me anymore. She was thinking. Her eyes moved from left to right, as though her thinking process was laid out before them and her eyes were following it step by step. When they reached far right, she looked at me and nodded. "That means we need to work fast, hon, if we want to find the killer first."

"That's what I thought, too."

"And you know what I always say. There's nothing like lighting a fire under a cop to get things going."

The loom house fire got a lot of people going, and most of them stopped by the Weaver's Cat that afternoon. Debbie, thank goodness, said she could stay until four to help the "real" customers while Ardis and I dealt with the rest and figured out our next move.

"Our next move is as simple as A-B-C," Ardis said. "Alibis, bad guys, and criminality. Figure those key parts out and we're home free."

"Let's not talk like that in front of the customers, though. Did Ernestine and John get hold of Prescott?"

"They did and they made an appointment. He said he would meet them at the mercantile at ten, but he left them standing on the sidewalk like brides at the altar. He did not return further calls."

"Neither Dan nor his boat was at home. Where would he go to fish?"

"With a boat like that? Boone Lake or Watauga," Ardis said. "I wonder if we can get Joe to—"

"Get Joe to what?" the man himself asked.

"Find a fisherman," said Ardis. "Or anyone who saw him this morning. You heard about the fire at the Snapp place?"

"I came by to see for myself that Kath has risen like a phoenix from the ashes. And to let you know the café's having a special on flame-roasted stuffed peppers to take advantage of the excitement. Mel's telling folks it's to celebrate your survival, though, because it sounds less grasping and commercial. You look good. No worse for the wear?"

"No, a little smoke and panic never hurt. It might have made my hair curlier."

He studied my hair. "It looks nice."

"Thank you."

"Cole's telling everyone you saved his life."

"That's an exaggeration." Telling *everyone*? I hoped that was an exaggeration, too.

"Maybe. He's happy about it, anyway, so thanks."

"Any news about the Tent of Wonders?"

A Joe Dunbar–patented single-shoulder shrug for answer.

"Are you tied up at the café all day?"

"No, thought I'd go fishing. Maybe start at Boone."

"In your red canoe?" I asked. We'd had a sort of date in his canoe. Nice canoe. Nice sort of date. Up to a point.

"It's a lot of water to cover," Joe said. "Cole's lending me his johnboat. Less flashy than Dan's, but it'll do."

Ardis rapped her knuckles on the counter. "You can play double agent, Ten Dunbar, but only so long as you deliver information to each party in an equitable manner. Now tell me, are you working on our back door early-warning system?"

"I'll have something for you soon. Bye." He smiled and ambled out the front door.

"Did his accent just get stronger?" I asked. "It sounded like he said 'baa.'"

Ardis didn't answer. She swept past me, zipped around the corner, and was gone. And Shirley and Mercy came in.

"How does Ardis know the Spiveys are here before they even get through the door?" Debbie whispered as she slipped past me to ring up a customer cooing over skeins of wool for a baby sweater.

"Her Spivey senses tingle."

The twins were back in sync; their outfits matched. They marched, in sync, up to the counter to tell me they were glad I was alive.

"And to forgive you for your insensitivity to our maternal—ow—to Mercy's maternal plight." That was Shirley, then, standing to the left of Mercy's elbow. "We realize that asking insensitive questions, as you do and as we are sure you will continue to do, is a necessary part of an investigation."

"We also realize that your plate is full, what with a

murder and avoiding being murdered yourself," Mercy said. "And while we appreciate your offer to help find Angela, we think she'll be safer if you don't."

"We'll do it ourselves," said Shirley.

"What are you going to do?"

"What you suggested," Mercy said. "Visit area hangouts. Bars and whatnot. Ask around. We'll keep you posted."

They turned and marched out. Women on a mission. I wished them well.

After the Spiveys left, I felt entitled to do my own disappearing act. Argyle was curled like a skein of cat wool near the great wheel in the front window, but I hadn't seen Geneva. I didn't want her to overhear a more colorful version of the fire, in case she overreacted—all over the shop. Ardis did her post-Spivey reappearing act and I dashed up to the study. I didn't see Geneva in the room and or in the cupboard—*her* room. But not seeing her didn't mean she wasn't there. I wished she could explain the mechanism, explain why sometimes she was visible and other times not. She said she didn't know, that it was most likely something to do with my end of things. That didn't explain why she sometimes appeared out of thin air when I called her.

I called her then, with no luck. Sighing, I turned to go back down, and nearly walked through her.

"You are lucky to be alive!" she stormed.

"Yes, I am and I'm glad you care."

She had her ghostly hands on her ghostly hips and was swelling in preparation for more yelling when I noticed something.

"Did you know you sound an awful lot like Ardis when you're all fired up? You might look like her, too, if I could see you more in focus."

I hadn't expected to deflect her tirade, but the comment had that effect. Geneva drew back, closed her mouth, and stared at me. Meekly, she followed me downstairs and floated over to balance on top of the great wheel. Argyle said, "Mrrph," but Geneva didn't say another word.

Ardis didn't mind hearing about the twins the way she minded being anywhere in their vicinity, so I told her about their plan for finding Angie.

"May their mother- and aunt-love give them strength," she said. "Do you think she took up with Dan again?"

I told her I liked that idea better than the one I'd had last night about a near-desperate real estate agent knocking off a new rival. Then I told her about looking for signs of Angie at the house, with no conclusions drawn. "Even if we don't think Angie would pull a trigger, though, what if she provided the kick in the pants that Dan needed?"

"She might not know she provided it," Ardis said. "Isn't that an awful thought? Angie's pattern in love and life is full of trouble, hon. I don't know how effective Mercy and Shirley will be, or how much they have to answer for Angie being the way she is, but right now I'm glad she's got them on her side. And I pray they find her alive and ready to cut their warp threads."

"Is this a bad time?" Sally Ann was in front of me at the counter. Her thin shoulders were hunched inside the flannel shirt she'd worn the night before. I took a step back.

"Sally Ann, no, not at all. Um, bad time for what?" I looked around. What had I forgotten now? Apparently it *was* a bad time for my brain. Debbie had straightened out the cash register twice in the last half hour because of mistakes I'd made. Ardis thought I might be suffering from delayed shock and she'd gone to get me a glass of ice water and a cup of hot tea. She came back with them as Sally Ann was explaining.

"You said I could come over for a one-on-one lesson, but maybe it is a bad time or you didn't mean it. But this is about the only time I could get here. I can't stay off work too many more days."

Ardis looked at the clock. Three. That gave us another hour of Debbie's time. She leaned her elbow on the counter like a barmaid and asked, "What's your pleasure?"

Sally Ann loosened up and laughed at what she thought was a joke. Little did she know; our fibers and fabrics and notions were every bit as addictive as bottles behind a bar. Once entangled in the web of our wares and wools, she would never be the same.

"Spinning?" Sally Ann asked. "I like the idea of it being something different from what Mama taught Reva Louise."

"Then this is the perfect time," Ardis said. "Debbie's here and she's our resident expert. We'll go find her and you two can use TGIF's workroom. Kath, honey, you drink your ice water, then drink your tea. It's peppermint. And don't operate any heavy equipment while I'm gone."

At some point during the afternoon, Geneva had

moved from the top of the spinning wheel to a corner of the window, but otherwise she hadn't moved or made a peep. When Ardis left with Sally Ann, she floated over so that she was taking up the narrow space between me and the counter.

"I want you to know," she said, "that if I were your business manager, I would let you operate heavy equipment anytime you want." She floated back to the window and must have felt happier for having gotten that off her chest, because she sat on top of the spinning wheel again, kicking her heels and enjoying the sun streaming in.

J. Scott chose that moment to reel in. He'd obviously spent time at a bottle-purveying type of bar, because he was quite drunk. And angry. I wanted to say, *Sir, you are both pissed and pissed. Please remove yourself.* Instead I reached for the phone.

"No," he said. "No need to call the consflabularly. I am perfly safe and within my rights to be in a public knitting place of businesses."

I was angry, too. "You had *no* right to be in my private study. You had no right to look through cupboards. I know you were up there. What were you doing?"

"Up there in the ratfers?" He tilted his head back and had to pull it level again with both hands. "Is that your airy, aerie eagle's nest? The door was open, if I'm not m'staken, so don't accuse me of tresspesspiss. Old buildings are my business."

"Oh yeah. Right. And you were just taking a professional snoop. "

"Fessional and business inrest. 'Cept my busisinesses turned against me and they're amok. The wretched murk, the m-m-mercantile is infested with fleas. Hoppin' like hotcakes and you can't sell hotcakes like they wanna sell hotcakes if the place makes you itch. I myself am eaten into inches of my life." He stopped to scratch his shins, which didn't help his stability.

"Bug bomb to lil' smithereens the lil' vermin might work but now's too late. My business cards are smithereens. The deal's sunk. An' I'm drink. Drunk. Someone else can kill 'em."

"Kill *who*?"

"Misser and missus Flea an all their lil' flealets. I gotta go."

"Wait. What was the mercantile deal?"

"Shhhh." He tried to put his finger to his lips but gave up. "A secret so I dint tell you she wanted a nook to cook her own."

"Who? Will you try to focus for a minute, please, and make sense?"

"Reva Evil Louise. *She* sounded like sense. She talked a good hotcake an' led me on a merry menu path. But dint have a griddle to rub together for a down-home payment, an' now she's dead an' your 'steemed mayor says pig plays are nevermore an' so am I. I came to smell you. To tell you good-bye. But I *do* smell you and I did. Up there." He waved at the ceiling without trying to look up again. "Dead mouse. I only caught a squiff of it. Unmistapleable. Definitely something dead. Unless you lied when I asked you about the drains. Reva Eva Lee lied. You all lie in Blue Lump. Good riddance, I say. I will turn around slowly so as not to vomit and be gone with me."

He did turn slowly but only so far. He stopped when he was facing the window. And he stared at Geneva. She waved at him.

Chapter 29

J. Scott didn't scream or say anything that sounded like "ghost." It's possible he saw nothing more distinct than a collection of dust motes or a cloud of gnats. He saw something, though, because Geneva decided to float around him in a wide circle and he followed, his eyes on her the entire time. Ardis came back and saw J. Scott's half of that weird dance.

"What the heck?"

"Drunk," I said. "Possibly on gin."

"And never on gin agin," J. Scott said. Geneva followed him as he reeled for the door. We let him wrestle with it and go. Geneva waved good-bye and came to perch on the shoulder of the mannequin that stood near the counter. Debbie had dressed it in a new seed-stitch wrap that shaded through a range of summery yellows and oranges. Geneva added a touch of summer rain to the look.

"You should have called the police," Ardis said.

"I had her back in case of rough stuff," Geneva countered. "We were fine on our own."

"You're right," I said, covering both their comments. "But I'll call them now. Prescott's a danger to himself on foot and everyone else if he gets in a car. Besides, he called Blue Plum 'Blue Lump.' "

"Then he deserves to be locked up," Ardis said.

I made the call then drummed my fingers on the counter. "There might've been some sense in his nonsense, though. Maybe. About the clearest thing he said was that he smelled the drains. You smelled something last week, remember?"

Ardis tool a few inconclusive sniffs in different directions. "Nothing now. We'll get Joe to take a look. What else did Prescott say? I can see the gears up there in your head trying to turn, but they're not getting very far."

"They're probably slipping in puddles of gin. *I* need coffee to sober up after that. His thoughts were definitely following a drunkard's path. Let me see if I can lay the gibberish out straight before it evaporates. Along with his fumes. He said he was snooping up in the study out of professional interest in old buildings. I can believe that. Then he said the mercantile is infested with fleas. Could that be right?"

"It happens in some of these old buildings when they're unoccupied except by rats and mice."

"Ugh."

"That's what flea bombs and rat traps were invented for. What else?"

"The mercantile deal. I think Reva Louise was trying to finagle a way to open a restaurant. Maybe a breakfast place? He kept talking about hotcakes. But he said she lied to him, possibly about a down payment. Did I tell you there was restaurant equipment in the loom house? And remember the theft Mel reported? Joe said it was a box of recipes. Except he wasn't supposed to talk about it, so I shouldn't have told you ... and I just thought of something. There was a box at the back of a drawer in a filing cabinet in the loom house. Wow, what if she 'borrowed' Mel's recipe box?"

"Would Reva Louise do that to Mel?" Ardis asked. "And could she pull off a business deal like that? She didn't have any money."

"Maybe the box wasn't Mel's recipes. Maybe it was full of embezzled or stolen cash. But it doesn't matter if Reva Louise could pull it off or not. Prescott thought she could and he's feeling Reva Louise-ly screwed."

"Enough to kill her?"

"How about if there was a better reason to kill her? What if Reva Louise and Dan were in on the mercantile deal as a couple and Prescott found out that Dan would have plenty of money if Reva Louise was out of the picture?"

"I've heard crazier schemes," Ardis said. "But I haven't heard anything about Dan Snapp that lets me believe he's really interested in owning his own business. I'd rather believe that Prescott, ham actor that he is, is suffering from Macbeth syndrome, wandering around getting crazier with remorse for a deed most foul. Did he happen to say anything about trying to kill you this morning by setting fire to the loom house?"

"No."

"Shame."

"Yeah." But as much as I disliked Prescott, I did believe in his love for old buildings, and I couldn't see him setting fire to one. "Sally Ann didn't say anything about the fire when she came in."

"Maybe she hasn't heard," Ardis said.

"And it's the center of my universe right now, but not everybody's." Although the Spiveys had heard and stopped by. "How's Sally Ann doing with the spinning?"

"I wouldn't say she's a natural. Debbie's going to send her home with a whorl and some roving to practice. She was sticking to it and that's what it takes."

My car wasn't in the parking lot. That's how out of it I was. I forgot that I'd walked over after showering and changing clothes. Just as well. If I was that out of it, driving even the short distance home would have been dangerous. I wasn't so out of it, though, that ideas didn't keep spinning in my head.

Two blocks from home, I looked ahead to the next corner and saw a nondescript pickup at the stop sign. *Nondescript vehicles.* How had the person who lit the fire gotten there and gotten away? That was a good question. And how had that person known where to find yet more gasoline at that gasoline-ridden place?

I looked ahead and the pickup was still at the stop sign. Or maybe it was another nondescript pickup with another guy behind the wheel. *Another.* Maybe there was another person we hadn't considered. Someone other than Dan Snapp, Angie, or Prescott. Who?

The pickup was still there with the guy. The creepy guy watching me. I slowed, reached for my phone, thought about crossing the street. Maybe I should take a picture of the truck. Or the creepy guy. I was practically not walking at all I was going so slowly. Then the creepy guy waved.

"Hey, how about that beer?" Creepy Clod.

*   *   *

We went for pizza. I'd been serious when I'd said make mine a whiskey, but Clod being Clod hadn't believed it. He had beer. I had ice water. I saw the symbolism. Then I saw the Spiveys. The twins, goggle-eyed, skirted our table and didn't stay to chat. A not insignificant point in Clod's favor.

"What kind of pizza do you like?" he asked.

"The spinach and mushroom sounds good."

"After a day like we had? We'll have the gut buster," he told the waitress.

I could have stood up for myself, but after a day like the one I'd had, I didn't feel much like causing a scene.

"Did you know Shorty's a volunteer firefighter?" Clod asked. "Well, it doesn't matter. Wouldn't matter who went back behind that shack."

"Loom house."

"Whatever. Wouldn't matter who hosed down its backside and checked for hot spots. The cow parsnip back there is up to your keister with no way around it. Up to *your* armpits, probably, and Shorty's, too." He thought that was pretty funny.

"That bad, huh?"

"Oooh yeah," he said. "Cow parsnip? You have no idea."

He was right—I had no idea at all—because I didn't know what he was talking about and wasn't about to ask. He carried most of the conversation, at the same time eating most of the pizza. That was fine with me. His topics, the gut buster, and the fact of our being out together were all out of my comfort zone.

When I did get a question in edgewise, I tried to steer

it toward asking about the drunk and disorderly Prescott. I wanted to know if he'd been picked up. Clod cut me off with a long story he thought was a thigh slapper about "picking up a puking drunk" when he was a rookie. The story was way too long. And vivid. To counterbalance it, my next question was short.

"Will you please take me home?"

He didn't object to going and he didn't comment on the half-eaten slice I left on my plate. Those were two more points in his favor. But the points didn't add up to this being an experiment worth repeating.

On the way to my nice little yellow house, where I lived quietly and alone, I decided that before I got out of Clod's truck, I would ask him what he'd meant the day before, when he'd said, "Mistakes were made." Did he mean that he and his colleagues had made mistakes in their investigation of the shooting? Or in searching the Weaver's Cat? Or had he made a mistake in not taking our broken window seriously enough? I did want to know, but also, like my glass of ice water, I liked the symbolism of the phrase.

When we got to my house, he hopped out to open my door. Rats. And when I climbed out, he pulled me into an enveloping hug. Double rats. Except that I felt absolutely nothing. Nothing. No animosity, no friendship, no love, no hate, no lust, no dislike, no revulsion. No mix of any kind of emotions. There was an absolute blank. A dearth. How odd. As though I was being hugged by a slab of Formica. Unfortunately, while I was marveling over that, Clod, who did feel something, kissed me.

I pulled away and, like an embarrassed teenager, looked around to make sure no one had seen. Looked around in time to see Joe, at the edge of the yard, turn and walk away.

Ardis called half an hour later. She said Joe had stopped by. He'd told her he hadn't had any luck fishing for any-one who'd seen Dan Snapp out fishing. That was incon-clusive, as everything in our case was proving to be, because there was a lot of fishable water in our part of the state. Ardis said Joe seemed kind of down about it, though.

I went to bed feeling kind of down, too. Almost down enough to wander over to the Weaver's Cat to see if a pajama fiesta with Geneva and Argyle would cheer me up, but not quite.

I woke up thinking about Granny. It had taken me a couple of months, but I'd finally started sleeping in her bedroom, in her wrought-iron bed under a coverlet she'd woven. A pretty blue-and-white double weave. It made me happy to wake up and look at the ceiling she'd looked at when she planned her days. She was a great one for plans and she hadn't put up with moping. She understood about depression and sadness and grief, but self-indulgent misery didn't cut it with her. *If you're so miserable you can't make yourself happy, don't put the blame where it doesn't belong. Turn your-self around. Go out and make someone else happy,* she'd told me. *Sometimes doing things the other way around is the best way.*

So when I woke up still feeling down, I decided the best way to deal with the Dunbar Debacle of Love, or whatever it should be called, was to go out and catch a killer. And maybe the best way to do that was to turn the problem around or turn it over.

I fingered the double-weave coverlet, looked at the pattern on one side, and flipped it over to see the negative pattern on the other. We didn't know who the killer was; the killer certainly knew who we were. Searching for the killer meant casting a wide net and hoping he or she wouldn't slip through; inviting the killer to come . . . Inviting the killer *anywhere* was completely insane, but it was that notion that made me realize something had been missing from the murder scene.

"Her phone, Ardis. We didn't see it."

"And I am blind with early-morning sleep deprivation, so it's no wonder I don't see what you're talking about. Kath, please do not make a habit of calling me this early."

"Quit complaining and listen to me. Saturday, when we were standing in the tent, after the shot but before we realized what had happened, we heard a couple of people talking. They thought Reva Louise was one of the actors. One of them scoffed at her shoes and—"

"Her phone." In the background, I heard the creaking that meant Ardis was sitting up and taking interest. "But weren't we around there pretty quick after we heard the scoffers? That would've been a mighty small window of opportunity for someone to take the phone, hon."

"Then where was it?"

"Considering the larger picture of Reva Louise lying there in her own blood, we might have missed a small detail like her phone."

"The details of that scene are seared in my memory, Ardis."

"Well, and into mine, too, now that you mention it."

"That's how the killer knew she would be there at that time. The killer called her there to that spot. Reva Louise waved to the killer in the window."

"Now you're just being fanciful. We need to stick to the facts."

"It's one of the details," I said, waving away the minor detail of that information being provided by a ghost no one else could see and also the detail of Ardis not being able to see *me* waving over the phone. "The story of what happened is in the details, Ardis. The solution is in the details."

"Mm-hmm. I've heard something about the devil being in them, too."

"Speaking of the devil, will you do me a favor? Call Cole Dunbar just to make sure they didn't find the phone and I really am making a mountain out of a detail?"

"You don't want to make that call yourself?"

"No."

"Mm-hmm."

Thea wasn't as cranky or insinuating as Ardis when I called her. That was mostly because I waited and called her at the library.

"I thrive on digging for useless information," she said when I told her what I wanted her to look up.

"I hope at least some of it *will* be useful."

"Then I am on it. I'll get back to you as soon as I can. Toddler Time comes first, though. We're doing the hokey-pokey in case you're interested."

My call to Mel was short. I asked her if she would find out from Sally Ann if she knew what kind of phone Reva

Louise had owned. Mel asked me if I wanted a ladle up my nose with that. Given that bit of hostility, I didn't ask her for a description of her missing recipe box that I wasn't supposed to know about.

My call to Mercy was shorter. She cut me off at "Hi," slipped in a terse, tear-laden "Your taste in men is questionable," and hung up. I took it Angie was still missing.

Shortest was my call to J. Scott Prescott—the same number on each of his cards. He didn't answer.

Ardis called as I was about to unlock the back door and let myself into the Cat. I waited, key in hand, as she told me Clod hadn't wanted to part with information about the phone.

"But, hon, from the way he blustered and *obfuscated*, I don't believe they knew there was a phone to wonder about in the first place."

"They do now."

"And that makes this the perfect time to say, 'The game's afoot.' Hon, I don't like the idea of you being there alone this morning. I'd cancel Daddy's appointment and be there in a second, but it took so long to get this one. We're spinning a web. I don't want you getting caught."

"Nothing's going to happen so soon, if at all, and I'll only be alone for the hour until Debbie gets here. You know someone from TGIF is bound to come in. Or if you're worried, you can call someone. Call Ernestine."

"I'll call Debbie and see if she can be there early."

"And who knows, maybe Joe will swing by."

After a pause the length of a small sigh, Ardis said, "Watch out for yourself, hon."

*   *   *

I let myself in the back door, ready to get the business day going. Ready to get this investigation into Reva Louise's murder finished. I locked the door again behind me. And something caught my ear.

A woman singing.

Chapter 30

For the second it took me to think — *Singing? Woman? Who?* — and for my eyes to practically bug out of my head — I was frightened. Then I recognized the voice and the tune, if not the exact words.

"My body lies over the ocean, my body lies over the sea." Geneva floated down the stairs, followed by Argyle. "Where do you suppose my body really lies? Probably in a bog and not any place so romantic as over an ocean or sea." She settled on top of the refrigerator in an artful heap. "The real tragedy is spending eternity without a forwarding address."

"I'm sure it is. Geneva, do you think your body is somewhere near the cottage where we met?"

She shrugged and watched me tip kibble into Argyle's dish and give him fresh water. He added another layer of fur around my ankles in thanks and I tried to remember if there were any marshy areas near the Holston Homeplace Living History Farm. But maybe she'd been singing with poetic license.

"Your beau was here this morning," she said.

"What? Who?"

"Who, *she has to ask? Who knew you had so many? Joe, Mr. Haiku.*"

Argyle looked up at her and trilled.

"He was experimenting with an electronic contraption at the back door; it made a noise like someone realizing she'd stepped in something unpleasant. Neither Argyle nor Mr. Haiku liked it, so he took it away again."

"Do you know when he's coming back?"

"I am not your social secretary."

She followed me through the store as I went through opening procedures. It was still dimmer than usual in the room with the boarded-up window. Joe had said he was looking for a source of old glass to replace the broken pane. *Replace.* Was Angie replacing Reva Louise? What evidence did we really have for thinking that? Had J. Scott Prescott done away with Angie because she was a budding real estate agent who would replace him? Again, what evidence?

"Lights, fans, action," Geneva chided. "You're falling behind in your duties. Why are you just standing there?"

"I'm thinking about our investigation. We might have some action here later today."

"By action, do you mean women of a certain age sitting quietly making things out of yarn? I might watch Argyle take a nap instead."

"If it's more dramatic than that, I'm sure you'll notice. Geneva, will you try to remember what you saw when Reva Louise was shot? You saw her wave and then you saw her fall. What did you see after she fell?"

"You ran."

"And Ardis."

"You were more athletic."

"Thank you. But I didn't run to her right away. Did you see anyone near her before I got there?"

"There were a lot of people around. I didn't know most of them. I don't get out much."

"Would you look at some pictures to see if you recognize anyone? See if you remember seeing anybody who was near her body on Saturday? Thea made a slide show and I can set it up on my laptop in the study—"

"Like TV? Let's go."

I put the Mug Shot Show on a continuous loop and left Geneva raptly watching.

To show that I had learned a thing or two about precaution, I didn't unlock the back door after I flipped the open sign on the front door. No back-alley surprises for me. But then I flashed to the panic of being trapped in the loom house behind a blocked door. Not the same as a dead bolt, but in a panic . . . And a dead bolt also kept help from getting in. . . .

What was I thinking? I had my own personal perfect alarm system. I relocked the front door and ran back up to the study to tell Geneva plans had changed. I relocated her and the laptop to the kitchen table, setting the computer so she was facing the door, and asked her to please let me know if anyone came in.

"Interrupt my viewing pleasure?"

"It's a loop, Geneva. You've probably seen it five times already. Just please let me know if someone comes in, okay? You don't even need to move. You can shout. No one else will hear. Just until Debbie gets here. There won't be that many customers this early, anyway."

"What would you like me to shout?"

"How about 'man' if it's a man and 'woman' if it's a woman?"

"Uninspired. I'll see if I can do better."

"Have you recognized anyone in the slide show yet?"

"No, but I'm fascinated by the shoes number seventeen is wearing. *They* look lethal."

I hadn't noticed and was tempted to fast-forward to see what she was talking about, but someone knocked on the still-locked back door.

"Incoming!" Geneva shouted in my ear.

"Thank you."

"I thought you'd like that."

Sally Ann peered anxiously through the window in the door, and I went to open it for her.

"Are you all right?" she asked before the door was fully open. "The front door's still locked, so I came around here. You looked like your head was hurting. Do you talk to yourself like that a lot?"

"Yes to most of that. Come on in."

I was glad to see she wasn't wearing the flannel shirt from the evening at Mel's. She was wearing another one and cargo pants in a slightly different shade of olive. She was very thin and her eyes certainly looked more haunted than mine did.

I left the back door unlocked and went through to open the front again. The hair on the back of my neck didn't quite stand up, as Sally Ann followed me, but I hadn't expected results from the various phone calls to arrive on my doorstep so soon.

"How's the spinning coming?" I asked

"I dunno. I think wool makes me itch."

"You can try cotton."

"Maybe. I dunno. Anyway, Mel called. She said there's something going on about Reva Louise's phone? Why would you need to know what kind she had?"

Okay, I hadn't thought that part of it through. Why *would* I need to know what kind she had? Why not the truth? "What I really want to know is who *has* her phone."

"Oh. The police, don't you think? Anyway, I don't know what kind she had. Something fancier than me. So I called Dan. Dang, *I* didn't know his shed burned yesterday. And you were in it?" She looked believably nonplussed, maybe even believably. "You are really something. I don't know what, but something."

From the kitchen Geneva shrieked, *"There's a man in here!"*

Brother. "Hello!" I called, surprising Sally Ann. "Sorry. I have ears in the back of my head. Someone just came in the kitchen door."

We both listened. Didn't hear anything. Then Geneva uttered an indignant "Hey!"

"Excuse me, Sally Ann. I'd better go see." I smiled, did a Joe Dunbar amble to the hall doorway, then sprinted to the kitchen.

Dan Snapp was there, watching the slide show in Geneva's place. Geneva had moved over to the counter and sat in a huff like one of Thea's two-year-olds whose toy had been taken away. Ardis would be both pleased and alarmed with the web we'd spun. We'd lured two of our invitees, the problem being that I was the only itsy-bitsy spider currently at home. Now what? Keep calm and carry on? I couldn't think of anything better.

"Oh, hey," Dan said, looking up. There was a glint of moisture at the corner of his eye. He needed a shave.

Probably some sleep. "I hope you don't mind. The saddest day of my life, but they're real nice pictures. You're Kathy, right?"

"Kath."

"I came to say that I'm very sorry for the trouble my shed caused you yesterday."

"I'm sorry it burned."

"The least of my worries, although I do have to wonder what you two were doing in there."

Not *And I have to wonder who trapped you in there and set the place on fire*? My phone rang before I could decide whether to ask him that. It was Thea.

"Excuse me, Dan. I'll be right with you." I pulled the phone from my pocket and walked over to the sink. "Hey, Thea."

"Are you ready for the hokey-pokey?" she asked. "Interesting item in a back issue of the *Bugle*—way, way-back issue—it might shed light on your Mattie and Sam."

"Holy cow. Holy *cow*." I was repeating myself. How appropriate for a double murder. I looked sideways at Geneva and was careful not to use names. "You found an article?"

"Nope."

"Thea!" I took a breath and spoke more softly, but still urgently into the phone. "Explain. Please."

"Not an article, exactly. Back then, people used the personals the way we do Twitter or Facebook. I found one asking Mattie Severs to, quote, 'Please forgive and contact the ones who will always love you.' A week later, there was another, asking anyone having seen Mattie Severs or knowing of her whereabouts to contact a PO box."

I heard the back door open and looked over my shoulder. Debbie coming in early, thank goodness. She swished in, wearing one of her long skirts and embroidered tops, her hair in a braid down her back. She waved. I waved back. She was humming happily, smiled at Dan, and went on through to the front room. I heard her say hi to Sally Ann.

"Kath?" Thea chattered on in my ear. "It sounds more like runaways, to me, or an elopement. I don't know where you got the romantic notion of a double murder. Anyway, it might be your Mattie and Sam. Or maybe Mattie was a common name back then. Oh, and the cow parsnip you asked me to look up? Here's a tip, courtesy of your local library and horticultural early-warning system. Do not go wading through cow parsnip. It's as bad as poison ivy once you get it on you and expose it to sunlight. You'll be itchin' and bitc— Oh, sorry. Patron calling. Gotta go."

Itching? I knew two people who were itching. I disconnected and turned around. The kitchen was empty and I heard raised voices out front. Dan Snapp's and Debbie's. And Sally Ann—the itchy woman.

Chapter 31

Should I call 911? And tell them what? There's a woman in the yarn shop who is either a killer or allergic to wool?

I ran down the hall, phone at the ready, careened around the corner, and stopped myself with a hand on the doorjamb. Dan was sitting in one of our overstuffed comfy chairs, head back. Sally Ann had grabbed a pair of shears from the counter and was standing behind him, holding the point of the shears to his throat. She'd jammed his mouth with a wad of wool roving.

I pressed 911 and slipped the phone onto the counter, hoping the operator would hear whatever happened next.

"You don't have to do this," Debbie was saying. "*I* don't want you to do this." She stood in front of the chair, her hands together, pressed to her lips.

"Yeah, I think you really do," said Sally Ann.

"Why?" Debbie pleaded.

Sally Ann wasn't listening. "Don't move, Dan. *Don't* move. Kath, get over here. *Now!* And help Debbie tie his hands."

Debbie whimpered and scrambled for a skein of thick yarn. I moved toward them, looking for something I could grab, something to disarm or disorient Sally Ann. *Disorient.* Where was Geneva when I needed her billowing fog? There was movement over our heads and I quickly looked up. Geneva was wrapped around the blades of the fan.

"Don't forget to tie the frock-coated poltroon's feet, too," she called.

"Kath!" Sally Ann shouted. *"I am not kidding."*

While Debbie tied his hands, I started on his feet. He tried to kick, but Sally Ann pressed the shears harder against his throat and he quit. I couldn't bear to look at his face, in his eyes.

"What's going on, Sally Ann?" I asked.

"It's all your doing, Kath." Her voice was chillingly matter-of-fact.

"How? How is it my doing?" I tried to match her tone, hoping to draw this out until help arrived. If it did.

"It was all you. Asking about Reva Louise's phone. Stirring things up. It worked. But maybe better than you thought, and now look."

"This isn't going to work, Sally Ann."

"Yes, it is. It already has. Debbie, go on over there and stay out of the way." Sally Ann nodded to the other side of the room. "If it hadn't been for you, Kath, Reva Louise's phone might've *stayed* lost."

I heard a siren by then and braced myself for Sally Ann's reaction when it registered with her. I wondered if I'd be able to fend her off, or tackle her if I had to, to protect Debbie or Dan.

She flicked a cool glance at me. "You called nine-one-one? Where's your phone? *Where is your phone?* Get it. Call 555-7185, quick—555-7185."

I grabbed the phone, dialed, then held it away from

my ear, not sure what to expect, and definitely not expecting what I heard. "That's Reva Louise's ringtone, isn't it?"

Frank Sinatra was singing "My Way" in Dan's pants.

"But I had it *backward*," I whispered to Ardis. "I was being so clever turning things around that I ended up *backward*."

"Only at the very end, hon, and at this point it doesn't matter. Turn yourself around one more time and look at Sally Ann over there."

Sally Ann looked tired, but more sure of herself than I'd ever seen her. She tucked loose hair behind her ear and listened to whatever Clod was telling her, her shoulders square, her arms and hands relaxed, no itching or twitching from nerves or wool. Debbie stood beside her giving moral support, but she wasn't really needed.

Ardis and Clod, his lone siren wailing, had arrived simultaneously and both tried to get through the front door at the same time. Ardis won. Sally Ann had refused to give the shears to Clod until I'd explained what was going on. She seemed to think I'd known what I was doing all along, and when I looked at it the right way around I saw that she hadn't threatened Debbie or me at all. She'd enlisted our help to hold Dan until the police got there. Geneva was happy to fill me in on what I'd missed while I was in the kitchen on the phone with Thea.

"Yon Snapp slithered in and sat down," she said, reveling in the details. "Sally Ann was all sweet worry and concern. She said she supposed he'd already asked the police about Reva Louise's phone. He claimed grief and said it hadn't occurred to him, but he betrayed himself

with a sly look at his pocket. Sally Ann saw and so did I.
I am sorry I didn't recognize him in your slide show, but
I only saw him from behind that day. The back end of
him is not very distinctive, and the sooner we see it, the
better, I say."

Clod listened to us with his professional, unim-
pressed cop face. Dan Snapp had nothing intelligent to
say for himself; no one had taken the wad of roving
from his mouth. Ardis was triumphant and enjoyed rubbing it in.

"And so, my dear Coleridge," she said, producing the
slightest wrinkle of a wince in his starch, "we have solved
another crime for you. Our good work here is done.
Please take the garbage out when you go. One question
before you do, though. Were you even close to an arrest
before we took over for you?"

"Would you like me to quote the statistics on how
women are more likely to be murdered by their hus-
bands than perfect strangers?" Clod asked.

"And yet," Ardis said, "here we are."

"May I ask Dan a few questions?" I asked. "I think he
owes some of us and the Weaver's Cat some answers."

"He isn't obliged to say anything," Clod said. "And
when my backup gets here, he's gone." Clod took a pair
of latex gloves and an evidence bag from a pocket and
removed the makeshift gag.

I did look into Dan Snapp's face then. I wanted to see
the eyes of a man who could shoot his wife and trauma-
tize a town, call it the saddest day of his life, and then buy
himself a boat. But there wasn't anything special in them.
Not even the tear I'd seen earlier. He looked past me out
the front window.

"Why did you bother to come back here today? What were you planning to do?" He didn't answer, but his eyes shifted from the front window. They flicked to his hip pocket, then toward the stairs and overhead. "You were going to hide the phone upstairs? Really? That's so uninspired."

"Zing!" Geneva said.

"And your eyes give you away," I added. "Why didn't you just get rid of the phone?"

His eyes spoke for him then, too. They didn't have nice things to say.

"But it was you who threw the rock through our window, right? And came in to hide the guns?"

"Ask him if he heard Mattie singing," Geneva said.

Why not? I did and *that* question got a response.

"What?"

I didn't look around to see if his opinion of the question was mirrored on anyone else's face, but as long as I'd gotten something out of him, I decided to try one more question. "Why did you set fire to the loom house and try to kill Deputy Dunbar and me?"

"Pest control."

Clod shifted by the door but didn't say anything. Sally Ann came and stood next to me, arms crossed over her narrow chest. "Dan, you're about the laziest man I know," she said without any emotion. "And now I know you for the evilest. Reva Louise said it took a prod in your posterior just to make you pick up your feet, much less pick up after yourself."

"She did, did she?" He didn't seem interested.

"And that makes it hard for me to believe you did this on your own."

"Believe what you like, Sally Ann."

"And that's the problem right there," she said. "You can't even stir yourself enough to make someone else believe in you. So, no, I don't think you could've done this. Not on your own. I don't believe it." Sally Ann's voice was rising. "Reva Louise did everything for you. She organized your life for you. And someone else is leading you now. Who?"

"Ms. Jilton." Clod touched her elbow.

"There *is* someone," Sally Ann insisted, yanking away from Clod. "Because Dan Snapp wouldn't move a muscle to swat a mosquito if it was biting his—"

"Wrong, Sally Ann," Dan said. "*That* is where you're wrong. And that is where you're just like her. You will not stop. *She* would not stop. She. Would. Not. Stop. And it always had to be her way. So yeah, you're right. There was someone else in charge, someone else responsible. Reva Louise. She did it to herself. None of this would've happened if it hadn't been for her. So I showed her I *could* do something. I called her and I told her where to stand and I shot her. But *she's* the one to blame. And you want to know why I kept her stupid phone? Because in the end, I did it *my* way."

Clod's backup was there by then. He and Clod got Dan to his feet and started for the door. I called one last question after them.

"How did you get through the cow parsnip behind your building when you set the fire? That stuff's like poison ivy. Why aren't you itching?"

"There's no cow parsnip back there," Dan said. "Where'd you get a fool idea like that?"

We watched as Clod and his partner hustled Dan out.

Then I turned to Sally Ann, a question still niggling in my mind and a risk I needed to take—I put my hand on Sally Ann's shoulder and felt nothing but the soft warmth of the flannel shirt and Sally Ann's thin shoulder.

"Can I ask you a weird question, Sally Ann?"

"About singing?"

"About the shirt you had on the other night at Mel's. Remember? I asked if it was Reva Louise's."

"I don't know why it matters to you. I told you it wasn't."

"I know. Sorry."

"She borrowed it when I left it at the café one day. It took me a while to get it back. You asked what she was like as a kid? Like that. Big on 'borrowing.' And in the end, she borrowed a whole lot of trouble, didn't she?"

Mel heard from her source in Knoxville that J. Scott Prescott returned there and was being treated for a hellacious number of infected flea bites. He was resting uncomfortably at his parents' and applying for jobs. When she called to tell me, I mentioned the curious box I'd seen in the loom house.

"I don't know what was in it. But the place didn't burn to the ground, and the box might've been protected enough that it survived."

"And you mention this to me, why?" Mel asked.

"The box intrigued me. I'm nosy. She was your sister. Maybe you can get access."

"Not because Joe told you I kept my mother's and grandmother's recipes in a box?"

"No, he didn't tell me that."

"Good. Thanks, Kath."

*   *   *

It was the spinners, Jackie and Abby, who said we should try one more time to celebrate with our own mini Blue Plum Preserves at the Weaver's Cat.

"'Preserves' has almost the same letters as 'persevere,'" Jackie said. "And it never hurts to do that."

Ardis, Debbie, and I agreed and we planned it for that Saturday. "It's short notice, but the sooner we get all this behind us, the better," Debbie said. "Because the world keeps spinning, and that's what we need to do, too." We didn't care if we attracted a crowd or not; between the other demonstration spinners and all of TGIF, there would be crowd enough.

Joe stopped by to ask if we'd like live music. "It's someone new," he said, "who lost out when the festival was shut down early."

"That's a fine idea," Ardis said.

"There's a short intro act, too," Joe said. "You'll like it. Oh, and I'll bring your new back doorbell over then."

The day after we trapped Dan—it didn't seem possible it was only Wednesday—I took Geneva a present. She smelled the gingerbread before I was halfway up the stairs to the study.

"I truly do think I've died and gone home to my mama's kitchen," she said, swirling around me. "Mama would have been the first to tell you that you are gooder than any angel."

"Sometime will you tell me more about your mama's kitchen? And your mama?"

"Yes, but hush. Not now."

I cut the gingerbread into squares and put one piece

on a plate for her in her "room." I took the rest down to the kitchen and froze the pieces individually so she had spares for days or weeks to come. When I went back up to the study, she was curled around the plate in the cupboard, crooning.

Thea had given me copies of the personals she'd found in old issues of the *Blue Plum Bugle*. They'd appeared in the October 7 and October 14, 1872, editions. I didn't show the copies to Geneva or tell her about them. Her distress over Mattie and Sam was real whether or not her vivid "memories" were. Somewhere, somehow, sometime she had internalized a traumatic incident and she absolutely believed that she'd seen Mattie and Sam lying dead in a green grassy field. I wanted to help her. Gingerbread therapy was probably a lame start, but maybe there was something more I could do. I took Granny's private dye journals, with their supposed hocus-pocus, from the shelf above Geneva and went to sit in the window seat.

Toward the end of the second journal, I found a sample of warm yellow wool. The name for the accompanying recipe, written out in Granny's neat hand, was "Wax Myrtle and Hellebore, Sweet Memories Evermore." Geneva wouldn't be able to feel or touch warm yellow wool, so I wasn't sure what good this would do—I wasn't sure about *anything* associated with Granny's dye journals—but how could it hurt to knit a pretty, warm yellow shawl and lay it on the window seat? If nothing else, Argyle would look handsome curled up on it.

Saturday was a whirl—a "whorl," as Debbie said—of spinners and spinning wheels on the porch and in almost every room. Abby came wearing shorts and a T-shirt and gave herself the title "Mobile Advertising Manager." She walked from one end of our block of Main Street to the other, showing off her drop spindle prowess with non-stop spinning. She told us she'd silk-screened the T-shirt especially for the day. It said SPIN, IT'S IN on the front and THE WEAVER'S CAT IS WHERE IT'S AT on the back. Ardis and I offered her a part-time job on the spot.

Ernestine circulated through the rooms, stopping a couple of times to ask the mannequin if it was having a good time. Geneva, sitting on the mannequin's shoulder, answered politely that she enjoyed a good mob scene. John manned a table of cookies and lemonade Mel sent over. Sally Ann sent her regrets. Mel had lent her the money to go see her mother down in Florida. Argyle thought it better to nap in the study.

Thea set herself up as a recruiter for Fast and Furious. She sat in one of the comfy chairs, surrounded by the plastic bins full of our baby hats. While she worked on another of her favorite red-and-white-striped beanies, she encouraged people to guess how many hats we'd already made.

"It's a story problem," she told one child. "If a librarian and her friends set out to knit one thousand hats between January first and December thirty-first, and if they aren't hit by a freight train driven by Curious George going east at fifty miles per hour, how many hats have they knit by the middle of July?"

Joe wouldn't tell us anything about the musician or opening act, saying only that the show would start at eleven, on the front porch, and if well received, be repeated at two. I would say that he and I were shy of each other since "The Night of the Dead-End Kiss" as I liked to think of it, but we didn't have a history of being much more than shy with each other. I was working up the nerve to change that.

Clod had stopped by the shop once and I'd repaid Ardis for all the times she did her Spivey-induced disappearing act. He might have called, too, but I'd turned my phone off and wasn't checking messages.

At five minutes of eleven, Joe shooed Ardis, Debbie, and me out to the kitchen.

"It'll be best if you go out this way and around so you get the full frontal effect," he said. "Ready?" He opened the back door.

"Baaaaa," said the door.

"What do you think?" Joe asked. He closed the door and opened it again. It baaed beautifully each time. "I used a recordable sound chip."

Ardis grabbed his head and kissed his brow.

Aaron Carlin, in bowler hat and sleeve garters, stood at the top of the front steps as we rounded the corner.

"Welcome to Dr. Carlin's Porch of Incredible Wonders," he said as we approached. "For the next ten minutes I will astound you with exhibits and artifacts the likes of which you never thought you'd pay to see, and for this onetime, limited-edition show, which will be repeated at two o'clock this afternoon, you indeed haven't. At great personal expense and risk to my personal reputation, I have acquired these items, gathering them from the six corners of the globe. Everything I am about to show you is real—including the six-foot-tall man eating chicken—and everything I say is true."

"Lord love a duck," Ardis whispered, "the man's a raving genius."

Aaron delighted the crowd with, as he said, "but a tiny fraction of his vast and incredible collection," bringing his exhibits one at a time from behind a trifold screen in a corner of the porch. He showed us vials that had contained not two, but three, identical snowflakes—alas, no longer in their solid state. He had the skulls of Japanese dragons, the skull of Charles Darwin, *and* the skull of Charles Darwin as a boy. He described the world's largest jackalope antler but didn't have it with him. "No room," he said.

"Now, what you've all been waiting for. Ladies and gentlemen, please stand back if you are easily frightened by poultry. I give you, the six-foot-tall man eating chicken."

Joe stepped from behind the screen, gnawing on a drumstick.

Shirley and Mercy had joined the crowd on the sidewalk at some point, unamused. They sidled over to say they'd been coerced. Ardis sidled away. Joe took her place beside me and handed the twins each a wing and me another leg.

"Mel doesn't need you today?" I asked.

"She hired someone. Started right off the bat this morning. Doing a split shift today." In-the-know Joe. "Look," he said, nodding toward the porch.

Aaron, with a guitar now instead of the bowler and sleeve garters, sat down on the top step and started playing a haunting melody. And Angela Cobb stepped from behind the screen. She held the edge of it for a moment and then she walked to the top step, held her arms wide, and sang.

"Oh, my angel," Mercy murmured.

"She'll need to be back at the café for the supper shift," said Joe. "Been taking a restaurant course at Northeast State, couple of singing classes. Impressed Mel with her tarts and crème brûlée."

"She wasn't studying real estate?" I asked.

"Apparently not. She and Aaron kind of hooked up last weekend. Sort of 'clinched' the deal inn the Tent of Incredible Wonders Saturday night."

"Ah. Where've they been since?"

"Aaron said they pitched the tent down in the Smokies. Incommunicado."

Ardis sidled back over, at that, unable to take her eyes off Angie. "It's beautiful," she said. "Her voice is absolutely haunting."

"Haunting," I agreed. "Oh my gosh."

"Hush," said Shirley and Mercy.

Much as I hated to leave in the middle of Angie's beautiful song . . .

Geneva, Argyle, and I sat next to one another in the front window listening to the end of Angie's two o'clock set. The sun was slipping through the window and puddling around the ghost and the cat. I'd moved over to be in the cooler shadow.

"Mattie had a beautiful voice," Geneva said. "But I like Angie's better. She sounds the way I so often feel. I could listen to her singing all day. Could you?"

"I could . . . oh . . . oh my." I could also smell "the

drains." "Geneva, honey, do me a favor? Go see if John has fallen asleep in that chair, will you?"

She floated away and so did "the drains." Oh my. I could see the label now: "Ghost—keep out of direct sunlight." I'd have to tell her, but not just then. I scooped up Argyle and wandered out to the kitchen. Joe was there with the door open, making adjustments to the new alarm.

"Hey," he said. "I was just about to take off."

"Oh, well, thanks for everything—all your help and for finding Angie—and especially for that." I nodded at the alarm.

"My baa-ck door alarm. Glad you like it."

"Before you go, can I tell you about a theory I've been working on? It kind of fits in with part of the investigation."

"Sure." He stuck his screwdriver in his back pocket and leaned against the open door.

"At the museum, I used to tell the curators that there's correct information and sufficient information. For example, in terms of the investigation, cow parsnip causes a poison ivy–like rash. That's correct information. But it wasn't sufficient information for identifying Reva Louise's killer. So my theory is that correct isn't always sufficient and making decisions based only on what's correct isn't necessarily the best path. What do you think? Does it make sense?"

Joe thought about it, nodding, arms crossed, hands tucked in his armpits. "Sure. Yeah. You could sum it up by telling a guy, one of your curators, for instance, not to jump to conclusions. About something he saw, for instance."

"That's it. You've got it."

"But you and Cole. Correct or . . ."

"Insufficient, Joe."

Argyle looked up and mrphed. Joe scritched him between the ears.

"You want to go to Mel's tomorrow night?" he asked. "Test the new cook?"

"Love to."

He hesitated for a second, then bent forward and gave me a kiss so quick it was tantalizing. I didn't realize I'd closed my eyes. When I opened them, Joe was gone, and the door closing behind him said, "Baa."

Ghost Finger Puppet

MATERIALS:

About 10 yards of sock yarn, fingering weight yarn,
  or baby yarn* (recommended gauge for yarn
  should be about 7–8 stitches per inch)
US size 1 needles (a pair of double-pointed needles
  will do)
Tapestry needle
Scraps of contrasting yarn* or embroidery floss,
  beads, or small buttons for features
*For a classic ghost, use white yarn for "body" and
  black yarn or floss for eyes/mouth.

ABBREVIATIONS:

K = knit; K2tog = knit two stitches together (decrease);
SSK = slip next two stitches knitwise, one at a time,
and knit them together through the back (decrease)

INSTRUCTIONS:

Cast on 21 stitches.
Row 1 (right side): Knit
Row 2: Purl

Repeat these two rows until work is about 2½ inches long, ending with a purl row.

Shaping Row 1 (right side): K3, K2tog, K1, SSK, K4, K2tog, K1, SSK, K4

Shaping Row 2: Purl

Shaping Row 3: K2, K2tog, K1, SSK, K2, K2tog, K1, SSK, K3

Shaping Row 4: Purl

Shaping Row 5: K1, K2tog, K1, SSK, K2tog, K1, SSK, K3

Shaping Row 6: Purl

9 stitches remain. Cut yarn, leaving a 10-inch tail. Using the tapestry needle, run the tail through the remaining stitches, removing them from the knitting needle, and draw them up tight. For additional security, you may run through the stitches a second time.

Sew seam and weave in ends on the inside of the puppet.

With the seam at the center back and with the right side facing, embroider the eyes and mouth onto the front with contrasting yarn. You may add hair or other features as desired. If you want your puppet to have arms, you could knit an inch or so of I-cord for each arm or crochet chains of the same length and attach them in the appropriate locations.

Baked Black Bean and Spinach Burritos

Serves 4

INGREDIENTS:

canola oil
2²/₃ cups cooked black beans, drained
2 10-ounce packages frozen chopped spinach, thawed
    and pressed dry
4–6 cloves garlic
²/₃ cup shredded Monterey Jack cheese (about 2
    ounces)
¹/₃ cup pine nuts, toasted
1¹/₃ teaspoon ground coriander
²/₃ teaspoon ground cumin
²/₃ teaspoon ají amarillo chile powder (or cayenne
    pepper)
¹/₃ cup chopped fresh cilantro
¼ cup fresh lime juice
salt to taste (about 1 to 1½ teaspoons)
¾ cup crumbled feta cheese (about 4 ounces)
8 10-inch flour tortillas
1 cup salsa (optional)

DIRECTIONS:

Preheat the oven to 350°F. Lightly coat the bottom of a

9-x-13-inch baking dish with canola oil. In a large bowl, combine the beans, spinach, garlic, Monterey Jack cheese, pine nuts, coriander, cumin, ají amarillo chile powder, cilantro, lime juice, and salt. Toss to blend. Add the feta cheese and toss again.

Place 1 cup of the mixture in the center of a tortilla. Fold up one-third of the end of the tortilla facing you, then fold in the sides and roll up the tortilla. Repeat with the remaining tortillas and filling. Place in the oiled dish and bake, uncovered, for 10 to 15 minutes or until heated through. Remove from the oven, top with salsa, and serve at once.

Mel's Rhubarb Sourdough Bread Pudding

INGREDIENTS:

*12 ounces sourdough bread ripped into pieces
    ranging ½ to 1 inch
4 tablespoons butter
1½ cups milk
5 eggs
1½ cups sugar
1 tablespoon fresh orange zest
4 cups rhubarb, chopped
¼ cup crystallized ginger, chopped
½ cup raw sugar (or brown sugar)
¼ teaspoon salt
¼ cup pecans, chopped*

DIRECTIONS:

Spread bread on a cookie sheet and lightly toast, then place in a greased 3-quart casserole dish. Melt butter with milk, pour over bread in casserole.

Mix together eggs, sugar, salt, and orange zest. Stir in rhubarb and ginger. Stir rhubarb and egg mixture into bread mixture. Top with raw sugar (or brown) and pecans.

Bake at 350°F 55–60 minutes until set.

Read on for a sneak peek
at the next Haunted Yarn Shop Mystery,

PLAGUED BY QUILT

Coming in December 2014 from Obsidian.

"**B**ut where will we find the *real* story behind the Holston Homeplace Living History Farm?" Phillip Bell asked his audience of two dozen high school students. "Where will we find the *dirt*? Where . . ." The end of his sentence disappeared as he paced the stage in the small auditorium, hands clasped behind his back. I watched from the door, where I could see the students' faces as they tracked his movements like metronomes.

Bell, who couldn't have been ten years older than the youngest student, screwed his face into a puzzle of concentration, shoulders hunched, as he continued pacing. He brought one hand from behind his back to stroke the neat line of beard along his chin. He would have looked like a freshly minted junior professor if he hadn't been dressed in mid-eighteenth-century farmer's heavy brogues, brown cotton trousers, a linen blouse, and a wide-brimmed felt hat. If he'd had a wheat straw between his teeth, it wouldn't have looked out of place. The students' reactions to him were as entertaining as Bell himself.

Without warning, Bell jerked to a stop, swiveled to face the students, and flung his arms wide. *"Where?"* he asked. "Where are the *bodies* buried?"

Startled, the teens in the front row jumped back in their seats. The boy nearest me recovered first. He slouched back down on his spine, stretching his long legs out so his feet rested against the edge of the stage. He smirked at his neighbor, then turned the smirk to Bell.

"In the cemet—" the boy started to say.

Bell flicked the answer away with his hand. "No, no, no. Not the cemetery. Boring places. Completely predictable."

"Unlike Phillip Bell," a woman's voice said behind my left ear. "Full of himself, isn't he? What a showman."

I glanced over my shoulder to smile at Ruth Wood. She'd crossed the carpeted hall from her office without my noticing. She didn't return my smile. She was watching Bell as raptly as the students and gave no indication that she expected an answer to her comment. I turned back to watch, too.

"No," Bell said to the students, "there's someplace better than cemeteries. That's beside the fact that no living Holston—or anyone else—is going to let us dig up his sainted uncle Bob Holston or aunt Millie Holston from the family cemetery. And you can bet *that* is chiseled in stone. Not chiseled on a gravestone, though." The students laughed until they realized Bell wasn't laughing, too. When their laughs died, he turned and stared at the boy who'd brought up cemeteries. "You aren't a Holston, are you?"

The boy started to open his mouth, then opted for a head shake. Under Bell's continued stare, the long legs retracted, and the boy dropped his gaze to the open notebook in his lap.

Bell looked around the room. "Are any of you Holstons? Last name? Unfortunate first name? Anyone with a suspicious H for a middle initial?"

Students shook their heads, looked at one another.

"Just as well," Bell said. "The Holston clan might not like what I'm about to tell you. Have you got your pencils ready? Take this down. Two words. Two beautiful words describing some of the most interesting places on earth. Some of my favorite places. Much less predictable than cemeteries." He turned a pitying look on the formerly smirking boy. "And that makes them so much *better* than cemeteries. Where are we going to find the *real* stories? Two words. Garbage dump." Bell nodded and rocked back on his heels. "Yes, sir, I love a good old garbage dump. 'Old' being the operative word."

"Will your ladies and a crazy quilt be able to compete with Phillip and his garbage dump?" Ruth asked in my ear.

"I think we can hold our own, although 'crazy' might be the operative word in our case. Is he always on like this?" I nodded toward Bell, who was describing the contents of a nineteenth-century household dump in loving detail.

"You should have seen him when he interviewed for the position," Ruth said. "He wore a purple frock coat. He looked like the Gene Wilder version of Willy Wonka, and he gave the search committee a tour of the site like they'd never heard before. As I said, quite the showman."

"I'm glad he's not wearing the purple coat today. It would clash with his garbage dump."

"It was really more of a deep plum," Ruth mused.

"Anyway, it worked. You hired him."

"Not on the basis of how he looks in a plum coat, but yes."

There was something in her voice that made me turn my back on Phillip Bell's theatrics and look at her more closely. What I saw was the usual, impeccable Ruth Wood, longtime director of the state-owned Holston Homeplace Living History Farm. "Slim, silver, successful, and sixty" is how my friend Ardis Buchanan summed her up. "Sparkling" would usually suit Ruth, too, but the sparkle was missing today.

"How's he doing as assistant director?" I asked. "Are you happy with him?"

"*I* am," she said. "He's only been here two months, though, and the Holston jury is still out."

"Ah."

Ruth's unease was easy to understand. For years, she'd lobbied the state legislature for funds to hire a full-time, professionally qualified assistant director, and for years her efforts were fruitless. Then one day she'd mentioned her wish to a well-heeled Holston visiting from Houston, Texas. That Holston knew other Holstons, who in turn knew more Holstons, and apparently they all knew how to make things happen—privately raised funds, a new foundation, and Phillip Bell were the results.

"They've been miracle workers," Ruth said. "They're kind and generous people."

"But that generosity comes with hidden costs?" I asked, thinking of the strings a powerful family might attach to the money they donated.

"You will never hear those words from my lips," she said.

"Ms. Wood?" Phillip Bell called. "Ms. Rutledge? Coming on the tour?" The students hesitated at the edges of their seats, waiting to be released and probably willing to follow Bell anywhere.

Ruth stepped past me into the room. "Unfortunately for me, there's a meeting I can't miss. But I'll see you all back here in an hour or so. We'll have snacks and cold drinks in the education room, and then we'll get down to the nitty-gritty of Hands-On History." She paused. "Unless by then you've buried yourselves in Mr. Bell's garbage dump and can't pull yourselves out."

The students laughed. Bell didn't ask again if I planned to join the tour and didn't wait to see if I tagged along. Without looking back, he led the students out the door on the opposite side of the room. I turned to Ruth, but she'd already disappeared across the hall into her office and shut that door. I turned back to the auditorium in time to see the door closing there, too. Drat.

Getting to that other door either meant walking around the solid block of auditorium seats or threading my way along the row leading straight across the room. The shortest distance won, but not without complaints from my knees as I banged them on upturned seats along the way.

"Yes, thank you," I said, feeling grumpy. "I'd love to take your tour."

"That's not what I was going to ask you," a voice said from the stage. "But I'll be happy to show you around, if you want."

I jumped and banged my hip against a seat back. I looked, and there was a young woman standing in the middle of the stage, hands in the back pockets of her jeans, short dark hair pushed behind her ears.

"Are you one of the students with . . ." I pointed to the door Bell and the student had gone through. But the room had been empty. I'd watched them leave.

"I'm a volunteer," the woman said. "You're Kath Rutledge, aren't you? I recognize you from your shop. I've been in a few times. I love the Weaver's Cat." She looked down at the front of her T-shirt. "And I forgot my name badge again. I'm Grace Estes."

"Where did you just come from?" I asked, ignoring her pleasant greeting and proving to myself, once again, how clumsy my manners could be when something puzzled me.

Grace didn't seem to mind. She looked over her shoulder at the wall behind the stage, hands still in her back pockets. I followed her gaze. Of course. There was a discreet door in the wall for backstage entrances and exits.

"The education room's through there," Grace said with a nod. "I was setting out the refreshments."

She hopped off the stage, and I resumed my trek between the rows of seats. We met at the door.

"Won't it be great if the money for renovations comes through?" she said. "It wouldn't be the highest priority, considering the need for better storage, but maybe they can bump out this wall, add seats, and improve the traffic flow in here." She grinned. "Do I sound like I'm doing a building-usability study?"

"Are you?"

"Practicing, anyway. I took a class in building and design for historic sites last semester, and I'm still psyched. Were you serious about taking a tour?" She opened the door. "Come on. We can catch up with Phil."

"It's nice to meet you, by the way," I said, falling in beside her and offering my hand.

Up close, it was easy to see she wasn't the high school student I'd first mistaken her for. She fit somewhere in age between Phillip Bell and the teens, but how close to either end was hard to tell. Her warm smile and her hands slipping into her back pockets again made her look confident and comfortable. I liked her. I liked the humor in her eyes.

We followed a brick path across an expanse of lawn toward the site's dozen or so historic buildings. The two-story antebellum clapboard house—the centerpiece of the Homeplace—sat on a rise to our left. Straight ahead, I spotted Bell and the students leaving the log corncrib and heading for the barn—one of east Tennessee's distinctive cantilever barns.

Grace nudged my arm with her elbow and leaned close. "The whole overhanging-cantilever thing isn't my favorite look in a barn. Don't tell anyone."

"Sacrilege. So you're studying site management?"

"On again, off again," she said. "Small problem with cash flow, but I'll get there, eventually."

"Stick with it. Of course, the cash-flow problems will stick with you, too, if you stay with the public-servant side of sites and preservation."

"Oh, yeah," she said. "I've got firsthand experience with that. I worked part-time for a couple of years at a site in West Virginia. So, yeah, I've been there, but it's what I love, so I plan to keep doing it."

"Good. That's what it takes. Were you really looking for me earlier? You said you were going to ask me something."

"When I put the program handbooks together, I saw that you're talking about signature quilts."

"Signature quilts and crazy quilts. We're going to piece one that combines both forms, although I don't know how far we'll get in two weeks."

"I'd love to sit in on the discussion, if you don't mind," Grace said. "Or if you have room for extra hands, I'd be happy to help with the quilting. I've done a few small pieces of my own. A table runner. A wall hanging. Nothing fancy. If nothing else, I can thread a needle."

I laughed. "And that's not always a given. Sure, if you have the time, TGIF will be happy to have you."

"Teaching Eyeff?"

"Sorry," I said. "TGIF—Thank Goodness It's Fiber. It's the needlework group that meets at the Weaver's Cat. Some of the members are quilters, and they're going to do most of the work with the students on the quilt. I'm just giving the kids some historical background on textiles."

"Oh, right. 'Just,'" Grace said. "Ruth told me about your textile and museum background. It's very cool. She also told me that she asked you to apply for the assistant director job. She says you could've had it pretty much just by asking for it."

"Ruth said that?" That didn't sound like impeccable, professional Ruth. She *had* asked me to apply for the job when the funding came through. And maybe I could have had it without any fuss, if I'd said I wanted it. But why was Ruth discussing her personnel decisions, or mine, with a volunteer? But, then, where else would Grace have heard it?

"So, why *didn't* you ask for the job?" Grace asked. She shook her head. Maybe in disbelief at my lack of drive or desire. "I'll tell you what," she said. "You're a heck of a lot more modest than Phil has *ever* been. As soon as he saw the position posted, he *owned* it. So what gives? I know you're still dealing with fibers and textiles at the Weaver's Cat, but they aren't historic. They don't have the *stories*. Have you really given up museums?"

She looked genuinely distraught at that idea. But there wasn't time to tell the whole, long story of my professional fortunes—what I'd come to think of as my professional yarn—before we caught up to the tour. And I didn't feel like justifying my decisions on such short acquaintance, anyway. Instead, I channeled my dear, late grandmother. She'd been a master of the subtle arts of deflection and misdirection.

"If you know about Phillip Bell's lack of modesty," I said, "does that mean you knew him before he came to work here? Where'd he come from, anyway?" Granny's trick worked perfectly on Grace, and in a more interesting way than I'd expected.

"Phil?" she said. "Oh yeah. You could say I've been there and done that, too. He came here from West Virginia. He's my ex-husband. Look, he just caught sight of me. Do you see the look on his face? Now watch this." She waved her whole arm and called over to him, "Hey, honey! Hi! I've got a straggler for your tour." She nudged me again with her elbow. "He hates that I'm volunteering here," she said with a wicked chuckle. "See you later. Have fun."

ALSO AVAILABLE
FROM

Molly MacRae

LAST WOOL AND TESTAMENT
A Haunted Yarn Shop Mystery

When Kath Rutledge comes to the small town of Blue
Plum, Tennessee, to settle her grandmother Ivy's will, she
learns she's inherited Ivy's fabric and fiber shop, The
Weaver's Cat. She also winds up learning the true
meaning of T.G.I.F.—

the name of the spur

artists founded by I

determined to help

gran

But when Kath learns

suspect in a murder,

important thing on he

to do it alone. She's g

on—and she's about t

from